Vision of Darkness

By Dawn Wilton

Vision of Darkness

Cover art Created by John M. T'lustachowski.

Fan email can be received at dawnwilton@aol.com

For my Husband, John, who reminds me that joy knows no bounds and through the good and bad times, we can still find reasons to smile, laugh and dream.

For my kids, who keep me far too busy and remind me life is too short.

For my Mom and Dad because well, I'm here and this book exists because of your love and dedication as parents.

For Gretchen, Aimee and Brenda—thank you all so much for your friendship. It means the world to me.

For Joe and Meri who took the time to read this before it was even published and told me it was something worth getting out there.

For Charlotte Burnette, Alta Dunst, Jeannine Villars and Verlene Potter, all of whom told me how tenacious and ambitious I was and whom I hope will be pleased that they can finally read one of my works in print. Ladies, you were the best educators I could have ever asked for. Thank you.

For my friends in second life who keep me grinning and laughing on a daily basis.

For Melendy Britt, Alan Oppenheimer, Christina Pickles and Frank Langella—your work is so inspiring!

For whomever reads this because I'm a reader too.

In Memory of Mary Travers, Linda Gary, Dragon and Oscar.

Prologue

Thunder crashed outside. Lightning flashed again followed by another frightening clash of thunder. Bael Fiorad sat up, his heart racing. Violet eyes narrowed as he tried to make sense of what he had seen. Beside him in the bed, his wife was sound asleep. He looked down at her, glad for her presence tonight after what he'd seen.

"Thank the Gods one of us can sleep through a thunderstorm," he said softly as he rose from the bed. Slipping on his breeches and tunic, Bael walked as silently as he could into the next room and closed the door behind him. Facing his scrying mirror, he cast a spell, reaching out to a fellow wizard by the name of Grenan.

"Bael, have you seen the Vision?" Grenan asked, his dark eyes wild with fear. Grenan was an Orc and had long tusks and dusky blue skin. Red short cropped hair topped Grenan's head and in the dim light, Grenan looked both formidable and frightening.

"I've had a vision, yes. Dark forces are stirring and seek to destroy Axrealia. The entire world is in grave danger. What have you seen?" Bael asked as he pulled his long blonde hair back out of his eyes.

"A dark cloud, eclipsing the skies and spreading over all the world. Then I heard the cries of women, children and men as they died in that cloud. But I sensed powerful magic in it, like nothing we've ever seen before. It wasn't natural, Bael."

"We need to summon the Council, then. If two of us have had this vision—"

"Uh, five others have had it, Bael."

"Who else?"

"Egrid the Elf, that blasted wizard of Floating Stone Mountain Pethis. Qualet of the Hive Clans, Sektet of the Desert tribes, Hebith the Gryphon and Uthos the Giant."

"Then all of the most powerful in our land have seen it," Bael replied as he sighed. "I was hoping it was a fluke, not a true vision. Summon the Council to the old Castle in the wasteland. Tell everyone to leave their affairs in order. Apprentices need to be given greater status if they're ready for it."

"Bael, you don't mean—"

"I do. If anyone doesn't wish to help, they are permanently excused from the Council. Anyone who wants to see our world live, tell them to get their affairs in order and prepare to cast the End of Days spell. We'll create a powerbase and merge to both protect it and to fight the Evil that's coming," Bael said gravely.

"But you just got married! Your wife—"

"Will understand. She's a warrior. She'll go on without me. I'll tell her to find another man and settle, or to go on and make her own mercenary company like she wanted to before we got together. Either way, she'll live. Knowing she'll live is consolation enough for me."

"All right. I'll contact the others. When do you want us there?"

"Tomorrow night. We begin at sundown."

"We'll be there. Grenan out," the Orc wizard said, a sympathetic look in his eyes as he cut off the contact. Bael closed down the spell and sighed, running his fingers through his hair again.

"No one said that being a wizard would be easy. Being the head of the Wizard's Council…the *last* head of the Wizard's Council is harder than I thought," Bael murmured. More lightning flashed and another crash of thunder echoed through the manor house he had built with his wife. He looked back to the bedroom and sighed as he went and slipped into his bed with her for his last night of freedom. His wife stirred and groaned softly in her sleep as he curled around her, holding her close to him. His lifeline. His solace.

"When I'm gone, dream of me and I'll be with you," Bael whispered into her ear as she slept. He didn't go back to sleep, but merely held her. Bael didn't want to sleep. He would be gone soon enough and every last moment was now more precious to him than power or gold.

Chapter One

Rain drizzled down over the woman as she made her way as she ran through the dead forest. She was focused, having made her decision and wouldn't turn away. Soaked to the skin and shivering, she continued on her path towards the center of the forest.

In the center was a wasteland. Baked hardened ground let the water run freely over it as she hurried down the path. Dead trees swung their skeletal limbs about as the wind picked up as she reached the edge. Nearly flattened, she fell to her hands and knees. Her metallic quarterstaff clanged against the ground and she looked up with tears in her eyes, looking desperately on through the darkness.

I've got to get to the castle! I can't let them do this! Ezra Coren though frantically as she forced herself back up to her feet. Water sluiced down her leather armor as she forced herself onward towards the path. She had been here only once in her lifetime. *I never thought I'd be here again. Last time, it was because the Seekers were marching to war in the Devastated Plains!* Ezra paused, gasping as lightning again streaked the sky, lighting up that one single building in the far distance.

Ezra picked up the pace, trying to run and slipped and fell again. The wind whipped her long braid of brownish red hair as she moved, forced to slow to a walk. She wasn't tall, but she wore high heeled boots in an attempt to hide her true height. Her quarterstaff hit the ground over and over with a clang as she used it to keep balance each time she slipped. Hands and knees blossomed bruises and ached from the cold. At last, after what felt like an eternity, she found herself standing before the castle.

The castle at the center of the wasteland was old, so old the marble had begun to crumble. The towers that were once twisted spires had begun to fall apart, leaving random piles of stone here and there. The battered horns of the two Unicorns that formed the facade of the castle looked down on her with disapproval as Ezra walked forward, hurrying across the battered drawbridge.

Inside, she heard chanting from men in the darkness. A faint glowing ball hung in between them in the center of what had once been a throne room.

Ezra paused, looking frantically again and finally spotted the one person here she knew.

"Bael, you can't do this! You promised me! We were supposed to have a life together! Why would you give that up? What's so important that you'd give me up?" Ezra asked frantically before she looked at the others. No one had stopped chanting, but some were looking at her as she spoke. "You can't give up your lives for a foolish purpose! What will you save if you aren't here?" Ezra asked, desperate to stop them from carrying out their spell. Bael was looking at her now and he motioned for the others to continue.

"Ezra, get out of here! It's too dangerous!"

"Please, please, stop! Bael, you can't do this!"

"I told you earlier. Darkness is coming, Ezra! This is the only way we can save our world."

"No! There must be another way."

"Get out! Hurry, before it's too late!"

"I'm not leaving you!" Ezra cried as she came to stand beside Bael. She touched his shoulder and looked to the center, determined to be with him until the end. The glow was brighter now and the orb was beginning to pulse. Ezra watched it, filled with dread as it grew and grew.

"Fine! Then on your head be it! The spell's nearly complete!" Bael went back to chanting, all of his attention centered on his task. The other wizards continued on, their voices rising together as they focused. Ezra stole looks at all of them. An Orc, a giant, an Elf. Even a Dark Elf was here. A large brown and black gryphon stood across the room, making signs and sigils as he chanted. She spotted one of the large wasp-like creatures from the Hive Clans before she spotted a man with orange skin and horns. Her eyes widened as she realized she had finally seen her first half-dragon! All of the Wizards chanted together, their minds on a single purpose. Hair rose on the back of Ezra's neck as her green eyes turned once more to the orb in the center.

All of these people were here, apparently to give up their freedom in the name of the greater good. All were powerful, all had strange powers. But none were more powerful than her husband, Bael. Green eyes widened in horror as the glowing ball exploded in a thousand pieces. A shockwave flared out, blasting everyone in the room! Ezra was thrown back into a wall. A scream was torn from her lips as she hit the cold stone before falling limply to the floor. Pain shook her like a dog shakes its prey before it tossed her into the darkness.

"Ezra, wake up," a strange voice called to her. Ezra lay on something cold and smooth. Consciousness was slow in coming. Her head pounded when she tried to open her eyes, pain echoing with each beat of her heart. The room spun and Ezra shut her eyes again, trying to will the pain to go away. Along with that voice.

Ezra groaned as she moved a little, feeling her entire body ache.

"Gods I hurt," she murmured to herself as she tried to remember what happened. Ezra started with simple things as she'd been taught since she was a child. Moving her fingers, one by one, checking herself for the source of the pain. She followed that by moving her toes. "This wasn't the smartest thing I've done, I think," she murmured as she tried to remember what had happened.

"True. Very few people would have tried to interfere with an End of Days spell," the voice said somewhere above her. "Most would have stayed away, as they were told to."

"Couldn't. Bael was too important," she said softly as she shifted on the stone.

"No one person is more important than the world, Ezra. Besides, the spell threw you into a wall. Was it truly worth it?"

"Bael?" she asked as she finally got her eyes open and looked up into a familiar face.

"Not anymore, I'm afraid. Bael is no more. The Wizard's Council, in its entirety, is gone, Ezra."

"Bael, what are you talking about—"

"I am not Bael. I am the Spirit of the Council. They are all within me. The spell changed us. All of us. Including you." Ezra blinked up at that familiar figure and then began to see differences.

The man that stood before her was translucent. His hair was long and blonde, but his eyes were orange. His skin looked almost a dusky blue. She could see right through him, but he was taller than Bael had been and far more muscular than Bael had ever been in his life.

"What do you mean 'changed us?'"

"All of us. The Council, the Castle. Even you."

"How?"

"The Castle is alive. The spell merged the Council and brought me to life. And you…"

"What did it do to me?"

"You will be the Light to fight the Darkness, my new Sorceress."

"I'm not a mage—"

"You are now. It's why you are feeling so poorly. Your body is still integrating the magic that has fused with your very being."

"Please tell me this is a dream."

"You know it's not. You were an unexpected complication. Bael should have known you would come after him." The spirit's voice had changed again, becoming sterner as he glared down at her. Ezra gasped as she felt a surge of anger coming from the spirit and rubbed her head again.

"I couldn't let him go."

"Thus, why he changed the spell once he realized you weren't going to go as you were told. Move slowly at first, my new Sorceress. Plans have been changed, but we will proceed as if you were meant to be here from the beginning."

"Plans?"

"As I said, you will face the Darkness."

Ezra groaned again as her pulse pounded in her ears. She turned and touched the wall. Memory blossomed as she touched it. The blast had hit her. She had been thrown back. She looked up at it in disbelief before she looked towards the throne room again.

Piles of ash were now in each of the places where the Council members had stood. Ezra looked at them in disbelief, their black substance in stark contrast to the now-white marble floor beneath them. She looked up again after a few moments, noting how much the Castle had changed.

The marble was no longer crumbling. The roof no longer leaked nor had holes. All of the random piles of stone were gone, and she looked up and saw the twisting spires of the towers were again whole.

Gargoyles and Angels looked down at her along with the eyes of the Unicorns that now each sported a new horn. She could see them down the hall at the Entrance, where the drawbridge was. The drawbridge's wood looked fresh, newly stained and no longer looked rotten or full of holes.

"What do I call you?"

Vision of Darkness

"I'm the Spirit of the Council, a ghost of what the Council wished to impart in these walls."

"I must've hit my head harder than I thought."

"You *were* thrown into a wall. Would you like help getting up?"

"I don't think I could get up if I wanted to. I feel dizzy and I'm seeing things!"

"That's the magic you've absorbed. You're feeling your new powers. Telepathy, empathy, the ability to move things with your mind. That's only the tip of the iceberg. We will start with small things at first. Your system has had a shock, but it will adjust. For now, let's get you to your Chambers." Hands pressed below her elbows and Ezra looked up at the spirit. He looked solid!

"How can you—"

"Help? I can become solid for brief periods of time. Come. Walk with me and we'll get you to bed." The voice had changed again, sounding soothing now as those hands pressed up again. Ezra gave in and struggled to her feet with real effort.

"This has to be a dream."

"This is no dream. You're no longer mortal. The Council had a vision of darkness and the future that may yet come. You weren't expected nor foreseen. As such, the full consequences of your actions here have yet to be realized."

"Why do you sound so cheerful? The Council died—"

"Not quite. They became One. They created me. Your chamber isn't far. Walk, Ezra. You were a warrior. You can make it." The Spirit looked sternly down on her again and Ezra looked towards the hallway. Leaning against him, she made her way, step by shaking step, out of the throne room.

"Your voice changes—"

"It depends on what I need to tell you. Which Council member chooses to speak moment to moment. It will pass as we all adjust. Sometimes, it may be Bael that speaks. Other times, it may be Grenan, Qualet or any one of the other sixteen. Now, I won't be able to stay solid for much longer. Can you walk a little faster?"

"I think so. Just let me lean against the wall," Ezra replied. After a moment or so, the Spirit did that, taking her to the wall and Ezra leaned her weight against it for a few moments. Her heart was pounding with the effort to stand and her head was spinning again. Clinging to that wall helped, but not much. Finally, she turned and leaned her shoulder against it and continued on. The spirit had resumed his translucent appearance, but his eyes watched her with a fierce determination, as if he were willing her to keep moving.

"Do you have to look so much like him?"

"My appearance is not my choice any more than yours is, Ezra. Why does it matter?"

"Because I loved him. He was my world. We had built a manor! We were planning for children—"

"I know. I have his memories. He loved you more than he loved his own life. He did this for you, so you would live."

"I couldn't live without him."

"Yes, you could. You chose not to. You've made a choice. Bael made his. Come on, just a few more steps and then we'll turn the corner."

Ezra forced herself onward, wishing for her quarterstaff. Suddenly, she heard a metallic clang as it hit the wall next to her. Ezra caught it, barely, and leaned on it before she managed to get herself around that next corner.

"I have to get home."

"You are home, Ezra. You gave up your freedom when you refused to leave."

"Great. So, I'm cursed."

"If anyone cursed you, you did it to yourself. No one else tried to get the Council to stop their plans. No one else tried to get them to stop casting that spell. Only you and your actions caused this. Like me, you are bound to this place. You can leave it for short times, once you learn how to use your magic. But, only for short periods of time. This place must be guarded from now on. Otherwise, the Darkness will win. And our world will die."

"What exactly is this darkness?"

"The Council members only saw a black cloud enveloping the world and consuming it, down to every last creature. No one knows what it is, but it's far more powerful than anything anyone on our world has ever seen."

"When it is coming?"

"No one knows for sure, but it will be a long time before it arrives. The vision gave us time to prepare."

"If it's not coming now, then why the haste?"

"We must prepare. The world must be ready to face it."

"The world is going to face the darkness?"

"Yes, through you."

"I need a drink," she muttered as she took a few more steps.

"Your Chamber is the next door on the left. Easy, Ezra. Easy," that soothing tone to his voice was back and it sounded so much like Bael, Ezra nearly lost control over her tears.

After what felt like ages, she reached the door. It opened on its own and she found herself looking back at the labyrinth of hallways she had traversed. She looked back in through the door and stumbled across the threshold. Falling to her hands and knees again, she winced as flesh met stone. A gasp left her lips as she looked at the opulent room before her.

The bed had a canopy with white and silver fabric flowing down the sides, front and back. The bed itself was covered in cushions, pillows and a rich burgundy colored coverlet. A vanity stood against one wall with simple cosmetics and perfumes. A mirror caught her eye as she struggled back to her feet. Catching her reflection, she paused at the stranger reflected back at her.

She had arrived in the castle in a cream-colored tunic, brown leggings and boiled leather armor and boots. Her hair had been brownish red. Her eyes had been green.

Now, she was clad in a white and silver silk dress with a white linen chemise. Soft white leather boots adorned her feet. Her hair was as white as snow and loose. A silver headdress with a glowing blue stone flowed along the width of her forehead and down the sides of her face. The color of her eyes had been changed to a clear ice blue. Those eyes caught her off guard the most and a cry left her lips.

"What did you do to me?"

"Bael changed the spell when he realized you wouldn't go home. He made it possible for you to survive the change. This is what the spell did to you. It made you into an immortal woman. A Sorceress."

"He should have let me die."

"In a sense, he did. He allowed you to be reborn. To be able to fight."

"Why?"

"You know why. He loved you as much as you loved him. We are going in circles, Ezra—"

"I can't handle this. I'm not a mage—"

"Yes, you can. Come. Rest for now. In a few days, we'll begin your training—"

"And what if I'm not interested?"

"It's too late for that, Ezra. If you don't use the power, it will use you. And if you're to protect this place from the wrong hands, you need to know what you're doing. Simple as that."

"What am I to call you?"

"I'm the Spirit—"

"I can't call you that. You need a name."

"Perhaps you'll give me one then. Come, lay down. Let your body rest and adjust."

Ezra sighed as she turned from the mirror and walked to her bed, leaning on her quarterstaff. She crawled onto it at last, feeling the last of her physical strength giving out as she tugged off her boots and let them fall to the floor. She reached up, feeling that unfamiliar weight there and tugged it off, looking at it.

"What's this for?"

"It's to protect your third eye from attack from anyone who might try to control you. You'll want to wear it when we have visitors. It will also help you to focus your magic until you can control it," the Spirit replied. Ezra lay back against the cushions and looked up at the ceiling, noting the little touches that was in the room as she put the headdress aside. She touched her neck, feeling another weight there and tugged off a wide choker. Like the headdress, it was silver and had another stone that would sit over her throat. Both were beautiful in their simplicity and made her fingers tingle as she touched them. She put the choker aside with the headdress, feeling overwhelmed.

Her eyes returned to study the ceiling again. It was beautiful. Silver and blue pictures adorned it, depicting runes that she knew were magical in nature along with trees, clouds and a sphere to represent the world. More spheres with different runes and symbols were marked about the edges of the room. Bael's mark was in every inch of this room she realized and that brought tears to her eyes. The beauty of it, the opulence of every item. It was everything Bael had spoken of when they had spent long nights talking about their future. Tears began to flow in earnest and Ezra was helpless to stop them as she turned onto her side. Sobs began to wrack her body as she realized that here was everything that she and Bael had ever wanted.

And it was too late to share it.

The vase smashed instead of levitating as it was supposed to.

"I'm never going to get this."

"That's why you keep smashing it, Ezra. Clear your thoughts and believe. Magic is like making a wish and letting yourself have it. Desire and intent are the building blocks of magic. Now, ground, center and try again," the Spirit replied, unrelenting.

"I've been at this for four hours."

"And once you succeed, we'll stop for the day. For now, try again." The Spirit was endlessly patient, never scolding her when she balked or hesitated. He was also an endless task master, refusing to let her leave the work room until she had accomplished her lesson for the day. Ezra sighed and clenched her fists in frustration, feeling her nails biting into the palms of her hands. Taking a breath, she relaxed her body before looking to the blasted vase. She took a moment, looking inward for a balance that she hadn't realized she needed until she found it. Once she found it, she let her energy run into the ground, connecting to the power that was in the ground beneath her. Or in this case, the Castle. Ezra watched as the Spirit magically fixed the vase yet again and willed it to lift off of the table.

"Hooriash sana flaurias." The vase turned slightly, then rose seemingly as light as a feather to float above the table. Ezra breathed a sigh of relief, continuing the slow and steady stream of energy that fed the spell. It was already taking a toll on her, making her both sweat and feel weak in the knees. "I did it."

"Very good. Now, lower it down again with control."

Ezra kept her eyes on the vase, willing it not just fall as she breathed. "Fausia sana flaurias." She concentrated on lower it down slowly and the vase obeyed, floating down to lightly touch down on the wood of the table. Ezra let go of the spell and the energy feeding it simultaneously and sank to her knees, feeling drained to her core. "Why would anyone use this spell? It'd be easier to just go and pick it up!"

"Sometimes the object you need to lift will be bigger than you can lift physically. Like a boulder for example. You did very well," the Spirit said as a wine glass came to float before her. Ezra took it, grateful that the Spirit had thought to take care of her needs at the end of each lesson.

"Two weeks we've been at this and I can barely cast a spell."

"You never had magic before. In time, you'll be able to do far more than this without growing tired so quickly."

"We don't have time. The darkness could be here at any time."

"We have years to prepare for its arrival. By the time it does, you'll be ready."

"I'll never be ready."

"Yes, you will. This path wasn't one you were supposed to have, but you're doing well with it."

"That I doubt. And you never give me enough time to train with my quarterstaff or my sword. How am I going to be able to fight physically if it comes down to that?"

"It shouldn't—"

"It could. And you still need a name."

"Give me any name you'd like." Ezra sighed and looked up at the Spirit and he was giving her a very sympathetic look. Such looks were a rarity from him. She looked down and thought on it, then said the name that was on the tip of her tongue.

"Baelios, then. Because you were Bael…and others before."

"Baelios it is then, Ezra. Thank you."

"Don't thank me. It's what I would've named our son, if we'd had one." Ezra said as she forced herself back up to her feet. "I'm going to go and train for a little while. I need to clear my head." She told Baelios as she took her wine and headed for the door she knew would lead out to the labyrinth of halls, some of which led into hidden courtyards.

"Would you like me to come with you?"

"No. I need to be alone for a little while."

"As you wish. Call me if you need me." He vanished and she continued through the hallways. The first week she had been constantly with the Spirit that had once been the members of the Council. Now, she was craving time alone, to grieve. Today she felt angry and the anger was making it difficult to concentrate on magic. However, it would give her a little energy boost in her training. She needed something familiar, not more frustration.

For those first few days, she had argued with Baelios until she pointed out that she would rather have breeches and leggings, both of which were easier to run or walk in than a dress and chemise. After two days, he had helped her to change the wardrobe he had apparently assembled for her into something more acceptable to her. So, her white leggings and tunic were no longer made of silk, but they were a soft linen. With a wave of her hand, she changed the ones she was wearing from linen to soft white leather. Magic couldn't solve everything, but she did enjoy using it as a short cut at times. There was soap in the laundry to clean the leather or the linen. She preferred to save the velvet or silk versions for more formal occasions. She had hung the original dress up in the closet, off to one side but she wasn't intending to wear it unless it was an occasion that would warrant it.

"Doubt I ever will have such an occasion," she muttered as she picked up the familiar weight of her light metal quarter staff from the weapons rack and breathed in the fresh air outside. She looked at the pells she had insisted be set up out here and began her exercises. This was familiar. This was what she had done since she was old enough to walk.

Her mind and body relaxed as she moved through the familiar motions with the pells, hitting, dodging, and ducking as if she were fighting several enemies. *I don't know if I'll be able to keep up my edge without anyone to train with, but at least I won't get as rusty if I train for a short time each day,* she thought as she moved from one exercise to the next. Finally, an hour later, she was drenched with sweat and feeling more at peace than she had in the past two weeks.

"Feeling better, Ezra?" Baelios asked from behind her. She jumped and whirled before she realized who it was, then relaxed and lowered her quarterstaff.

"If you have his memories, then you know I do. Please don't sneak up behind me, Baelios. It's rude, not to mention it causes me to practically leap out of my own skin!"

"We can't be having that, of course. I drew you a bath if you'd like to soak and dinner will be ready in an hour." Baelios looked at her sheepishly, his expression showing he hadn't wished to frighten her even as his mixed array of thoughts thundered at her with amusement at her reaction.

"Why are you taking such good care of me, Baelios?"

"Because you are the Guardian of this place. And I'm here to guide you and help you in any way I can."

"Too bad the Council didn't think of hiring servants in their haste to put this together."

"No need at present. It's easy to grow food for one and just as easy to keep things clean with magic. I have no need to sleep since I'm a Spirit."

"Nor to eat. They didn't plan on me being here, or they might have planned things a bit better. Oh well. It's probably for the best. It's not like anyone knows we're here anyway." She put her weapon back on the training rack and turned to go back inside.

"True, but people will come eventually. What the Council did here caused currents through the magical energy of all of Axrealia. Other Sorcerers will come to check to see what happened. And others will follow them," Baelios replied, with a bit of sadness in his translucent eyes.

"Wonderful. All potentially wanting to take the Castle and try to kill me, right?"

"Or coming to see if they can help. We'll find out as they each come."

"Thanks for the ray of sunshine, Baelios. Knew I could count on you to remind me of how inadequate I am."

"You aren't inadequate. You're the only one who can protect this place and prepare for the Dark times to come."

"Please don't remind me. I'm going to go and soak."

"Might I also suggest studying—"

"I'm not studying another book of magic today. If I read anything today, I want it to be for the pure pleasure of reading and just to relax. *Nothing* related to magic." Ezra turned on her heel and headed to her chambers to bathe.

"As you wish, Ezra."

* * *

Ezra jerked awake, feeling the water had turned cold around her. She looked around, her hair dripping around her face. She coughed, realizing she must have gone under the water as she had fallen asleep in the tub.

"Ezra, are you all right?"

"Baelios! Yes, I'm fine!" Ezra snapped back at him before she rubbed her hands over face, trying to keep her heart from leaping out of her chest.

"I'm sorry, I know you wish privacy when you're in your chambers, but I sensed that you had fallen asleep and I wanted to make sure you—"

"Didn't drown? Thank you. I'm sorry, but I don't think I'll ever get used to all of this."

"You're not mortal, Ezra. You wouldn't have drowned, but I'd rather not risk it."

"If I'm not mortal, then what am I?"

"You're immortal. As I told you that first night. If you're hurt, you'll heal. Most wounds will heal fairly quickly, though it will depend on the wound itself. I can heal you when necessary."

"Can I be killed?"

"No. But you can be changed, captured, and weakened. Worse fates than death could happen to you."

"Leaving the Castle unprotected."

"Yes, which mustn't happen. In the wrong hands, the power here could destroy or enslave everyone on Axrealia."

"I understand. Guess I can't just run away from all this, hm?"

"Hardly. Besides, I'd always know where you were."

"Thanks for the warning," Ezra said as she rose out of her bathtub and took up her towel to dry herself. She turned to get dressed and found Baelios standing there, her nightgown in his hands. "Thank you," she said again as she took it from him and moved behind her changing screen to change into it.

"You're welcome. I found a history you might like. It's about a woman who was much like you, though she was a mortal. I thought you might like to read it tonight," Baelios offered as Ezra came around her the screen to move back into the main room of her chambers. Ezra paused and looked at him, carrying her headdress in her hands.

"That might be fun. Thank you, Baelios."

He smiled at her and bowed himself out before disappearing. Ezra sat down on her bed and took up the book, then curled up in her covers to read it. It was a wonderful tale, featuring a heroine Ezra had heard about throughout her childhood.

Completely absorbed in it, she relaxed for the first time since she had been changed by the Council's spell.

Far too soon though, Ezra found herself nodding off after a couple of hours. With a weary sigh, she put it aside and blew out the candles before closing her eyes to finally sleep.

"What happened to the ash?" Ezra asked as she walked into the throne room and noted the spotless floor. She hadn't come here since the night of the change, but today Baelios had insisted.

"I gathered it up and sent the remains back to their families. So, they can be remembered by their people as heroes," Baelios replied as he appeared next to a door that was just behind the dais of the throne.

"I see. What about Bael's ashes? He didn't have any family, other than me."

"That's what I wanted to show you. Come," Baelios replied as the door opened behind him. Ezra studied him for a moment, trying to read his thoughts before she moved past him and through that door.

"I haven't seen this room before."

"It didn't exist until an hour ago. The Castle being alive certainly has some interesting side-affects," Baelios replied with a rare chuckle. Ezra glanced sharply at him. "Surely you felt the tremor—"

"I did but I didn't think it was the Castle. I thought maybe it was an earthquake, that my spell had woken up a fault or something."

"No, you weren't working anything so dangerous nor will you be up to that for some time yet. Look."

The room was simple, mostly just a decent sized room. But at the far end, there was an indent in the wall and on it sat a small urn. Beneath hung a small plaque.

"Here rests Bael Fiorad, last Head Wizard of the Wizard's Council of Axrealia. He and the Council gave their lives so Axrealia Could Live," Ezra read the inscription out loud and paused to reach out and touch the smooth copper container. "Baelios, you didn't have to."

"I wanted you to have a way to remember him. He may be part of me, but he and the others deserve to be remembered by all. Do you like it?"

"Yes, thank you, Baelios." Ezra lowered her hand and hung her head, letting a couple of tears fall as her heart seized up in her chest for a moment. "I still can't believe he's gone."

"I know. It should get easier with time."

"Heads and hearts don't heal at the same pace, Baelios."

"Yes, but they *do* heal, Ezra. It's all right to grieve for him, to be angry and sad. I know what we're doing here hasn't given you much time to think, much less grieve, but—"

"It's all right, Baelios. I've never had a chance to dwell much on anything that's ever happened to me. I lost my parents when I was very young, I lost friends when I was taken to the Temple of the Warrior Goddess. Now I've lost Bael. Nothing's changed. I've lost more than I've gained over the years."

"Not true. You have gained powers and skills. You've gained friends—"

"And lost them when I came here. No one knows where I am, Baelios."

"I do."

Ezra sighed and turned, forcing herself back upright. She needed to get on with her day.

"I'll be in the courtyard for a bit. Thank you, Baelios."

She strode out quickly before he could stop her. She wanted to lose herself for a little while.

A year had passed. Ezra stood on the turrets of the Castle, called Ammora Castle. She and Baelios had discovered the name of the place as they had explored its walls together. Over much discussion, they had both decided that it was best not to change the name of the Castle, as it had once been a place of great importance in Axrealian history. Baelios still got on her nerves, but he no longer made her wish to cry or feel as inadequate as he once had.

"A whole year has gone since Bael died," Ezra noted softly as she looked out over the wasteland that surrounded her new home. A soft wind was blowing, making the dead trees seem to wave their twisted limbs around in an odd macabre dance. She did pause, noting the butterflies that flew by, seeking flowers briefly before moving away towards the forests that grew to the South. Ezra sighed, but looked up as she saw a pair of bright plumaged falcons flying in circles overhead, looking for prey. "And life has gone on as if nothing ever happened."

"True, but you have grown in this past year, Ezra. As has your control and understanding of magic."

"My skill as a warrior is starting to suffer, Baelios."

"I could help you practice."

"No thank you. Besides, you can't maintain solid form long enough to get a decent bout in anyway. No, it's all right. I'll make do as best I can and hope that I can find a solution to that before we have unwanted visitors."

"We have time."

"Supposedly. It's been a year, and no one has come calling yet but, that could change any day now. I know you don't want me to stop preparing, but I need a few days here and there just to relax."

"You have nearly learned all you need to know."

"And still you push me."

"I push because you have balked in the past."

"I don't balk anymore. I've mastered every spell you've thrown at me. I've read almost every history and strategy book in the library."

"Yes, and soon you'll need to begin watching the rest of the world as I taught you."

"Why?"

"You must be aware of what's going on if you wish to help delay the darkness and to find others who might help you."

"I won't recruit anyone to come here. It's too risky."

"That may change in time."

"Doubtful! I don't need friends here. I don't need lovers or a husband. I don't want any distractions. And I don't want anyone else. It hurt too much when Bael died."

"Bael wasn't the only one who died, Ezra."

"No, but he was the one most important to me."

Vision of Darkness

"You can't stop feeling, Ezra, or you will become like the very darkness we are trying to stop."

"If I don't feel, I can't get hurt."

"If you don't feel, you can't feel compassion or empathy or even love. You can't shut off your feelings, Ezra. Even immortals must feel."

"I can choose not to, Baelios."

"Why do you fight me on this, Ezra?"

"You know why. Part of me died with him. I can't bear for that to happen again. It hurts too much, knowing I'll never be with him again."

"You are with him every single day, Ezra, through me."

"It's not the same."

"It's never the same when you lose someone. But there can be others and other loves, both small and great. Ezra, you're immortal, but you're not made of stone." She felt a pair of strong hands touch her shoulders and she bowed her head, trying not to cry.

"I won't change my mind, Baelios."

The ground began to shake, and Ezra scrambled to grasp the rocks of the turrets. She looked down towards the moat and the closed drawbridge and blinked. Down below, a single man stood, looking up at the Castle as he held his hands before him. He was chanting something. She saw his lips moving but couldn't hear the words.

"He's trying to open the drawbridge, Ezra."

"He's not going to!" She gasped as she braced herself for balance and began a counter spell. She chanted the spell over and over, reaching for the all too familiar feel of the power inside of her. She also drew power from the Castle itself, adding strength as Baelios had taught her, to keep from collapsing. The shaking ceased and the blonde mage below dropped his hands and looked up in surprise. Ezra stepped forward to where the Sorcerer could clearly see her and put one hand on her hip as she rested the other against the stone parapet. "Who are you and why are you trying to break into my home?" She called loudly down to the man below, knowing he would hear her.

"I'm Maelcon. A year ago, I sensed a disturbance in the fabric of the magic of our world and came to investigate."

"I'm the Sorceress of Ammora Castle. This place was created a year ago to prevent a darkness from destroying our world. Now you know what happened. Is there anything else you wish to know?"

"I sense great power here. I will have it!"

"You will not! I have already kept you from entering Ammora and I can keep you out!"

"Arrogance won't save you, Woman!" Maelcon replied acidly before he began to chant again. This time, the ground wasn't shaking, but she could sense the drawbridge itself being forced downward.

"I need to get down there!" She gasped to Baelion.

"Teleport down there, Ezra. The spell is simple. Think of where you want to be...and then—"

"Wish to be there and let myself have it. Thank you, Baelios!" She closed her eyes and envisioned the hall where the drawbridge was located. She reached, strained and felt magic warp and stretch, then opened her eyes to find herself there! She raised her hands and began to chant again, feeling the power rising in her as she willed the drawbridge to remain shut! She pulled even as Maelcon pulled. *He's so strong! I can't let him in though, he'd use Ammora's power for all the wrong reasons,* Ezra thought as she kept pulling, forcing the drawbridge to remain shut. Ezra reached and pulled more power from the Castle, knowing it would replenish from the knot of power that existed naturally beneath it. She kept at her task, refusing to let him win. Finally, just as her own strength was about to give out, she felt Maelcon's strength give out. The drawbridge ceased trying to open and she fell to her knees, shaking with exhaustion.

"I'll be back, Sorceress of Ammora!" She heard Maelcon cry. Magic rippled outside and she felt his presence vanish.

"He's gone. He made a portal and left, Ezra. You did well for your first magical duel," Baelion said as he appeared beside her. His hands lifted her up as he had so many times and Ezra sagged against him.

"I feel so tired!" She gasped as she leaned against his temporarily solid shoulder.

"You used much of your energy in fighting him. Time to get you to bed and I'll bring you food and hot wine to help you replenish what you used up in fighting."

"He's going to come back!"

"He's mortal, unlike you. He'll try again, but unless he gets help, we know he can't beat you. Others will come as well; they'll have felt the battle miles away. Relax and sit here," he told her as he helped her down onto her bed. Ezra lay back, feeling drained and exhausted as she sank against the many cushions and pillows. After a couple of minutes, Baelios was back with hot spiced wine and a plate of cheese, bread and fruit. Ezra struggled to sit up and drank the wine eagerly, realizing how thirsty she was. After a moment or so, she forced herself to stop.

"You put herbs in it along with the spices," she noted, looking down into the goblet, feeling her hand shaking.

"To help you renew your strength. Eat and finish drinking. I'll pour you a hot bath to warm you. Then we'll get you back to bed to rest for the rest of the day."

Ezra nodded and managed a small smile. "Thank you, Baelios. I would've just collapsed in the main hall without you."

Baelios smiled back at her. "Perhaps the Council should have thought to have had you as part of the original design they had for this place, Ezra. We make a good team."

"Yes, we do." She gave him another smile as she began to eat, feeling how weak she was still. She forced herself to finish the small plate, despite feeling barely strong enough to lift each piece to her mouth. When she was finished, the goblet and the plate both whisked themselves away and Baelios reappeared. He picked her up as easily as if she were a rag doll and carried her into the bath chamber. Ezra couldn't even keep her head up, and groaned as she felt him lay her down on the lush rugs next to the bathtub. He removed her headdress and her clothing with gentle, skilled hands, then lifted her up and lowered her down into the warm water.

"I'll fall asleep in the tub again," she warned him, barely able to utter the words. Her eyes were already trying to close as she realized how cold she felt.

"I won't let you slip under the water, Ezra. Rest. I'll do all the work and put you to bed."

"I don't think…I have…a…choice," she whispered as her eyes did close on her and she began to doze.

Baelios gently stroked Ezra's hair back from her face, a tender look in his eyes. Inside of him, Bael was stirring. Bael sighed at the sight of the woman he loved, despite what the spell had done to change her. The Spirit began to bathe her well-muscled body, taking care of her. As drained as she was, if she had been alone, she would have been easy prey.

"We should have planned for her to be part of this from the start," One of the other Wizards, Grenan, inside of him spoke up, noting with admiration how much she had learned and how hard she had fought to keep their one hope safe.

"Yes, and I had told you that very thing. She didn't want this power, yet she protects it just as we would," Bael said with unabashed pride. Baelios chuckled, hearing the wizards who had become one to create Him all debating again as they had daily since Baelios had been born. Baelios finished bathing the woman and lifted her from the tub, wrapping her damp hair in a towel and her body in more towels before he lifted her again to take her back to her bed. Once in her main chamber, he dressed her and tucked her into the bed. Baelios let go of the power that kept him solid for this short time. He felt tired himself but went back to the parapets above to keep watch.

Maelcon, after all, was going to be back. He would not let Ezra be caught unawares while she recovered.

Chapter Two

Ezra looked down at the messenger that had arrived at the Castle with the dawn. Three years had passed since Maelcon had attacked, but thus far he hadn't returned. Ezra kept her guard up, expecting more visitors of his ilk, but thus far things had been very quiet.

Until now. Even through the quiet days, Ezra had drilled relentlessly with magic and her weapons. But even she needed sleep. At night, Baelios kept watch over the Castle. It helped, but Ezra still slept uneasily most nights. Ezra rubbed her eyes as discreetly as she could as she looked down at the messenger from the dais and tried to fathom how she could be of help.

"I understand your concern for the disappearances in your town, but whores and the homeless do tend to be transient, Sir Ethos. Is it possible that they didn't just leave town to pursue a better life elsewhere?"

"No, Sorceress. The people who have disappeared didn't leave the city. Zethos has walls and guards. All people coming and going from the city are recorded at one of the Gates," Sir Ethos replied, his cape swishing a bit with his frustration as he twined the corner of it between his fingers. "Those who are in the poorer districts thinks it's a demon, but no one has seen the culprit. And there are now at least two bodies that have been found. They were brutally murdered."

"Have you consulted with your local mages, Sir? Surely someone who is more familiar with your city would know if something was out of place."

"The mages that tried to investigate went missing, Sorceress. One of the bodies that showed up was the body of one of those mages. Most of the mages have left the city, fearing for their safety as a result."

"I see your dilemma then, Sir. I'll investigate the matter to the best of my ability, and I will try to help as best I can. I will not tell you how, but I'll send word if I'm successful. For now, return to your city and act as if you were unsuccessful in your efforts to recruit me, please. I'd rather have it not spread to ears that I interfere in other realms of Axrealia," Ezra replied very carefully, not wishing to reveal how she intended to help or investigate to this man. *"I must be very careful. I don't want any other mages knowing that I can leave this Castle unattended, or else they'll be here attacking while I'm off dealing with other places problems,"* Ezra thought to herself, trying to keep her expression calm and serene.

"Thank you so much, Sorceress! Thank you!" Sir Ethos bowed himself out and Ezra flicked her fingers, lowering the drawbridge to let him out. This was the first such messenger she'd had, and it had her concerned.

"How in the world did he know who I was, much less that I was here?"

"Another mage perhaps, Ezra. We must be careful. This could be a trap."

"It could easily be a trap and that's why I'm worried, Baelios. Maelcon hasn't returned yet, but it's just a matter of time. He's the only one who's come here in all of this time until today. So, either he's a very sore loser who has spoken to someone—"

"Or the messenger was from him. Clever. What do you intend to do, Ezra?"

"I'll need to go to Zethos to investigate these claims either way. I'll brave the trap, but I'll go in disguise. I could scry, but that could tip Maelcon off if he's behind this. If he's not, it could tip off whatever creature or mage is behind this. That wizard was clever, but arrogant and lacking in moral fiber. He'd do anything for power. But, if it's a demon or some other creature…"

"Thus, why you intend to investigate and get to the bottom of the matter. I can craft illusions in case anyone comes and make them think you're still here. So long as you check in with me as often as you can. How do you intend to travel?"

"Preferably by horse, if I can buy one. I'll have to start out on foot. I never have had luck with sky chariots or flying vehicles. I've never been comfortable with flying in general. I'll return by portal once I've finished there though. I just don't want to tip anyone off by arriving by portal."

"A wise precaution, Ezra."

"How could I check in with you though? Without scrying that is."

::Telepathically of course. Your telepathy is as strong as mine is, perhaps stronger. We can check in this way and magically, you'll be invisible to other mages, Ezra:: she heard clearly in her head as Baelios smiled at her. It was a rare thing, seeing such a smile on his face. She studied his dusky blue skin and his orange glowing eyes and chuckled.

"That will take getting used to. I knew I could hear your thoughts when I was first changed, but I was beginning to think—"

"Nothing just goes away, Ezra. Especially magically. Couldn't you hear the messenger's thoughts?"

"Yes, but I felt his fear more than I heard his thoughts. He is afraid, regardless of whom sent him. It's why I decided I have to go."

"A wise choice. When do you intend to leave?"

"As soon as possible," Ezra replied as she rose and made her way down the dais. The messenger was gone, and a flick of her fingers raised the drawbridge to secure the castle. "I'm going to go as a warrior who's looking for work and down on her luck. Zethos isn't further than a fortnight away even on foot, so even if I can't get a horse it won't take me longer to get there."

"There's a farm on the southern border of the Dead Forest. And last I knew, there were horses there," Baelios told her as he fell into step beside her at the bottom of the dais. Ezra briskly walked for the labyrinth of hallways that would lead to her chambers and Baelios chuckled as he hurried to keep up.

"Good. Let's hope the farmer will part with one. I had some coin on me the night of the Change. I'm not sure it'll be enough for the trip though."

"There's more coin. I gathered that up when I cleaned up the throne room after the Change, Ezra. Most of the Wizards had a coin pouch on them. They carried it out of habit. It should be plenty for your trip and for a horse."

"I hope so, Baelios. I'd rather not waste time living off the land if I can avoid it."

"My headdress—"

"I have a plain one that will match your leathers, Ezra. It'll add to your look. I'll get out your old leathers and I'll bring your weapons to the Entrance Hall," Baelios added.

"Good. I'm going to dye my hair, too. A nice black should suffice. Or red. I want to look as different from myself as possible. Too bad I can't hide my eyes."

"You can use a low-level disguising spell for that, Ezra. No one will detect it if you do," Baelios added helpfully as they turned the final corner that took them to Ezra's private Chambers. Ezra paused and gave Baelios a look before she went inside and began to get to work.

Two hours later, Ezra finished pulling on her disguise. A bit of a paste made from dried leaves that created a brownish stain on skin had dyed her hair back to its original brownish-red. A low-level disguising spell had changed her eyes to a pale green. It helped add to her look as she donned her original cream tunic along with leather breeches and boiled leather armor. Ezra ran a brush through her long hair, then braided it before pulling on her boots. Then she paused to stretch before she pulled on the new leather band that crossed her forehead and tied it behind the back of her head. Ezra studied herself in the mirror for a moment before she picked up the now-full coin pouch that was hers and tied it onto her leather belt. She turned and walked out, ready to get her weapons and start off.

"How do I look?" Ezra asked Baelios as he appeared with her sword and quarterstaff by the Entrance Hall.

"Like a warrior. No one would know that you were a mage at all," Baelios assured her as he passed over her sheathed sword. She pulled the leather strap across her body, securing the sword against her back. She then took her quarterstaff from him and leaned on it as she studied him. "Very convincing, Ezra. If you get into trouble, make a portal and return. I'll cover for you while you're gone if anyone comes near the Castle."

"Thank you, Baelios. What's that?"

"A pack. Soap, extra clothes that look just like what you're wearing. A cloak just in case it rains. And a bit of food to start you off. Everything a warrior would have with her, but very light so if something happens, drop it and run."

"I don't run from bandits, Baelios. I've never had a problem stopping them even when I was mortal and alone. But I'll keep it in mind. Thank you. It's been so long; I didn't really think about what to pack."

"It's been a long time since you were a mercenary, Ezra. Be careful and check in as often as you can. I'll let you know if anything happens here that requires your attention," Baelios said as she flicked her fingers and lowered the drawbridge.

"Good luck to us both then. I'll…miss you, Baelios. Talk to you soon," Ezra said before she walked across the drawbridge that she hadn't crossed since the night of the Change. She turned at the end of the bridge and looked up at the twin Unicorns and their crossed horns, then at Baelios before she flicked her fingers again. The drawbridge raised itself and she turned to walk away with an of excitement. She was leaving Ammora for the first time in three years! She felt elated, joyful and yet…sad. *Must be because I'm alone. Completely alone for the first time in three years without even a Spirit looking after my every move. Gods, Baelios probably feels the same way! Well, this trip will be over before I know it. Best to get back as soon as I can but…I still can't help but feel that I'm walking into a trap,* Ezra thought to herself as she walked down the path that would take her to the south of the Dead Forest. The Skeletal looking trees shook their limbs as she walked past them and into the waste land. Hard baked ground still bore traces of her passing from the night of the Change. It rarely rained here, but she chuckled as she noted where she had fallen in a couple of places before she turned to the Southern path. From a distance, she knew no one would know who she was. Just another warrior, down on her luck.

Ezra paused as she came across a farm just where Baelios said it was. She had been walking for several hours and her feet was starting to ache. Her legs were all right, but she hadn't been quite this active in years.

I need to step up in my training and exercise more, Ezra thought as she walked through the gate for the farm. In the distance, she could see the neatly plowed fields and several people tending to the crops. At the farmhouse, she could see a sliver of smoke rising from the chimney so she approached the door and hoped that there was someone home. She tapped on the door lightly and waited.

"Hail and fine day to you, Warrior," the woman who opened the door greeted her warmly. She was older, but her face bore a friendly smile and a twinkle in brown eyes that warmed Ezra's heart. Long red hair streaked with gray was coiled in a long braid that hung down the woman's back. A kerchief covered the top of her hair. Her face had a streak of flour across one cheek and she was wiping her hands on her apron, having washed them. Ezra could see the dough the woman had been working sitting on a table in the kitchen behind her.

"Hail and fine day to you too, Lady. I'm looking to purchase a horse. I haven't much, but I'll give you a fair deal if you have one that you can part with."

"As a matter of fact, I do! My brother was killed and left me his war horse! I can't do a thing with it! Would you be able to handle such a beast?"

"Yes, I've had war horses before. Mine was killed when I was guarding a caravan and I haven't had a chance to replace him. I've felt lost without one, to be honest. I'll treat him as well as your brother did, if not better. May I see him?" Ezra asked, her hopes rising within her like the sun.

"Come with me and we'll see what he makes of you then, Warrior." The Farmer came out with a grin and she motioned for Ezra to follow her around the back of the house. Ezra spied the stable and was impressed with how neat everything was organized and how clean each of the stalls were as she passed them. No stale smells of feces or urine. That meant good healthy animals! "He's a bit unruly and bored with us. He needs a chance to do some honest work, and he's far too head strong to be just a plow horse," the Farmer continued on as they paused at the last stall.

Inside was an animal so dark it was blue-black. The horse stamped one strong hoof and looked at Ezra with one black eye that held amusement in it as it studied her. He was well muscled, healthy and well groomed.

"How long ago did your brother pass?"

"Four years ago. Just before that big flash of light in the sky on the other side of the forest. That old castle must have been destroyed in a monstrous storm of something. For the best; it was getting dangerous anyway. My brother passed just a week before. He was home visiting and bandits came to call. He drove them off, but they got him in the heart."

"I'm very sorry for your loss, Lady. May I?"

"Of course!"

Ezra opened the stall and slipped into it, leaving her weapons and pack with the Farmer. She approached the animal carefully, staying on the angle so he could see her and began making soft clicking noises as she approached. She laid her hands on him and began running her hands down each of his legs, checking for injuries or scars. Each hoof was picked up and examined.

"You've been taking good care of him. His hooves are trimmed, and his feet are well shod. How old is he?"

"Not sure, I think no more than ten though, Warrior. Quite a beauty, isn't he?"

"Yes, he's in very good shape for a war horse that hasn't been worked in a while. What's his name?" Ezra pried the beast's lips open and examined his teeth, then rewarded him with some scratches in his itchiest places before she rubbed him down with a soft cloth. He leaned into the attentions and began to rub his nose against her.

"Old Black. He likes you!"

"Yes, he does. I can offer you two silvers for him, Lady, if you're willing to part with him."

"I'll take five coppers for him and give you some fodder for him for a few coppers more, Warrior. The coin isn't important to me, it's that he has a proper home."

"I'll give you two silvers anyway and I won't take no for an answer. He's a fine beast and I think we'll get along just fine. Do you have a saddle and tack for him?"

"On the shelf behind you, Lady. That's all his."

Ezra fished out two silvers and put them into the Farmer's hand. A flash of a vision hit her, showing her how the woman and her family had been struggling of late to keep themselves and all of their animals fed. She slipped an additional five coppers into the woman's hand.

"For the fodder. What's your name, Lady?"

"I'm Seila, Warrior. Thank you. It'll be worth it to see Old Black off to a good owner who will treat him right and aye! Make him work for his supper!"

Ezra chuckled and turned to begin tacking up her new horse.

"As for that Castle in the forest. It wasn't destroyed. In fact, it looks brand new. There's a Sorceress there who is kindly to those in need. I would've stayed, but she didn't have work for me. But, if you ever go there, tell her Cara Ezroth sent you," Ezra told Seila as she tightened the girth strap on the saddle, then began to put a hackamore on Old Black's head instead of a bridle with a bit. He seemed touchy in the mouth and she knew he could put those teeth to some wicked use on bandits if they should be attacked on the road.

"Thank you, Warrior Cara! I'll see that Sorceress in the next moon or so and we'll see if what you say is true," Seila said as Ezra led Old Black out of the stall. His tail was up in a flag behind him and he pranced with excitement as Ezra strapped her pack and a bag of grain onto the back of his saddle pad. Ezra swung up into the saddle and hit a button her quarterstaff. It slid into itself, becoming something more manageable that she slid into a saddle bag. Her sword was still in easy reach, as was her dagger. Ezra led him out of the Stable and swung up into the saddle for the first time on this beast and sat there for a moment, letting him get a feel for her weight.

::Baelios, if this woman, Seila, comes to our door, let her in. She had a war horse, one who is exactly what I need. If she ever needs help, I'll gladly give it. Old Black is very good natured for a War Horse. He's positively radiant at the thought of being with a Warrior again. Can you see if there's any place in the Castle where we could keep him? I'd like to keep him for when I have to go out like this."

::Of course, Ezra. Good luck on your journey. I think I know just the place. I'll see if there's any place where we can plant fodder for him and grain, but maybe the Farmer can help us with that.::

::I'll see what I can arrange when I get back,:: Ezra sent telepathically before she again looked to Seila. Old Black was fidgeting, anxious to be on the road. "There there, Old Black! We have miles to go before we rest tonight. Thank you again, Seila, and Good day to you!"

Ezra turned Old Black to leave the farm and Seila waved.

"Thank you again, Cara! If you ever pass by this way, drop in for a cup of tea!"

"I will! Thank you! Fare well!" Ezra touched her heels to Old Black's flanks, and he surged forward, prancing out towards the gate with a trumpet of excitement. Ezra laughed and slowed him down once they were on the road, not wanting to wear him out before sundown. "Easy there, Old Black! It's been a long time since I've been in the saddle and I'll need a little time to get used to it again. I think you'll enjoy being in Ammora once this errand is though. For now, let's get to know each other, hm?" Ezra looked forward to the journey now, her heart pounding as she thought on the days ahead. It felt good to be out in the world again…if only for a short time.

Six days later, Ezra rode up to the city gates for Zethos. She looked discreetly about her as she approached it on Old Black. Sky chariots, large flying vehicles that flew through the air using magnetic forces, zoomed overhead, racing over the walls and back to the roar of a distant crowd. "I'm Cara Ezroth. Warrior. I'm lookin' for work if there be any in your fine city. This be my horse, Ole Black," she said, putting on an accent with ease when the guards questioned her.

"It's the lean season, Warrior. Not much work available in town, but the inn would welcome your custom for a few days. Do you have any coin?" The main guard asked as he looked her over.

"Oh aye. I have coin, enough to resupply and rest before movin' on. Is there a Guild House for the Mercenary Guild here?" she asked.

"Aye. They'll give ye shelter for less than the inn, but their food isn't as good."

"I'll visit there before goin' on to the inn, then. Which way is it?"

"Down the fork to the left. Oh, and be careful goin' out at night. Lots of people have disappeared from the poor district. A couple of bodies has turned up. Culprit hasn't been caught yet."

"Has this been happening for long?" Ezra asked, being careful to sound wary and concerned.

"About three months now, Warrior."

"Any idea what's causing it?"

"None. No witnesses, nothing unusual other than the fact that only two bodies have turned up. Most of the people missin' just…disappear. Be careful now," the guard warned as they opened the gates to wave her through.

"Aye, I'll be careful. Thanks fer the warnin'," Ezra replied as she rode through the gates on Old Black. As she rode through the gates, Ezra looked at the town using her mage senses. Then she shut it down quickly.

::Baelios, something is definitely wrong here. The magic here feels wrong. Slimey. Corrupted,:: Ezra sent telepathically as she rode down the path on the left, heading for the fork in the road. She kept Black at a walk, not wanting to trample anyone nor to startle anyone. As it was, people turned to look at her as she rode, and she kept a closed expression on her face as she rode.

::Any idea what's causing it, Ezra?:: Baelios sent back a moment or so later. Ezra breathed a sigh of relief, having worried that she might not hear him so far from the Castle.

::No, not yet. I may be here a few days just investigating. Will you be all right if I'm gone that long?::

::Yes, but I'll let you know if anything happens that changes that. Take your time. Maybe try seeking out local mages that might be nearby?::

::The messenger said most of them left or disappeared. I don't like this. I'll look to see if there's any mages left, but I'm not counting on much in the way of help.::

::I understand, Ezra. Be careful.::

::Always,:: she sent back before she began listening for stray thoughts from those around her. She turned Old Black down the fork to the left of the road and watched for the sign for the Mercenary Guild house. She smiled a little in relief when she did see it and swung down, aching from being in the saddle for so long. She gave Old Black a pat and a lump of sugar before she tethered him up front. Walking around the posts, she walked into the porch and took a quick glance before stealing inside the door.

Inside, everything was spic and span. Nothing was dirty. Weapons were neatly arranged on their racks along the walls. The eating hall was simple, plain but ready for those who lived or visited here. An old retired warrior approached her, looking as fit for duty as he likely had twenty years before. He had shoulder length brown hair, very dark skin and had an eye patch over a scar that went across his eye. His remaining eye was a warm dark mocha and looked at her shrewdly.

"Hail to you, Warrior. What can the guild be doin' for ye today?" he asked with a gleam in his eye as she noted him taking stock of her.

"Hail to you, Warrior. I came to pay my dues for the year and to see if there's any work in the town that you know of," she replied, seeing no reason to explain further than that.

"It's the lean season. So, no work but we can take your dues and give ye custom if ye need it, lass," he replied as he led her over to a desk. He sat down, took out his roster and held it and the pen out to her. Ezra signed it with her alias, Cara Ezroth, and paid the fee of ten coppers. He slipped her a badge, which she pinned onto her sleeve for now. "Would ye like a cot and a place for ye beast? Or will ye be movin' on to the inn?"

"I'll be goin' to the inn, but I had some questions. The guard at the gate said some people have been murdered and others have disappeared. Do ye have any idea who might be behind it all?"

"I have an idea, but since the man was banished—"

"Unlikely he'd come back, but who do you think it is?"

"A wizard named Maelcon. Dark sorcerer, that one. He tried to sacrifice victims to a demon to get more power a few years back. The Prince found out and banished him. Gave restitution to the victims and their families. But the way those bodies were cut up…twas similar to when we caught 'im," the warrior replied, looking gravely at her with his one good eye.

"I see. Are there any other mages left in town? I was hoping maybe one of them could point the way for me."

"None. Nearly all of them have left. Whole place feels dark and…wrong. Like there's something in the air, but there's nothing to see."

::Baelios, I think I know who might be behind this. Maelcon was banished from Zethos. All of the other mages are gone. I have a bad feeling he might have come back here--::

::Be extra careful then, Ezra. He is not one to underestimate.::

::No worries there. I'm taking no chances. Tonight, I'll start hunting him.::

"Well, then I'll be on my guard. Thank you, Warrior," she said as she took her leave and headed for the door.

"If ye hunt him, lass…. I wish ye luck."

Ezra turned and studied the man.

"Why do you think I'm here to hunt him?"

"Ye just have the look of someone who doesn't stand for things that are wrong. If ye find that evil bastard, send for me. I'll bring enough men to ensure that he'll never get away again."

"I'll keep it in mind, Master—"

"Rowthen. Just Rowthen. Good luck to ye, lass."

"Good luck to you as well, Rowthen. Fare well," she said as she slipped out the door and headed to her horse. She untied the reins from the post and led Old Black down the street to where she could see the Inn's sign hanging just a few doors down. People passed her, some looking friendly. Others looked as though they were hurrying to get things done before returning to their homes for the evening.

The stable for the inn was around the back, so Ezra led Old Black along, giving him the subtle signals that he was to behave and not bite anyone here. She inspected the stables as she led him in with an experienced eye and nose. No stale urine smells and no piles of dung were in any of the stalls. All of the stalls had been scrubbed and had fresh hay. The stable lad was a good boy and came excitedly forward to take Old Black's reins from her. "He should be fine, just keep his tack in sight," Ezra told the boy. The boy's father was the head of the stables and came forward to introduce himself. Ezra paid him for Old Black's fodder, water, fresh hay and grooming. She gave Old Black the signal to relax and he leaned into the boy's brush strokes with a look of pure pleasure in his dark eyes.

"Oh, don't worry, Warrior. He'll be right spoiled by the time you're ready to leave," Wester, the boy's father, explained. Ezra laughed and added a couple more coppers to the pile she'd already given him.

"Good, he deserves a bit of spoiling. We've fallen on hard times, he and I," she explained.

"Well, the inn keeper used to be a warrior herself. She'll see that you're just as spoiled inside," Wester added before Ezra reluctantly left the stable to go back around to the main entrance to the inn.

The inn was as clean as the stables and just as well kept. The food smelled delicious and when Ezra inquired as to the prices, it was more than reasonable. Ezra paid for a week's stay, hoping it wouldn't be that long, and took her pack and her dinner upstairs. She ate far more quickly than she normally would have, glad that the food here was different from what she usually had at Ammora. There was a bathtub and plumbing in her room and she took her time in the bath, enjoying a nice long soak in hot water. She rose and dressed in fresh clothing and sat on the bed and waited for the sun to go down.

::Baelios, I'm at the inn. Old Black is in the stables and being spoiled by the Head Groomer's son. The magic here in the city feels wrong. It's almost like it feels slimy, and something is definitely out of balance here. I've felt ill since I entered the city,:: she sent telepathically, reaching for that presence that she had become so used to over the past three years.

::That's alarming that the city is so out of balance and no one has noticed it?::

::Those who have noticed it are either dead or fled, Baelios. I haven't searched yet, but I'm not feeling any strong magical presences in the city…yet. The one presence I do sense feels very foul. I'm thinking about taking a walk in the astral, to see if I can track that presence to its source.::

::Be careful not to be trapped by it, Ezra. Once you find the knot of the presence, go back. Don't investigate in the astral. Just find the location for tonight. Tomorrow, you can go there physically and investigate further.::

::Good idea, Baelios. Wish me luck. It's dark out and time for me to go out into the astral.::

::Good luck and be safe, Ezra,:: Baelios sent before he cut off contact. Ezra sat on her bed and leaned back against the pillows and the wall. She relaxed her body, starting with her feet and hands. As each body part relaxed in turn, her spirt drew up and stepped out of her body. She opened her astral eyes and looked back, checking that her tether was indeed going back to her body before she spread the angelic wings that sprouted from her back at a thought. Lightly she took to the air and began to fly through the streets of the city.

In the astral, the city looked very different! The colors were darker, grimmer and more foreboding than it normally would have been. She had gone into the astral to check things around Ammora from time to time, so Ezra was familiar with how things generally looked in the astral. In general, colors were normally brighter, more vivid and energy sources became absolutely radiant.

Here, there were very few energy sources and those that were immediately about her looked dull and grim. As she looked things over, she noticed that all of the energy in the city, with the exception of hers and Old Black's, was going towards the poor district. Following the reddish tendrils, she grew more and more alarmed as she finally spotted the source. A single building, an old temple that was crumbling and falling apart, had at its heart a large black and red power source.

That's it. Whoever is behind all of this, they've set up shop there, Ezra thought as she studied the name of the old temple. She turned and flew back to her body. Once there, she stepped back in and opened her physical eyes. ::Baelios, I've found it. Whoever it is, they're in an old temple of the Goddess of Night.::

::Those followers were nearly wiped out. Interesting that they chose that temple. Let me know what you find out tomorrow. So far, everything here is quiet, Ezra,:: Baelios reported.

::Good, let's hope it stays that way. Talk to you tomorrow, Baelios,:; she sent back before she closed her eyes and lay down on the bed to slip off into sleep.

The next day didn't bring much more information. Ezra discreetly asked around the inn, and in the marketplace. Finally, she just walked through the poor district, edging over to the old temple little by little. People didn't meet her eyes and hurried away the instant her eyes landed on them. She could feel the strain in the air, feel the pull of energy towards that temple as if it had come alive and was feeding on the city.

::Baelios, I don't like this. Not at all,:: she sent as she stood by a corner and just watched people walk by for a little while. She was wearing one of her more tattered and worn looking outfits, trying to blend into the crowd. The hood of her cloak was up, hiding her hair and most of her features. She was eating a plarmat fruit, a large purple fruit that had to be peeled before it could be easily eaten. Ezra took another small bite, relishing the taste of it as she continued to discreetly watch the sorts of people that lived and worked in this area.

::Poor districts never leave anyone with a good feeling, Ezra,:: Baelios sent back after a few moments.

::The flow of energy here is going directly to the temple. It feels as though something is feeding off of the people in the entire town, but it's worse here,:: Ezra replied as she continued to watch a pair of orphan boys as they each stole some fruit and ran past to wherever their current hiding hole was. The cart keeper shook his fist at them, but when Ezra flipped him a couple of coppers, he let it go with a sigh of exasperation. Ezra shook her head and chuckled inwardly at the boys' antics, but she remembered from her own childhood what it was like to be starving and alone in the world.

::Any sign of anyone going in or out?:: Baelios asked, his mental voice tinged with both curiosity and worry.

::Not yet. But, since I know where whatever this is is holed up, I think I'm going to see Guildmaster Rowthen and see if he or any of his students would like to go hunting with me tonight,:: she replied.

::Why tonight?::

::The people here are being fed upon so much, I'm afraid some of them aren't going to last much longer, Baelios.::

::I see your point then, Ezra. Good hunting then,:: Baelios sent back before she felt him cut off the connection. Ezra shook her head again and went back to people watching for a little longer, trying to formulate a plan.

"So you see, Guildmaster, I think I have located the source of the culprit behind your murders," Ezra explained patiently, trying to skirt around the truth as much as she possibly could. "The old temple in the poor district is giving me a foul feeling and I have heard that many of those that disappeared disappeared in that area—"

"How do you know all of this?"

"Coin, in the right hands, can loosen a few tongues. I asked around that area. Both murder victims were seen in that area just before they disappeared. Those that are still missing were last seen in the vicinity of that temple. Whatever is in there holds the answers to what happened to those that are gone or murdered," she explained. Of course, she had questioned no one, but used her telepathy very discreetly and had seen those who had disappeared. Afterwards, she'd done some discreet spell work back at the inn. Everything she had seen through that showed her answers and left more questions.

"I see. Why not go to the guard?"

"I have no absolute proof, Guildmaster. But I am going hunting tonight. I would prefer not to go hunting alone, lest I walk into a trap," she replied.

"A wise plan. I'll meet ye at the temple at dusk with as many hunters as I can muster," Rowthen replied, his one good eye having gone both dark and deadly. Ezra gave a nod and bowed herself out, glad that she had not been the one to rouse the man's anger.

Vision of Darkness

Ezra donned her brown clothing that night, knowing it would help her to blend into the darkness easier than just black would. Black could stand out in shadows if the shadows weren't quite dark enough. Brown blended easier, as did gray. She had checked in on Old Black and given him some attention as well as a couple of treats she'd saved from her lunch. Now, with the shadows growing long and dark, she made her way again on foot through the streets to the poor district and the Old Temple of the Goddess of Night.

It was less busy in the poor district now that it was nearly dark. Less darting bodies to keep track of. The children were gone, for instance, having gone to wherever they lived or squatted. Thieves weren't visible either. Those who were returning from work hurried through the streets to their homes, not even going to a local inn for an ale. That disturbed Ezra greatly. Working men often wished at least an ale or beer just to relax at the end of a hard week. It was the last day of the week; the working men and women should have been at the inn just a few doors down. The inn itself seemed deserted and dark.

Just as well, since that means less eyes tonight to see what'll be happening at the Temple. When this is done, I'm going to recommend that it be burned to the ground and salted, lest more trouble seek its shelter, Ezra thought darkly as she waited for Rowthen and his volunteers. She leaned up against the wall in an alley across from the Temple and just waited. And waited.

The shadows grew longer and longer. The darkness grew and grew. Finally, two hours past the time they'd agreed to meet, Ezra concluded that Rowthen must not have been able to find anyone.

"Cara?" she heard a whisper and looked towards one lone figure that was coming down the street.

"Here," she whispered back. The hooded figure came to her and brushed back his hood, revealing his face.

"I couldn't find any volunteers. It's just us tonight," Rowthen said darkly. He was angry and she didn't blame him. She gave his shoulder a pat.

"S'all right. Two is better than one, after all. Do you know the layout of this place?" she asked him.

"Best way to enter will be from the second floor. No one will see us going up or in," he murmured as he nodded across the street towards a drainpipe along the side of the Temple. Ezra gave a nod and she took the lead, walking towards it and glanced around. No one was in the street. She took a breath and tested the pipe gently before she began to climb it.

It was a long climb, slippery as well as it had begun to rain in the past half hour. Ezra took her time and gently tapped it twice when she got to the ledge. She felt along the wall and found the window and pulled. It opened easily. She waited, being patient as she heard the noises that told her that someone else was coming up the pipe. She held her hand out to Rowthen, who grasped it when he came into view. She pulled him up beside her, then opened the window a little wider before stepping in. She turned and saw that the inside of the temple was mostly open, with little more than a walkway for the second floor and a small library. Old books, gone moldy with disuse and too much moisture, lined the bookshelves around her.

Pity. What knowledge might I have found in these? she wondered as her hand ran over the volumes of books on one shelf next to her. She pulled her attention away and took out her quarterstaff as she and Rowthen edged at his gesture towards the rail. Crouching down, they looked below.

What had once been a beautiful temple of life had been corrupted into a perverse altar of death. A single stone table stood in the center of the room. Blood, both fresh and old, coated most of the surface of it and much of the floor about it. Runes for dark magic had been etched in the blood all around the edges of the table and around the circle of blood around it. Horrible depictions of human suffering had been hung about the room in perverse tapestries. Ezra felt her own anger growing as she saw the rivers of energy running to this room into a single black stone that was sunk into the center of the table.

"What i' the 'ell," Rowthen whispered next to her.

"I've heard of scenes like this. Dark magic. Everyone who's disappeared is likely already dead," Ezra explained to him softly, as she studied the runes. They were for both protection and for harnessing life force. She studied the spell surrounding the altar and felt sickened.

Someone was gaining more magical power by reaping death here.

"No wonder the mages all disappeared. They would've felt sickened by this."

"It's why the ones who investigated were murdered," Ezra explained, her anger rising by the moment. She went silent as she heard the temple door open and slam shut.

"Come, Child. I have need of you," a familiar voice rang through the air. Down below, a hooded figure walked, bringing along a young woman. A whore, judging by the girl's clothing that looked so light that the cold must've half-killed her before the man had caught her. He was tall, broad shoulders, muscular. The whisp of hair that caught Ezra's eyes cinched the identity.

"Maelcon," she whispered very softly as the hooded man dragged the paralyzed girl to the altar.

"Ye sure?"

"I'm positive. Go get the guard. I'll hold him here," she whispered.

"I'd rather stay and take his head."

"Get the guard, Rowthen. He's been gaining power from the death he's sown here. I'll stall him. Get the guard so he can be punished and brought to justice," she said in a warning tone. She opened her palm, letting a little magic flow and brought a flame into her own hand.

"Ye're not a warrior."

"I'm a warrior, but things are not all that they seem. Get the guard, Rowthen. He's clever and fast. I'll hold him here until help comes," she warned softly. Rowthen's eye glimmered darkly, but he gave a nod and crawled back towards the window, leaving Ezra alone.

Ezra looked down at the scene below and at her surroundings. As Maelcon began to chant a paralyzing spell, making sure his victim wouldn't be able to move, Ezra crept towards the staircase and began to make her way, step by silent step, towards the altar. She withdrew her metal quarterstaff from her pocket and hit the button, making it snap to full-size in an instant.

Maelcon whirled, alerted by the tiny sound, but Ezra was already on him. She hit him with physical blows of her quarterstaff while casting a counter-spell to release the girl.

He deflected the quarterstaff as if it were nothing and with a snap of his wrist, Ezra went flying across the room. She landed hard shoulder-first on the floor. Pain lanced up her side. Her quarterstaff landed with a metallic clang somewhere nearby. She forced herself up to her feet and turned to face him.

"Why, it is the Sorceress of Ammora. I'm honored that you came to investigate this matter for yourself, rather than trying to send someone else to do it for you," Maelcon purred as he drew back his hood. "In disguise, but you none-the-less. I sensed your power once you arrived. You're like a beacon in the darkness."

"There's a reason I'm a beacon in the darkness, Maelcon. To stop evil like you," she replied candidly, neatly sending a fireball right at him. He deflected it as if it were an insect and Ezra tilted her head.

"Impressive," he said.

"Just wait," she replied as she cast a blinding spell on him. He stumbled for a moment or so, but that was all she needed. She rushed him and tackled him, trying to draw her knife in the same instant. He kicked and sent her flying back while he rose. He barked three words and chains snaked out, trying to capture her limbs. Ezra jumped out of their reach and barked a spell of her own, trying to drain him of any power he'd raised by the spilling of innocent blood.

He reacted by raising a whirlwind. Ezra hit the wall hard and fell, tasting blood in her mouth as she landed in a heap at the bottom.

"Portharos Lumnaros!" She barked as he tried to blind her as she had blinded him. The spell, meant to make him melt into the floor, had no effect.

"I've shielded this temple against that sort of spell, Sorceress," Maelcon purred as she finally got her feet under her. He approached her, lazily approaching her as she spun and round-kicked him into the wall behind her. She whirled and got her knife out. He seized her wrist and plunged that knife blade hard into the wall, snapping it in two. Ezra whirled again and kicked him again, back into the wall. This time, his blinding spell hit her, and she stumbled, unable to see!

She immediately studied the spell with her mage-senses and found the weakness and broke it.

"Most impressive," he complimented her as he studied her while she studied him. "Your parlor tricks won't save you, or the girl, Sorceress. Once I've drained you, I'll take your pretty little castle for my own."

"Not if I have anything to say about it," Ezra replied as she raised her hands, power glowing in them.

Maelcon spat out three words and Ezra felt herself thrown backwards into the opposite wall. She hit her head hard this time and everything began to go black from a blinding spell he spat out.

"Ah much better. You're blind while my sight is clear, my dear Sorceress. Ammora Castle will be mine for the taking while you're incapacitated," he drawled as he moved closer to her. One fingertip caressed down her left cheek and fire burned in its wake. Ezra screamed while reaching for more power within herself even as chains crept like serpents to grasp her wrists and ankles. She began to create a shield between them even as Maelcon's blurry form moved away.

No guards yet. Rowthen wasn't back with them yet. Ezra's thoughts raced even as she worked on the weak point in the blinding spell, using her mage-senses to look for more weak spots in the spells on the room. She found one very big one, one that was all that was keeping the Temple standing. Ezra brought up her power as Maelcon began to cut the girl, nice and slow.

Then she reached out and broke all of his spells simultaneously. Maelcon whirled as the temple began to shake. The chains holding Ezra went limp and Ezra snapped them easily with a barked spell. She rushed Maelcon again, this time with another dagger in her hand.

She caught him by surprise in the stomach and jerked the dagger up from his navel into his sternum. Then she tilted the hooked knife and caught his heart.

He went limp and she pulled her dagger out again. Sheathing it, she ran to the girl and checked her quickly before pulling her from the altar. Pulling the girl up and over her shoulder, she turned and ran for the main entrance as fast as she could while dodging around falling stones. Seeing her quarterstaff on the floor, Ezra snatched it up and kept running. She finally made it out just as the temple finished collapsing behind her.

Rowthen and half of the guard pulled up short outside, clearly caught by surprise by her sudden emergence.

"Cara, what 'appened?" Rowthen asked as Ezra lowered the girl.

"He was going to kill the girl. He'd killed everyone who's disappeared recently from your city. I had to stop him," Ezra explained as she laid the girl down on the stones and put pressure on the girl's wounds. The cuts were shallow, not meant to kill the girl yet. "She's lucky. Maelcon intended to take his time with her."

"We'll get her to a healer. My men and I will go and collect Maelcon—" the guard started.

"He's dead. I killed him and the temple began to collapse. He was using magic to keep it together," Ezra explained quickly while one of the guards picked the girl up. The Head Guard offered Ezra his hand and she took it, getting up awkwardly. She picked up her quarterstaff again and leaned on it heavily.

"Then you've done Zethos a service. Maelcon had a bounty on his head of a ten thousand gold coins."

"Give it to the girl. And to the families of his other victims if they have any. I want her to have a fresh start, an education if it can be arranged."

"A phoenix from the ashes, Warrior?" the Guard asked with a smile.

"Yes. I have skills to sell. I don't need that much coin."

"Then we'll give you enough to at least get you through the lean season. The rest we'll give to the victims. Fair, aye?" The Head Guard suggested to her.

"That's fair, aye," Ezra conceded as she began to walk with Rowthen and the guards. "You should burn what's left of the temple and salt it. Or at least burn it and clear it. Maybe plant a garden there," she suggested as they walked out of the poor district.

"I'll suggest it to the King tomorrow morning," the guard replied as Rowthen chuckled.

"I told you she was a good 'un."

"That you did, Rowthen. That you did."

Ezra chuckled with the others as they walked along. When they reached the healer, the girl was taken in hand. Ezra declined the healer's services.

"The girl needs your skills more than I do. I only got a small knock to the head. I was lucky," Ezra admitted to the older woman. The woman studied her but pronounced her fit and well and turned her skills to the girl instead. As the guards and Rowthen escorted her to the inn, Ezra turned to them.

"You'll make sure she gets the coin I want her to have?"

"Aye, I'll make sure o' if meself," Rowthen reassured her. The Head Guard had disappeared, but now she saw him riding back on a spotted palfrey with a large bag of coin in his hand. He tossed her a small sack of coin, then gave the rest to Rowthen.

"That's your reward. You're sure you don't want it?"

"I don't need that much coin. I'd rather those that Maelcon harmed the most be taken care of," she replied. Rowthen gave a nod and went inside. When he returned, the sack was a bit smaller by a good amount.

"Most of the victims didn't have families. I gave the healer her fee and left enough coin for the girl to get a good life for herself. An education. The healer said she'd make sure the girl gets a new trade. The rest, I'll give to the few family members of the victims that were murdered," Rowthen explained. Ezra gave a nod, trusting him.

"Thank you, Guild Master. I'll see you all in the morning," she said as she moved towards the inn's entrance, still holding part of her reward in her hand. Ezra retracted the quarterstaff and went upstairs to her room, and barely got the door closed and locked before she collapsed on her own bed.

It was dawn when Ezra rode out the next morning. She saluted the guards, giving her name as she left and rode Old Black a good way away before she made a portal. Slipping from Old Black's back, she led him through and came out into the main hall of Ammora Castle.

"Well done, Ezra. I was watching as you fought Maelcon. You did well," Baelios greeted her as he took Old Black's reins from her. "I've prepared a place for him and grew some feed and fodder. There's a bath prepared for you. I'll be in shortly with a meal and wine," Baelios said warmly as he led Old Black away.

Ezra turned and walked to her familiar chambers and stripped off the leather clothes. She sank into the bath and gave into the sorrow that pulled at her heart. She bathed and rinsed out all of the dye from her hair, returning it with magic to its true color of silver before she rose and dressed. She picked at her food and finally collapsed on her bed.

Then she heard the singing. Baelios' ghostly arms came about her and became solid as he sang the same song Bael used to sing to her when she was upset. Giving into her sorrow, she cried herself out.

"He left you no choice, Ezra. He would have drained you, kept you weak and used you to gain Ammora's power, Ezra. You had no choice," Baelios said soothingly as he held her.

"I don't have to like it. Maybe this is why I was cursed, to the feel the pain and know—"

"No. You weren't cursed. Bael changed you to save you. In a sense you cursed yourself, but in his mind, he was saving you. He knew you would be able to make hard choices like these and yet still feel the sorrow of it. He knew you would be a beacon of hope in the darkness," Baelios reassured her. Ezra closed her eyes, oddly soothed as he began to sing again and, after a time, fell asleep in Baelios' arms.

"I almost failed." Ezra was sitting up in the middle of the night in her bed, having woken and felt unable to go to sleep.

"You beat him. And this time, he won't be back. Others will come, but you and I will defeat them together as we did today." Baelios was still next to her. No longer solid and back to his usual ghostly self, the spirit seemed determined to comfort her. As Bael would have.

"What if we can't? What if we aren't enough?"

"We'll find help, people who are willing to fight with you to protect this place as you do. You should rest and recover," Baelios soothed her, urging her to lay down again. Ezra laid back and after a long time, she fell again into a more restful sleep.

Baelios took up a comb as Ezra dropped off again and began to comb her long silver tresses. He used his magic to send her into a restful slumber as he sensed her starting to have a nightmare. He hummed a soothing tune, the same tune he'd sung to her before.

Inside of him, the Wizard's Council was arguing.

"Look at her, suffering more than those whose lives she took!" Egrid the Elf started in, amazed with what the woman had accomplished, yet disgusted by what he took as a sign of weakness.

"It's a sign of her strength and not a weakness," Bael argued back. "She suffers because she respects all life. To her all life is precious and she can't undo what she had to do today. She will accept what she has done, as she always has. But, for her, she feels the cost of it. She hates killing and always has. Who better to be our resident Sorceress than one who knows the difference between right and wrong, and the cost of the War ahead? She has fought many times as a mercenary Warrior. She's only starting to realize that she won't be enough and that she can't do this alone. She needs others, more than what we are. She needs people to trust and confide in, train with. She's been stubborn because she doesn't want anyone else to get hurt if it goes badly here, but she's starting to realize that things will go badly if she doesn't have someone else here with her. To be something more than what we can be," Bael told the others. The argument continued inside of him, heated at first, but gradually they came to a consensus.

Baelios chuckled as they continued to argue.

"The more things change, the more they stay the same, Ezra. We've both changed so much, yet you still feel the cost of the lives you take. He still argues that you are strong for it and sings to soothe you," Baelios murmured to her as his fingers ran over her hair and down her cheek before he put her brush away. He went back into his ghostly form and went up to the parapets to keep watch over the Castle so she could sleep.

Ezra was in the larger courtyard, working with Old Black on maneuvers and signals. He needed training and exercise to keep fit and she had found she both needed and enjoyed training with him. Training helped when she felt filthy inside and out no matter how much she bathed after a kill. She hated killing and hated the necessity of it at times.

Baelios is right. I know he was too dangerous to leave alive. He would've killed more and I have no idea how many he actually did kill in that temple, Ezra thought bitterly as she went through her latest maneuver yet again, rolling over Old Black's back while he was moving to land on her feet. Old black was coming along very nicely on her training and she felt they made as good a fighting pair as she and Baelios did with magic. Ezra didn't want to lose that possible advantage any time soon.

::Ezra, a visitor approaches,:: Baelios sent to her telepathically along with an image. Ezra smiled, recognizing Seila immediately from her clothing.

::I'll be right there, Baelios,:: she replied as she signaled for Old Black to come and get a treat. She slipped him a slice of apple and began removing his tack and brushing him down. "Well, Old Black, let's get you put out to graze for a bit. Least we were nearly done for the day, eh?" she asked with a chuckle as she continued to scratch his itchy spots and groomed him until he practically shone. Baelios appeared and took Old Black's reins to lead him to their "pasture," which was an overgrown courtyard that had very tall hay that had magically sprouted overnight and plenty of vegetables for him to pick at.

Ezra turned and walked through the labyrinth of hallways, cleaning herself up and magically changing her clothes from old brown leathers to a white leather tunic with light linen leggings. Seila was certainly a pleasant surprise! Ezra hurried her steps to arrive at the throne room just in time to walk up the many steps to her dais and sit down. She used her magic to detangle her hair and when she sensed that Seila was outside, she lowered the drawbridge and waited. Magic orbs lit themselves for Seila to follow and Ezra just settled herself, being patient as she knew this was Seila's first time here.

A few moments later, Seila shyly entered the hall and Ezra raised the drawbridge to keep out any potential enemies from following her in. She smiled kindly down at the farmer woman.

"Sorceress, I've come—"

"On the advice of a friend. Welcome, Seila, to Ammora Castle."

"Yes, I was told by Cara Ezroth, the warrior? She said if I needed help—"

"To come here and so you have. I've been expecting you. How may I help?"

"Well, I was wondering how the lady warrior knew of you, Lady—"

"Please call me 'Sorceress' for now. I am not a 'lady' for I am not of noble birth."

"But, how did she know you, Sorceress?"

Ezra looked down at Seila and telepathically examined her surface thoughts. The woman was honest, hard-working and would take a secret to the grave. Ezra made a decision and rose, walking down the long marble steps so that Seila could get a good look at her. As she drew near, Seila gasped.

"You're Cara Ezroth!"

"Actually, that's not my name, but please use my title. I use 'Cara Ezroth' when I go out in disguise. It makes things…simpler, Lady. You did a good turn for me by selling me Old Black when I was needed somewhere in a hurry. I'm willing to be of help to you in return," she explained with a smile, liking the woman and her up-front nature. Seila chuckled and returned her smile.

"You did me a bigger favor by taking him off me hands, Sorceress. He ate too much and was too rowdy! Er…where is he?"

"I've made accommodations for him here. Would you like to see him?"

"Yes, please!" Seila looked like a woman who was fretting over a babe and Ezra chuckled as she turned and motioned for the woman to follow. "How is he?"

"Quite well. I used to be a warrior before I became the Sorceress of Ammora. So, he's keeping me in fighting trim and I'm keeping him from dying of boredom. I think he's quite happy. He's groomed every day, has plenty to eat and plenty of training and exercise with me. Right about now, he's…ah. Here he is."

They turned into the courtyard turned pasture and in the center was Old Black, rolling in the grass like a silly foal! Seila took in the sight of him and laughed, looking delighted.

"You're right. He *is* happy!"

"Yes, he is. I told you I would take good care of him. He'll help me again should I need to leave the castle for a short while. And he keeps me company," she explained, not feeling that it was right to reveal Baelios' presence just yet.

"Why did ye leave the castle, Sorceress?"

"A messenger came to me and needed help with a situation in his city. A lot of people had disappeared and two had been found murdered. Anyone who investigated disappeared and all of the mages in the city had fled. I had to go and make sure that the people were safe. As it turned out, it was an evil Sorcerer, one whose eye has been on Ammora. He's been dealt with, permanently," Ezra explained as Old Black rose and trotted towards them with his tail up like a flag. Ezra chuckled and took out a sugar cube from her pocket and offered it to him while patting his neck gently. Seila joined in to pat the war horse, cooing to him as if he had been her lost babe.

"Good Ol' Black. I'm glad ye're happy," she said to the horse before the horse turned to trot back to the grass. He began to graze, and Ezra motioned for Seila to follow her again. "He definitely likes it here. I've never seen him so happy."

"I do my best to keep him occupied and out of trouble. He's made things easier for me here, in some ways."

"Ye're lonely," Seila noted. "Where d'ye get your food from?"

"I grow it here in one of the other courtyards. Enough to feed me and Old Black."

"What about in the winter?"

"I've shorted myself a few times when it gets really cold, but I do my best to preserve everything that grows, when I have time."

"Well, why can't I grow it for ye? We grow far too much food and we have no one to buy it from us! The nearest town is over a fortnight away and we can't eat everything we grow. We preserve as much as we can, but our stores are overflowing!"

"Why would you wish to help me, Seila? I was hoping to help you, but you haven't said what you need help with."

"That's what I need help with, Sorceress. Someone to buy up what we don't need for ourselves and…ye look like ye could use a friend," Seila noted as she tilted her head and looked knowingly at Ezra. Ezra shook her head and considered it.

::Baelios, what do you think?::

::She's right. You need a friend and we could use the help with our food supply. It was never intended for you to be completely alone. I try to be a companion to you, but I know I'm not enough. Don't turn what she's offering away, Ezra,:: Baelios advised her telepathically.

"Very well. How much do you wish to sell it for?"

"Five silvers should be fair enough for you and Old Black to get you through the winter and into the spring," Seila replied and Ezra couldn't help but chuckle at the look the woman gave her.

"I'll pay you seven silvers and I want assurances that you won't short yourself or your family. Do you have any children?"

"O' course! Two boys and a girl! Me husband and boys take care of the fields. Me girl and I, we care for the animals and house. I'll bring the deliveries to ye meself and should ye need more, all ye have to do is ask."

"Then we have a deal. Is your daughter like you? Trustworthy and honest?"

"She's practically me younger self!"

"Then bring her with you and I'd like to arrange for her to inherit your farm, if possible."

"Oh, that's exactly what she'd like. Me oldest boy wants to marry a girl whose father has no sons, so she has to inherit. Me younger son wants to go to the city and seek his fortune there," Seila explained, dimpling at the thought of her problems being solved in one go. Ezra gave a nod.

"Then that's what should happen. It'll solve your problems, and mine, quite neatly. When she weds, I'll host the wedding here for you. I have a courtyard that has so many flowers, it'll make a perfect wedding spot," Ezra told her as they made their way back to the main entrance hall.

"Oh, she's gettin' married next spring! She's engaged to a lad who's a younger son and won't inherit his father's farm. He loves the land and bein' a farmer as she does. They're a good match. Normally we'd just have the wedding i' the barn—"

"Nonsense. Bring them here to wed. I'll make it the most beautiful day. Let me know if you need more coin for her dowry," Ezra offered with a nod, settling the matter as she lowered the drawbridge.

"Thank ye, Sorceress. We'd pay for th' honor o' course—"

"I wouldn't hear of it. Consider it a wedding gift for them and a token of friendship between us," Ezra replied as she summoned a small pouch of coin. She slid it into Seila's hand with a wink. "Now, there's seven silvers for the crops at harvest that I need and a bit more to go towards her dowry and the cost of the wedding. Should bandits call, take this," Ezra slid a small necklace into Seila's hand, one set with a small stone from the Castle itself. "Just touch it and call for me and I'll come run off the bandits. If there's too many for me to fight, just come here with your family. I'll scare the wits out of them."

"Thank ye, Sorceress. How could I ever—"

"No need, my friend. Thank you. I look forward to getting to know you better," Ezra replied, feeling more cheerful than she had before Seila had come to call.

"And I ye. I need to get back. I'll see ye soon, Sorceress! With me girl next time!" Seila called as she made her way back over the drawbridge.

"Fare well, Seila. May the Gods shower blessings upon you and yours."

"Fare well, Sorceress of Ammora. May the Gods guard ye and keep ye safe!" Seila called back as she mounted her own palfrey on the other side of the drawbridge. Seila turned her palfrey towards the path and Ezra watched as they rode away, glad that she'd listen to Baelios' advice and her instinct to trust the woman.

When they were out of sight, Ezra raised the drawbridge and walked back towards the staircase that would take her to the library and the parapet above the crossed Unicorn horns on the face of Castle Ammora. It was getting late in the afternoon and Ezra was eager to get back to studying and to create a few new spells of her own.

That night, Ezra stood on the parapet again, looking out. The moon was full and lit everything up, tinting everything in pools of silver. She'd studied, but it had felt odd without Baelios coaching her. He had said she'd no longer needed such close guidance, but it still felt odd. She looked over the moonlit scene, thinking over the events.

"I know I can't do this alone forever and I certainly can't rely on Baelios for everything," she rued softly, thinking on how she might have suffered some of those "worse than death" fates he'd warned her about in the past.

"I don't mind taking care of you, Ezra. It's why I'm here, after all," Baelios said as he appeared next to her, his dusky blue skin and blonde hair making appear to glow in the moonlight.

"You shouldn't have to, Baelios. I'm grateful, please don't think I'm not—"

"Ezra, I never thought you weren't. You need people around, however. My presence should be kept a secret, but if you had had more help in Zethos, you might have not had to fight so hard to take out Maelcon," he pointed out.

"You were worried," she said as she saw how his expression had changed from cold and disconnected to one of ultimate concern.

"I still am. You can't not care for others and you can't not be cared for. You're too kind, loving and beautiful inside. Some, like Seila, see you and know that you're more than you seem because you are compassionate and caring. Others, like Maelcon, see you as a trophy to be displayed and toyed with before they destroy you. The years will be hard enough. Can't you enjoy the company of friends and companions, even if you know they'll eventually pass?"

"Yes, which is why I decided to be friends with Seila and her daughter. I want to build a friendship with them both.... for the future. You're right. I need friends and allies. I can't hide. I'll need friends, but I won't have more than that. It's too risky."

Baelios gave a nod and gestured for her to come back inside. "Let's go back downstairs. I have a meal prepared and some new reading material that you might enjoy rather than have to memorize."

"I'd like that. It's nice....to be home."

Chapter Three

"Ten years. How is it possible that it's been ten years?" Ezra asked as she looked about her throne room. Ten years she had been here as the protector of Ammora Castle. Ten lonely years.

"We've been busy," Baelios replied as he appeared next to her.

"Quite true. Three mages have come, all with varying intents. One Witch, who wanted to use the power here to find happiness. She was easy to help; we just helped her to find the missing piece of herself. After that, she went on her way. One Sorcerer, who just wished to see who was here and was glad that the power was being kept out of the wrong hands. And another like Maelcon, who wanted the power for his own. Mortals have come and gone, most just seeking something and thought that I could help them find it."

"Yes and don't forget the missing child you found for that Mother," Baelios reminded her. Ezra paused and felt that warm feeling she'd felt back then at the thought of their touching reunion.

"I'm just glad that I was able to help her find her son. I'd like to help more in the cities when I go out."

"How?"

"By seeing that orphans are given a place to build their talents. That they aren't kept hungry and cold. Those are most likely to become thieves. By giving whores a choice; that they needn't sell themselves for coin when they could give so much more to the world. By helping where I can, I'd like to help make a difference in Axrealia."

"You can't help everyone, Ezra."

"Yes, I'm well aware of that, Baelios. I know I can't save everyone. But I'd like to help, where I can. What else is this power meant for, other than to stand against the darkness? Perhaps by helping those who need it most, we'll keep the darkness--."

"Nothing will keep the darkness from coming, but we can make it less of a threat by making sure that those who need help the most are given it. I like your plan, Ezra, but we'll need to be careful how we go about it."

"I know, but we'll manage somehow. I think I'll need to make a few more disguises," she said with a sigh as she thought on it, then got up and headed down the steps.

"Where are you going?"

"To get started! Things have been quiet lately. Let's start making some new disguises and start…. traveling a little. Not a lot. I can make a portal to anywhere I need to go and be back in the same day or night. Come on. Let's go get started," Ezra called over her shoulder. Baelios laughed, the first laugh he'd ever made since they'd been together. Ezra turned and grinned. They stared at each other for a moment, then the laughs began. They turned and went upstairs to get to work, together.

As a team.

Ezra dodged and parried with the Sorceress who stood below. The mortal sorceress wasn't a match for Ezra, though she was quite good!

"Sorceress, I will be the one who defeats you!" the woman called from below.

"No, Perothia. You won't!" Ezra called back. Perothia growled and sent up a big ball of fire up at Ezra. Ezra shielded herself, blocking the spell easily before she sent down a spell of her own, one designed to sweep away Evil.

Perothia cried out, grasping the stone beneath her as the wind tried to sweep her away.

"I'll be back!"

"I'll be waiting!" Ezra chuckled as Perothia finally gave up and teleported herself out and away. Ezra leaned against the parapet for a moment, feeling elated and not worn down like she usually did after a battle.

"Fifty years has definitely given you more strength than you had when you were first changed, Ezra," Baelios observed as he appeared beside her.

"I'm not tired at all. Not even winded. How is that possible?"

"Perothia is perhaps the strength Bael was back when he was alive. You're stronger than both of them by far these days. Remember when you could barely lift the vase?"

"How could I forget, Baelios? That day, I felt as though I would pass out just from trying to lift it. Now…I know I could make it fly around the room without any effort if I wished."

"And you thought you'd never be able to master magic," he reminded her with an ironic grin.

"True. And I thought that I would never get used to being here. Or that I would ever be able to make a difference," she replied as she looked back out at the sky as she cleared away the sweeping spell. The sun came out from behind a cloud and the dead trees stopped their fearsome dance. For a moment, it looked as beautiful as it should be.

"You have made a difference and you'll make more of a difference in the years to come. At least I think so. You've helped children and women. You've helped people here and in cities all over Axrealia. And Ammora is still safe."

"Seila's funeral was beautiful yesterday. I'm going to miss her," Ezra said as melancholy rose in her again.

"She was a good friend. But her daughter has been a friend and her granddaughter adores you."

"And I adore her. It's good to see them happy," she said softly. "Well, let's go inside. I have more magic to go over and horses to attend," she said, shaking off the melancholy.

"It worries me that you push all of this aside so much, Ezra. You don't have to be alone."

"Drop it, Baelios. I'm not alone. I have you," she replied as she plopped down in her usual chair in the library and picked up a new book. This one was about magical constructs. She opened it and got absorbed quickly. Baelios sighed and allowed himself to fade again for the moment, worried that she was pushing too hard and not dealing with her sadness.

It hit a few days later. Ezra woke with tears in her eyes. For the first time ever, she just couldn't rise from her bed. Sobs wracked her as they had when she had first mourned Bael. With the loss of Seila, the loneliness again loomed and threatened to tear her heart apart.

Invisible hands touched her shoulders and after a few moments, she sat up long enough to bury her face into Baelios' strong chest. Normally he couldn't hold his form for more than a few moments, but today he was as solid as Bael had been when he'd been alive.

Fingers stroked her long hair gently and he hummed that same tune Bael had always hummed when she'd been faced with the weight of the lives she'd taken after a battle.

Ezra just took the solace for now, grateful as he held her long enough to sob herself out. He didn't insist she get up or do anything, but instead brought her soothing tea and comfort foods. She stayed in bed all day, just unable to bring herself to rise as she usually did. That night, she fell asleep after another bout of crying. Peace did come in this one's wake and the next morning, she woke and forced herself out of her bed. Tears fell again, but not as many as the day before. Baelios let her take her time and ensured that her horse was tacked and ready. Old Black had passed twenty years before, but he had sired a couple of foals. The one that Ezra had kept was a mare. She was as beautiful as her sire had been and called "Black's Get." The same shade of blue-black coat as her sire had been. It helped when the memories became too much to bear to have something familiar. Ezra mounted up, intending just to train when Baelios spoke.

"Why don't you take her for a ride outside of Ammora? Clear your head a bit. I'll be waiting when you return," he promised her. Where she went, he never did know. When she returned, he saw that she'd found a bit of peace within herself. Baelios surprised her with her favorite foods, favorite wine and a nice bath on her return. By nightfall, he saw that she would be all right and sighed a bit in relief. She would heal and continue on as he had known she would.

Ezra marveled as she returned home to Ammora. She had been gone just for a couple of days, but she had missed the sight of the Castle. She still felt melancholy whenever she passed Seila's farm, which now belonged to a great-great-great-great granddaughter's granddaughter. But when she came upon the sight of Ammora, she always felt a sense of awe.

"Five hundred years and I still feel like a novice when I return," she said softly to herself. She tugged on her horse's reins, Old Black's descendant. The stallion whickered softly, but moved along, plodding up the road towards the Castle. He was a calm one, and she had called him Stormsbane. It was ironic, because he could sit in a storm and just wait it out. She didn't care, nor did he. She lowered the drawbridge and led the horse across, relaxing as she crossed the threshold.

"Home."

Chapter Four

"C'mon, men! Put your backs into it!" Derik strained against the large boulder, helping to roll it away from where they were setting up their camp and into the moat. He and two others strained, muscles protesting as they shook long hair out of their eyes and pushed with all of their might. Finally, the boulder rolled over the edge and down the slope into the white castle's moat. Derik stared down after it, listening as he stared down into the darkness of what seemed to be a bottomless pit. After a few moments, he finally heard a loud crash as the rock hit the bottom.

"Not quite bottomless, but I'd hate to fall down there. Who lives here anyway?" he asked his fellow soldier, a man only known as Fao. Fao was tall and muscular with almond shaped black eyes and very dark skin. Otherwise, he was fairly unremarkable, but deadly with a sword. He chuckled and looked to Derik with an all-too-eager grin.

"Some woman. A Sorceress they say. She can't die, or so the tales claim. That can't be right, though. This place has been here for over a thousand years, but it looks brand new. Tall tales. Legends. Myths! Bah. Who cares! Tomorrow, I'm going to find me a nice servant wench in there to warm my bed!" Fao said with that eager grin that made Derik want to vomit. Derik was tall, but about a hand shorter than Fao. He was more muscular, all wire and sinew as he'd grown up with the sword in his hand from the age of eight. Before that, he was an orphan. He had long, curly red hair and blue eyes. He glanced around at their fellow mercenaries, all warriors from all sorts of races. Orcs, Goblins, a few Elves and a couple of Tribesmen from the Plains. Two hive warriors as well, though the humans seemed to fill most of the ranks. All scum, all from prisons.

All except Derik.

"You and your tall tales," Derik said as he looked up at the twin unicorn statues that formed the entrance to the castle. He shook his hair out of his eyes and began pulling it up into his customary braid at the back of his head. "Guess we'll find out for sure when we crack 'er open, hm?" Looking up, he thought he saw a figure standing at one of the windows, then it was gone as soon as he tried to focus on it. "Wonder if it's haunted."

"Who knows? No one goes in or out and those that do are said to never come out again. Maybe this Sorceress eats them!" Fao laughed at his own cleverness and Derik just shook his head.

"All I know is that mage, Juktis, is eager to get in there. He even brought a laser canon so we can break through that drawbridge if we have to. Anything that's in there is probably going to flee the minute we break in, Fao, and you know how I feel about raping prisoners. No servant girls, got it?"

"You take all the fun out of a good fight, Derik!"

"Just remember what I did to the last idiot that decide to rape and pillage in my scouts. No rape or there'll be no pay. Do it twice and I'll remove your genitalia with a rusty butter knife, just like I did to Sevin. Got it?"

"Got it," Fao grumbled as they went back to setting up the tents.

"Good. That goes for the rest of you. I catch anyone hurting an innocent and you'll be wishing you were never born," Derik reminded the rest of his scouts. His scouts grumbled but went back to their work. "We attack at first light tomorrow. I want everyone to get a good night's sleep."

Once their part of the camp was set up to Derik's satisfaction, they began to pass around the rations for their dinner and sat around a fire, joking with each other and teasing as soldiers often did. Derik sat alone, looking up at the white marble castle across the moat and wondering as he studied it. It seemed pretty but set in a dismal wasteland. Hard baked-clay ground surrounded it and a forest beyond the edges of that. The edge of the forest was pretty, but this part was pretty stark and bare.

Why would anyone build a castle in such a place? Derik thought as he ate his rock-hard biscuit and drank a swallow or two of water from his water-skin. He shook his head and went back to his tent and crawled in for a nap. At nightfall, he planned to stand watch. Most of his scouts were already sharing a wineskin. That meant a fairly sleepless night for him anyway. Derik draped an arm over his eyes and relaxed, trying to sleep.

* * *

Derik rose before midnight and went out to find his scouts had finally found their own bedrolls and gone to sleep. He shook his head and started his rounds, checking on things in the camp. He preferred to keep watch the night before a battle. His nerves were always too keyed up to sleep anyway.

Derik headed towards the sentry lines, or where sentries would be in most camps. Most of the other officers didn't assign them, so Derik ended up usually doing this job alone. He hated it, but there were precious few companies that paid as well as this one did. They had sixty men in their company and no women. Derik was just the head of the scouts, not the Captain, but the Captain did trust him more than most might have. Of course, Derik had saved his ass on more than one occasion. Derik smirked grimly as he walked around the perimeter of the camp, studying the Castle as he walked. It glowed blue in the darkness, practically pulsing with magical energy.

That's why we're here, I'll wager, he thought to himself as he walked. *What have I gotten into this time?* Derik continued to walk around the camp slowly, making sure they weren't taken by surprise in the dark by an enemy.

Around midnight, when he was thinking of heading to bed, he heard a noise. Most of the men were snoring and the Sorcerer's tent was dark. So far as he could tell, he was the only one awake and no one was really in any sort of condition to take over for him.

Derik turned, hearing the noise again. A foot fall. A cloaked figure was walking in the shadows around the camp. He barely spotted them as they were dressed to blend into the shadows as much as possible. Derik was used to battle lines, though. He hid behind one of the few boulders that was around the edge of the camp and as the figure passed, he tackled it.

The figure struggled, surprising him with a blow to the head from a metal quarter staff. He grabbed it, wrestled it from his enemy's hands and wrestled them down to the ground just as the moon came up from behind the castle. The stranger's face was caught in the light and he paused, stunned.

It was a woman. A beautiful woman with silver hair in a long braid coiled beneath her head and a young face. He grabbed her mouth quickly in case she tried to scream.

"Shh. I don't know who you are, but you picked the wrong place to be tonight. Tomorrow, we're taking that Castle. Don't scream. I'm going to let go of your mouth and you're going to tell me your name and why you're here. Understood?"

The woman was looking up at him angrily, but she gave a curt nod by way of reply. Derik slowly released her mouth and pinned her second arm back down.

"My name is Cara Ezroth. I'm a warrior seeking work—"

"There's no warriors around here. Other than this company and we don't take women in our ranks. Women are a distraction to these men. They don't respect women. They see them as only something to use or abuse, or to pay for sex. They're prison scum, released on the promise of gold and whatever they wanted so long as they served as mercenaries for this Sorcerer."

"Then why are you with them?" Cara whispered angrily, her eyes studying his as he spoke.

"The pay is good, even if the clients aren't. After this, I'm going to retire. I've had my fill of fighting," he admitted to her honestly, though he had no idea why he felt the urge to do so.

"And what if you're on the wrong side of a battle? What of the people you hurt in the name of your client?"

"I don't hurt innocents. Children and women are off limits and if I catch any of my scouts trying to kill or hurt anyone they shouldn't, I send them packing without pay. On a couple of occasions, I sent them without pay or genitals."

"How noble of you. What happened to their victims?" Cara whispered, still studying him.

"I gave them my pay to help rebuild their lives. Gave 'em their attacker's pay, too." He looked down at her, unsure of what was happening. Something about her made him want to tell her everything. Was it her beauty, or something else?

"Then you have more honor than the rest of the men here do. Who's your client?"

"Lord Juktis. Sorcerer. Don't know much else about him."

"Juktis? Don't you know how he got his power?" she asked.

"No."

"He stole it from other mages and killed them. He's committed atrocities across Axrealia to gain more power for himself. How could you stomach working for him, honest as you are?"

"It's good pay—"

"The pay isn't what's important. If he's after the Castle, he's after more power and he'll torture that poor Sorceress inside to get what he wants! You can't let him, Derik," she whispered, worry in her eyes.

"How do you—"

"Tomorrow, please...*stop* him! *Please!* Let me up and I'll go from your camp. You can go to sleep. There's no wild animals nearby and no one will stir from the Castle to attack you," Cara whispered, her tone showing worry and concern.

"I can't let you up."

"Of course, you can. You're the only one awake here other than me. Even Juktis is asleep. Listen. Everyone's snoring, but us," she pointed out. Derik paused and listened and realized she was right. There were no animal noises. Nothing but the sounds of snoring men.

"What about the Sorceress in the Castle?"

"She doesn't harm anyone unless she's forced to. Trust me. Let me up and I'll go, I promise."

Derik looked down at her, puzzled by the sincerity in her words. He rose, unsure of why he did it, and handed her back her quarterstaff.

"Go quickly. I'd better not see you here again."

"You won't. Thank you. Fare well...and may you make the right choice tomorrow." The woman turned and melted back into the shadows. Within a couple of moments, he couldn't even hear her foot falls.

"Fare well, Cara Ezroth," he whispered softly before he turned back to the camp. She was right. No one was awake, no one was stirring. There were no animal noises and his nerves had calmed significantly. He yawned and stretched and moved back to his tent. It was safe to sleep. He crawled into his sleeping roll.

All night, he dreamed of those beautiful ice-blue eyes.

Ezra turned and walked silently away from the man who had caught her. She'd allowed herself to be caught. It was easier to cast the truth spell on him and find out why they were here. Now she knew.

And it was one of her worst fears. Once she was back in the shadows, she hid herself magically from Derik and waited until he went to bed. Then she moved about the camp's perimeter, using magic and her wits to get a head count. Sixty-one. One Sorcerer, sixty fighters. She knew then that there would be no rest for her tonight.

She teleported herself back inside the Castle and magically changed into her white linen tunic and leather leggings. She added her headdress and white boiled leather armor that she preferred when facing an enemy and headed to the throne room.

"Baelios, we're going to need a plan," she called as she paced back and forth.

“This is a dangerous situation, Ezra,” Baelios stated as he appeared before her, watching her pace with his glowing orange eyes.

“Sixty-one men, Baelios. And one of those is an oddity. And I don’t mean Juktis. One of them is Derik. He’s an orphan I saved decades ago from the streets of Zethos. He still has all of his morals, all of the honor and pride that the Guildmaster and his teachers taught him. Yet he’s here with prison scum! He might lust for money, but he doesn’t allow the men under his direct command to rape or pillage. I don’t understand how he can be working for that sick bastard in that velvet tent!” Ezra kicked an empty bucket that she’d left in the throne room before she’d noticed their uninvited guests’ arrival. She growled and kicked it again, sending it flying in her frustration and anger.

“The odds aren’t in our favor, Ezra. You’re used to one-on-one duals with mages, or physical fights with maybe a small force. You’re not a one-woman army.”

“There’s got to be a way to hold them off, Baelios.”

“We’ll have to resort to some dirty tricks then. What will you do with Beauty?” Baelios asked, referring to her current war horse. Ezra stopped pacing and swore.

“He’ll torture her to death if he manages to get in. I’ll have to send her to the farm,” she said after a few moments of thinking. She needed to think, not react. She took a breath and thought on it. “I can use a portal to take her there. I can create illusions when I get back. What do you know about booby traps?” she asked him, a bit of a smirk gracing her lips.

Baelios gave a grim chuckle.

“Enough to know that I can build them while you’re gone. Be careful when you come back and watch your step,” he suggested as he disappeared. Ezra turned and went to go and get Beauty. She needed to hurry!

Half an hour later, Ezra banged on the door of Cephra, Seila’s descendant. The farm was passed down, by tradition, from mother to daughter. Cephra was the latest land holder here, and she was nearly Seila’s mirror double. Swallowing hard while holding Beauty’s reins, she waited as she used her telepathy to nudge Seila and her family awake.

The farm was dark and quiet, and Ezra knew they were usually fast asleep by this time. Normally, they would be safe. But, not tonight. Ezra tapped again on their door and sent another telepathic whisper, urging them all to wake. After what felt like an eternity, Cephra opened the door.

"Sorceress, what are you—"

"I need you and your family to gather what you can quickly. I need you to deliver a message for me to the Guildmaster in Zethos. Take Beauty with you. Hurry!" Ezra replied, giving no further explanation. Cephra disappeared back inside and Ezra could hear her waking the others, making them get up and get ready to go. A few moments later, Cephra, her husband and their three children emerged, the children still rubbing sleep from their eyes. Ezra began leading the way to their barn, where a new one had been built where Seila's barn had once stood.

"Zethos is a few days away—"

"I'm sending you by portal. You'll be there by morning when they open their gates. Please, Cephra, take this coin and just do what I ask. Each of you take a horse. Please, hurry," Ezra urged them as she took out a sealed scroll for the Guildmaster and her coin pouch. The family tacked up their horses and ponies, Cephra and her husband swung into their saddles while Ezra tethered Beauty to Cephra's palfrey's saddle ring. "There's an inn just a few doors down from the Guild Hall. Their food is good, their beds are comfortable. I'm giving you enough coin to get you all by along with the animals for a few days. I'll send for you when it's safe," Ezra told her as she handed over the scroll and the coin pouch and tucked both into Cephra's saddle bag.

"We won't let you down, Sorceress," Cephra promised.

"I know you won't." Ezra turned and made a portal that would take them to about three hours outside of Zethos. From the height of the moon in the sky, she could tell that there wasn't much time left before dawn. Cephra and her family rode into the portal and Ezra cast a spell on the animals, making sure none of them balked. When they had all gone through, Ezra shut down the portal and created another. She stepped through and back into the main entrance hall of Ammora Castle.

Ezra paused as she came through, watching where she stepped. True to his word, Baelios had set up more than a few booby traps. Ezra wound her way through them and began her part on this work, creating illusions that hid the illusions.

She was tired when she was done, but she was satisfied.

"That should keep all but Derik from being able to enter this place safely."

"Why Derik?" Baelios asked as he appeared next to her. Ezra didn't jump, she was completely used to him appearing and disappearing at will by now.

"Because he may be the key to turning the tide," she replied as she turned to go up to her throne.

"Good reason. There's still about two hours before dawn, Ezra. You should rest."

"No time for rest, Baelios. I'm going to dream walk for a little. Wake me before dawn, hm?"

"As you wish. Good hunting," Baelios wished her as she sat on her throne and leaned back.

Ezra smiled and winked.

"Thank you, Baelios. I'm sure I will."

Derik was lost in a green mist. In the distance, a white blob glowed with power. He turned, unable to find his way to it or from it. He turned again as he heard a chuckle.

"Cara?" he called.

"Yes, Derik. It's Cara. This seems a rather unpleasant way to be spending your evening," Cara replied as she appeared in her leather armor, leaning against a wooden post. She waved her hand and the mist disappeared to reveal the castle in the distance, pulsing with power, and moonlight shining down on the desolate surroundings.

"What're you doing here?"

"You tell me? It's your dream," she pointed out tauntingly to him as she studied him as he had studied her in the camp. He shrugged.

"What can I say? I'm clueless here. This castle…it seems alive," he told her as he looked at it, watching it pulse with power, almost as if it had its own heartbeat.

"Some say it is alive," she replied with a shrug.

"That's ridiculous. Castles can't be alive."

"Why not?"

"That's just in fairy tales."

"Maybe you're in one. Why are you here?"

"To do a job. Juktis wants this place taken and we've been hired to do it for him."

"That's why your fellow fighters are here for. Why are you here?"

"I don't know," he admitted, running his fingers through his long, curly red hair. "There's something about this place, though."

"It's very special. There's a legend that says it was created by a wizards council to protect against a threat to all of Axrealia."

"What's such a threat that could threaten the whole world?"

"I don't know, but maybe it's people like Juktis," Cara replied as she looked at the castle in the distance. Derik turned and watched her for a moment before she looked at him. "Haven't you ever wondered if you're on the wrong side?"

"Many times, but that's the job. We get hired, we fight, we get paid. I don't deal in politics," he told her as he watched the wind blowing through her long silver hair.

"This isn't about politics, Derik. Juktis is here, seeking power and he'll do anything to get it. You have a choice to make. You're a good man. I can't see why you would be willing to fight for a man like him."

"I told the Captain it was a bad idea, but…the Captain doesn't care. The highest bidder gets our services and Juktis had more than enough coin to promise the company just about anything the Captain wanted."

"Why aren't you the Captain?"

"Me? I'm nobody. Just an orphan with a conscience."

"Ah. But, maybe that's the difference, Derik."

"What? Being a merc with a conscience?"

"You didn't' say that. You said you were an orphan with a conscience."

"Why does it matter?"

"Maybe it does, maybe it doesn't. But, something's bothering you about this job."

"My gut doesn't like it. A woman living here, supposedly alone. It's not a fair fight."

"Fights are rarely fair, but you could change that by standing up to the Captain and his men."

"The Captain would just kill me and say good riddance. He calls me a pain in his ass every day I think."

Cara laughed at that, her laugh as melodious as a merry brook from his childhood.

"What's so funny?"

"I've been called that myself. It's nearly sunrise, Derik. Remember, one person can make a difference. They just have to try," Cara said as she faded from his sight.

Derik sat up and blinked at the light of dawn. His tent mates were up and dressed. They were putting on their arms and eating their trail rations. Derik rose and got his arms, having remained in his clothing from the night before. He grabbed his own trail rations and downed them, not tasting the bland biscuits they had daily.

"I'll be glad when this job is over," he told Fao. Fao tossed his long black braid and shrugged.

"Your conscience bothering you again, Derik?"

"How'd you know?"

"You were talking in your sleep again. Who's this 'Cara?'"

"Nobody. Just a figment of my imagination."

"No, I don't think so. But, maybe she's just a good lay, hm?" Fao laughed at what he thought was cleverness again. Derik shook his head, angry and disgusted at the thought of Fao touching that beautiful creature.

"As I said, just a figment of my imagination," he turned as the Captain walked out with his own armor and weapons.

"Scouts, get ready! Laser Canon, stand by!"

Juktis walked out of his own tent then and glared over across the way to the castle.

"Ammora is ours for the taking."

"Look, up there! It's a woman!" One of the men gasped as he pointed up at the parapets, where the twin Unicorn horns crossed. A woman, dressed all in white and silver, stood there with an orb in her hand.

"Ah, she shows herself!" Juktis grinned with sadistic glee as he stepped forward. "Sorceress, surrender and be shown mercy!" He shouted in a tone that made Derik's skin crawl.

"Never! Leave while you can, Juktis!" The lone figure shouted back. Derik's eyes widened a bit at the sound of that particular voice.

Cara? No! Derik thought, fearing for her safety!

"Not until I have all of the power of Ammora, Sorceress! And that includes YOU!" Juktis hurled a lightning bolt at the woman, who brought her arm forward as if she wore a shield. The lighting struck an invisible barrier at her arm and she replied by sending a bolt of energy right back at Juktis.

"You shall not take Ammora today, or any other day, Juktis!" She called back tauntingly as she raised the glowing orb in her hand. She tossed it up into the sky, releasing it. The orb rose higher and higher, then burst. A bright light flashed, and the orb was gone! Just as suddenly, clouds appeared above them and lightning rained down along with a freezing rain over the castle and the waste lands around it.

"Scouts, soldiers, attack! Laser canon, FIRE!" Juktis commanded and the Captain barked out orders.

"Seige engines, forward! Scouts, get up those ladders!" The Captain barked as a laser blast hit the drawbridge! Derik surged forward with the rest of the scouts, sending ladders that were folded up across the chasm and raced across as they had with many fortresses in the past. They started climbing up the wall, using axes and picks to make the climb as lightning streaked through the sky and thunder boomed over-head.

I'd better get double the pay for this one! Derik thought as he climbed, trying not to slip on the marble stone.

Ezra felt the castle tremble with the force of the laser canon's blows and looked below. She sent another spell streaking towards it, only for the spell to be deflected like a gnat by Juktis.

::Baelios, we're in real trouble this time!:: She sent telepathically as she tried again and again to get through Juktis' shields. Juktis only smiled coldly up at her and sent another spell up her way. She deflected it, barely, sending the flames he sent up at her up into the sky with a wind spell. On the walls below, she saw men grappling at the stones with picks and axes and watched as a few were blown away in the maelstrom the magic had caused. With relief, Ezra noticed that Derik wasn't one of them. Another spell made her rip her attention away and look back to Juktis.

::Don't give up, Ezra. Keep trying! Use as much of the Castle's energy as you need to; it's what it's there for!:: Baelios sent back and Ezra breathed a sigh of relief, then pulled more energy from the castle itself and tried again.

Wind picked up and a maelstrom swirled around them. Derik watched as several of his scouts were blown away along with others from the rest of the company. Fao hung on, barely, as did most of the others.

How is she keeping this up? he thought as he turned to see her exchanging spell after spell with Juktis below. The laser canon had splintered the drawbridge and some hooks had been thrown up to try to pull the bridge down.

The drawbridge didn't just lower, though, as Derik saw with surprise. The drawbridge resisted being pulled down! He looked up again at the parapet on the crossed unicorn horns and watched as the woman continued to batter Juktis' shields with stronger and stronger spells.

How can she be still standing? Derik thought as he took Fao's outstretched arm and climbed into what looked like a library. He had never seen so many books his life as he looked about in awe. Nothing was dusty; everything we neat, orderly and cared for. He looked around while Fao and the others charged down the stairs. A lone book sat out on the table, open to a page on, of all things, traps. "Fao, wait!" he cried only to hear sharp cries of pain from the stairway. Derik walked out, more carefully than the others had only to see his fellow mercenaries impaled on a trap! Fao was alive, barely, gasping out his last breaths as he reached for Derik. The sight angered him as he took Fao's hand.

"Give…that bitch…her…due!" Fao gasped before his eyes began to glaze over. A minute later, his hand went slack in Derik's and Derik turned his gaze to the sight below. More mercenaries had entered the castle and were wandering about, seemingly lost. Others were impaled on yet more traps or hanging from the ceiling like macabre dolls. They were dying by the score!

Derik turned and saw a staircase leading from the library up to the parapet on which the Sorceress stood and hurried up it. He could hear her voice and she was sounding tired. Grimly, he gripped his sword and moved out onto the parapet behind her.

Ezra was so absorbed with fighting Juktis, she didn't realize anyone else was there. She was getting tired and soaked to the skin to boot. She continued to fight, not giving up nor giving in to Juktis. The mercenaries had gotten the drawbridge open, but now they were facing the illusions and booby traps that she and Baelios had set up. They would have a very hard time of it until someone broke the illusions because she had designed them so they wouldn't see or hear each other, nor the traps until it was too late. The only one she had not allowed to be affected was Derik.

::The mercenaries are down by half, Ezra. Juktis hasn't bothered to break the illusions yet,:: Baelios' voice echoed in her mind. They had agreed he would stay out of sight until this was over. Ezra wouldn't give Juktis a single secret to carry away with him if she could help it.

::Good! There's still hope that we can win this then--::

::Ezra, look out! Behind you!:: Baelios shouted in her mind. Ezra winced and turned just in time to see a grim looking Derik coming up behind her.

"You have a choice, Derik! You don't have to work for this monster!" She exclaimed as she dodged another spell and drew out her retracted quarterstaff. Juktis' attacks were getting stronger, not weaker and she felt run down, even with the extra energy from the castle. She pulled more, trying not to take too much from the Castle. Ezra knew that Baelios would need that energy more if they won.

"It doesn't matter. It's the job I was paid to do," Derik replied as he attacked her, bringing his sword to bear. Ezra brought up her quarterstaff just in time to deflect the blow, hearing the ring of metal on metal. They began to circle each other in deadly contest, her attention split between him and the Sorcerer below.

"You can choose not to do this! You aren't like them!"

"Cara, you shouldn't be here!" He gasped as they struggled, blow after ringing blow traded between them. Down below, she heard Juktis laugh and realized the laugh was coming from inside the Castle!

::Ezra, Juktis is inside! Hurry, we have to keep him from breaking—AHH!:: Baelios screamed in her mind, making her hesitate as her head spun.

::Baelios? BAELIOS!:: she screamed mentally, unsure of what had happened as she whirled again, feeling Derik's sword grazing her side as she barely got herself out of the way of what might have been a killing blow to a mortal. Baelios remained silent as she sensed that while he couldn't die again, something was draining him.

Juktis.

Juktis was also draining the Castle. She could feel it, sense it as she whirled and kicked at Derik before running for the stairs. She fairly flew down them, then jumped past the buttons where a slew of mercenaries had met their end on a trap. She skidded down the last few stairs to the first floor.

Down below, Juktis had broken the illusions and the remaining mercenaries converged on her. A hand grasped her shoulder and forced her around. Derik's face was the last thing she saw as his fist collided with her cheek. Pain exploded in her head and she fell back with Juktis' laughter echoing in the halls and in her ears.

The woman went down, pinioned by his fellows after the final blow. Derik had won the day for them, but they had lost a great deal. Thirty-three men were dead, caught in traps that the woman had somehow managed to set up by herself. Outside, the thunder and lightning stopped along with the seemingly never-ending rain.

"Bring her to the throne room and chain her to the wall. I want to see her face when she wakes to her own defeat!" Juktis laughed madly as the Captain and officers carried the unconscious woman away. Derik watched, feeling sick with himself as the men began to cheer about him.

I don't know her! I don't owe her anything. But, why do I feel as if I've betrayed her? he thought as he turned to help the others with removing both traps and bodies. Half of the men left began to carry out the bodies and debris from the traps. The other half began to clean up the blood. Derik lost himself for a while in the cleanup process. Once the mess was cleaned up and the bodies were dumped into the waterless moat without ceremony, the men assembled in the entrance hall and waited for the Captain's orders.

"Good job today! Derik, you'll be guarding the wench when Lord Juktis isn't in the throne room with her. Reltus, you'll switch on and off with Derik. Since Derik looks dead on his feet, Reltus will take the first shift. Derik, go rest and report back in five hours for shift change." The Captain turned to issue more orders and Derik shrugged.

"See you in five hours," he said before he went to go and find a room to crash in. He wandered through the hallways, surprised at how quickly he could get turned around. Finally, he moved into a room that had a bed, a bathtub and nothing in the closet. He sighed with relief and closed the door and locked it before crashing on the bed with an audible groan.

He was so exhausted, even as upset as he still felt, he managed to fall immediately into sleep.

And still he dreamed of those ice-blue eyes.

Her hands hurt. That was the first thing she felt as she began to awaken. Ezra kept her eyes closed, sensing danger nearby through her telepathy. Thoughts washed over her, some so vile and obscene that she felt dirty just hearing them in her head. She pretended to be unconscious still, listening as Juktis gave orders to the Captain of the mercenaries.

Her arms were over her head. Her body dangled from something cold about her wrists. *Chains,* she realized as she hung there. Her feet didn't touch the floor. She was up off the ground, though she felt the cold marble wall behind her back. Using her contact with it, she carefully probed the Castle's energy and was dismayed as she saw the red drain of energy being fed now to Juktis.

::He's feeding on the Castle, Ezra. And on me,:: Baelios whispered into her mind.

::I see it, Baelios. How long have I been out?::

::An hour, maybe two. I'm not sure. He is planning to torture you to try to find out more about the Castle, Ezra,:: Baelios told her, his mental voice tinged with regret.

::I won't give him anything, Baelios,:: she promised as she studied how the Castle was being drained. It was being drained directly from the stones, but not from the source of power itself, hidden so deep in Ammora that Ezra herself had never seen it. If Ezra touched it now, Juktis would sense her wresting the power back. She dared not do that just yet. First, she needed to get loose.

::He's too close to you to try anything just yet. You'll need to wait, Ezra.::

::I know, I see him through the energy. Gods, he feels vile! Where's Derik?::

::Sleeping in the chambers next to yours, ironically enough.::

::Can you go into his dreams, try to talk sense to him?::

::Yes, but I won't hear you if you call--::

::Do it, Baelios. Do something! Please! I need a distraction, something, anything!::

::I'll do my best, Ezra. Stay strong. Think and stay alive,:: Baelios said before she felt his presence vanish.

Ezra listened a little longer before she finally dared to open her eyes.

Juktis, tall, muscular and very dark haired with crazy eyes that seemed to miss nothing was sitting on her throne. Her own ice blue eyes narrowed as she took in this sight. The Captain withdraw from the base of the dais and Ezra watched as Juktis casually turned to look at her with a wild smirk.

"Sorceress of Ammora, you have lost," he taunted her calmly.

"The game's not over yet, Juktis," she replied.

"Yes, it is. I have you. I have your Castle. You have no one to help you, no one to protect you. I will have your power and the power inside of Ammora. The Darkness will reward me well when it comes," Juktis told her as he rose and began to slowly walk down the many steps that led to the throne.

"The Darkness comes to destroy our world, Juktis. It won't reward you. It will destroy you as it will try to destroy everything else," she replied. Juktis laughed and leaned into sneer, his hand coming to rest on the stone next to her chained arm.

"I serve the Darkness because this world should be destroyed. I loathe it. The goodness of it—"

"Then why not ask the Darkness to take you to another world, Juktis? Or better yet, do it yourself with your magic? You're powerful enough. Why destroy everyone and everything?"

"Because I enjoy it, my Dear, sweet Sorceress. You're so sentimental—"

"And you are nothing but a cruel boy seeking to torment a pet!" she retorted, trying not to let him provoke her into anger.

"This cruel 'boy' sits on your throne, Sorceress!"

"As a wise woman once said, 'Without the right person to sit in it, a throne is nothing more than a simple chair,'" Ezra replied philosophically, trying to keep his mind on bantering with her than on seeking more power.

"And as my teacher once said, 'Never listen to a philosopher, they'll have you chasing your own tail!' So, Sorceress, shall we move on to the more interesting part of your captivity, hm?" Juktis asked as he reached up and removed her headdress and her choker. Ezra stayed calm. In the thousand years since she had first become the Sorceress, she had worked on her mental defenses. Even without the headdress, she could protect herself.

He dropped both to the floor and removed a single item from a pouch on his belt. A steel collar was shown to her and he opened it with a smirk and closed it about her throat. She heard the tumblers within the locking mechanism click shut ominiously.

"You and I will be getting to know each other very well, my dear Sorceress, and you are going to tell me everything, including your name," Juktis said softly into her ear.

"Never," she replied softly, feeling her anger boil just a bit and not daring to let it show.

"Never say never," he whispered as a knife appeared in his hand. He caressed it along her cheek, down her neck, then began to cut her through her clothing. Ezra screamed as he cut her in long shallow cuts that seemed to take forever. "What's your name, Woman?" he demanded.

"Sorceress!" Ezra replied, then screamed as he made another long shallow cut. Bit by bit, he cut through her clothing, revealing her body and rivlets of blood. He didn't remove the tattered clothes but left them hanging on her. He had cut her arms, her thighs, her feet and hands. He had cut her belly, carefully choosing each place before he cut it. Her breasts he cut as well, leaving several long red streaks across both of them. After an eternity, he stopped and leaned in, breathing hotly against her flesh.

"You will tell me your secrets, Sorceress, one way or another!" His hand closed about her throat and squeezed, letting her have very little air. Ezra gasped for breath, feeling her world narrow to just taking the next breath of air. "Your name!" He whispered into her ear, giving her a chance for a deep breath after what felt like another eternity. Her head was swimming with the lack of air and that one deep breath felt like a treasure as she took it. Then she felt it, his mind trying to worm into hers. Immediately she brought up her defenses, not letting him get a glimpse of any of her thoughts, her feelings. Nothing. He would sense nothing but a serene energy as she withdrew behind her own defenses.

"Cara, we need to stop doing this! I can't help you!" Derik shouted in his dream to the woman who looked at him accusingly.

"My name isn't Cara. Just call me "Sorceress," for now. Do you know what Juktis is planning to do to me?" she asked him, shifting to hop up onto a boulder and sit as he turned to look at the Castle in the distance.

"I don't know. It's none of my business," he replied sourly.

"Let's just say it's worse than death. But you can help, Derik. One person can make a difference here. Why do you refuse to believe it?"

"Because there's nothing I can do! I'm out numbered and I'm just a warrior!"

"You were taught by the finest Guild Master that Zethos has ever seen! Think, Derik!"

"How do you know about that?"

"Don't you remember me?" she asked as she disappeared along with the Castle. Suddenly, Derik was a little boy, starving on a winter's night in Zethos. Thinly clothed, no shoes, he was huddling next to bare stone, trying to keep from falling asleep.

A cloak fluttered across his cheek and a woman with a horse had paused. She was clad in brown; her hair was a dark brown but those ice blue eyes caught his attention as she knelt down to his level and studied him.

"I saved you. I found you starving and orphaned in the streets of Zethos," Cara's voice whispered to him in the dream as the woman smiled and picked him up. Next thing he knew, he was sitting on her horse and she continued down the alleyway, taking him somewhere. She paused and threw her own cloak over him to keep him warm and continued on. "It'll be all right, little one. By morning, you'll feel much better," she reassured him as she continued to walk on. The alley melted away and they were at an inn. Cara had given him a bath, the first he'd had in months and had gotten him fresh clothes. He put them on, suddenly nice and warm, though still hungry. Then she sat him down at a small table and gave him soup, cheese, bread and a small piece of fruit. "I clothed you, bathed you, fed you. I gave you the first good night's sleep you'd had in months," that voice whispered again as she tucked him into her own soft bed. She stayed with him, singing softly to him until he fell asleep, full and happy.

"The next morning, I arranged for your long-term life. Training with the guild, learning how to be a warrior. I made sure that you would want for nothing. Our world is in Danger, Derik," that voice whispered again as the scene changed from him being in the bed to being handed over to the Guild Master of the mercenary guild, Rethes. The old warrior clapped a calloused hand on his shoulder and smiled kindly down at him before it all melted away, showing the castle and Cara, this time in chains and hurt. "One person can save the world today, Derik. The choice is yours," Cara said softly before the dream ended and he sat up, a knife in his hand as he looked about, panicked.

He relaxed after he realized that it was just a dream.

"Gods, I need to get out of this mess," he murmured as he ran his fingers through his long red, curly hair. He got up and poured a bath for himself. He took his time cleaning himself up, luxuriating in the feel of hot water and soap after weeks and weeks on the road with the company. He took an hour, just soaking off the dirty before he used a cloth to scrub away the last of it, then washed his hair and got out to get dressed. He pulled on clean clothes and donned his weapons. His hair was combed and braided by the time he left his room and headed back towards the throne room.

He gave Reltus, a grizzled Orc with one eye and one hand a nod. The Orc tossed his black hair and gave a nod of his own as he left to go to his own rest and Derik turned to see Juktis and Cara.

Cara was against the wall, chained. Her clothes were in tatters on her body and streaked with blood from the cuts Juktis had inflicted on her. A steel collar hung about the woman's neck, marking her as property.

That made Derik's blood boil, more than the cuts and the treatment that the woman had already endured. What made that worse was that Juktis had his hands on her and Cara's mouth was open in a silent scream as tears streamed down her face. Derik's hands balled into fists as he leaned against the wall and tried not to watch.

Juktis finally lifted his hands from her, leaving her shaking in those chains. He was breathing hard and looked winded.

"We will continue this later, Pretty One. I'll have all of your secrets very soon," Juktis promised her as he turned to sweep out of the throne room.

In his anger, he didn't notice Derik.

And Derik's blood was boiling. As soon as Juktis was out of sight, Derik moved to where Cara hung. She lifted her head, jerking at first, then her eyes widened when she saw him.

"What in the hell?" he asked as he examined the collar about her throat, checking to see how it locked.

“He is trying to make me less than he,” Cara replied softly, her face calm despite what she was going through. Derik glared at it as he pulled a roll of bandages he kept in his belt pouch and began to dress her wounds.

“Why does he want you?”

“He wants Ammora’s power. I’m just a…fringe benefit, I suppose,” she replied coldly, her voice so soft he could barely hear it. Derik growled softly under his breath as he continued to dress her wounds.

Why do I have any feelings towards this woman? She isn’t anything to me! She might have saved me, but that’s it. It’s not as if she found me a family, she gave me over to a guild master. I can’t go against orders, Derik though angrily as he looked at her.

Then he was startled as he heard a voice within his own mind, one that wasn’t his own.

::This woman is the one you were destined for, Derik. Her heart is like yours, good and compassionate. Caring and honest. You must help her, for I cannot.::

“Who is that?” Derik asked out loud, startling Cara, who had looked away. She looked back to him, her ice blue eyes curious and yet filled with sorrow.

“No one is speaking, other than you, Derik. What did you hear?”

“A voice. One I’ve never heard before. A man.”

Surprisingly, the Sorceress chuckled, but sadly.

“He thinks you’ll help me to put things right.”

“Why would I do that? Who is he?” Derik demanded as he finished dressing her wounds and tilted her chin up so she couldn’t look away.

“One who is dead, yet not dead. Juktis is evil and nothing will stop him from hurting innocent people. From killing. He thinks you will help me to stop him,” Cara explained patiently, as if she were a teacher and explaining a difficult problem to him instead of being half naked and in chains.

“I can’t go against orders.”

“Then Axrealia is doomed. Juktis will seek to destroy everyone, everything, on our world. If we don’t stop Juktis here and now, all of our world….is lost.”

Derik swallowed as he looked down at her, then turned and walked back to his post. He said nothing else, heard nothing else. Cara looked away, closing her eyes and seeming to rest.

Derik began to pace, not able to really do anything but to while away the hours, thinking on what had been said and on what he had dreamed.

Chapter Five

Ezra walked through the hallways of Ammora. Bael was just ahead. She hurried forward, eager to stop the spell. Bael turned…

But it wasn't Bael. It was Juktis, standing there in his place and smirking at her as he reached for her. Ezra screamed, pulling back…

Ezra jerked awake, still chained. Juktis had been busying himself with exploring Ammora, but today it amused him to have her on a leash and chained so she couldn't move from his feet. He had gone to her library and was pouring through her books. She had been taken down from the wall last night, when Juktis decided to retire to her rooms. She had been chained, hand and foot, and leashed to a heavy table next to her own bed.

This morning, he had forced her to bathe in front of him, showing how well the cuts he'd inflicted on her had healed during the night. They had healed about halfway, but she could see the way he was eyeing her that he was looking forward to his next torture of her flesh. She was allowed only a tunic, no leggings, and the tunic had had the sleeves removed. It was of linen, and he'd ripped it in several places to show some of those half-healed cuts.

He wanted her displayed before the men. Her long silver hair had been brushed and pulled back, braided so that it hung down her back and coiled down over one shoulder. Juktis then had paraded her through the hallways so the men could see her. Now he had her at his feet, curled up on a cushion while he read her books.

Derik stood nearby, watching. Ezra looked up at him now and then, unsure of what she could do.

Juktis had begun to drain her power, in addition to the Castle's. Baelios didn't speak much, not unless he had to.

Ezra tried to read Derik's mind and found only anger at what he saw. He hated this. Hated having to watch while Juktis humiliated her.

That was something she could work with. Baelios had been trying whenever Derik slept. Ezra hadn't been able to sleep or concentrate enough to dream walk or astral project. She was growing weaker, but she wasn't done yet.

Vision of Darkness

Thus far, she had managed to keep Juktis out of her mind.

Now, she reached out with her mind while Juktis was occupied and touched Derik's again, this time sending him a vision.

Derik hated having to help guard the Sorceress. He was there to ensure she couldn't escape. His only relief was when Reltus took over for him and he could go to rest. Today, the Sorceress had been forced to wear a torn linen tunic, no leggings. No sleeves. Her entire body was practically on display. She'd been forced to do her hair as Juktis had pleased.

She hadn't complained, hadn't whimpered or whined. She seemed to be obedient and mindless.

Then she looked up at him and he could see she was anything but. Something was going on inside her head. She was thinking. Derik had been doing his own thinking and none of it he liked. All of it had to do either with going with or against orders. Thus far, he hadn't done so.

Oh, but he wanted to. Every minute of the day had become an agony of guilt.

Suddenly, he felt something touch his mind and then he was overwhelmed with a vision. All around him, the Castle was ruins. Everywhere he looked, things were burned, destroyed. Bodies. The world was dark, and everything reeked of filth and decay.

Just as suddenly, it was gone again. His eyes met those ice blue eyes of Cara's…and she gave a small nearly imperceptible nod.

She had shown him the future as it was now. What Juktis would do to the world if he was allowed to have his way.

::Derik, we must stop him. I can't do it alone. Please, help me,:: her voice echoed sadly in his head, showing her sorrow at what might be if nothing changed.

Derik had no way to reply. He wasn't telepathic, but he looked to her and just thought on what he wanted to say.

I'm just a warrior. I can't fight him for you, Sorceress.

She must've heard it. ::I only need a distraction, the right moment. I must strike at him before he becomes unstoppable.::

Derik balled his fists, frustrated and just tried to stand there as casually as if he'd heard nothing. After a time, Cara's head fell and she went back to laying quietly on her cushion.

"Derik, take the woman to the throne room and chain her as she was before. I'll be there shortly to question her again," Juktis said suddenly, sounding bored. Derik pushed away from the wall and began to take the leash from Juktis' hand.

"Yes, M'lord. Right away," Derik replied as he pulled Cara up roughly and began to escort her down the stairs.

Cara went quietly, to her credit. She limped her way down each step. He could see her cuts had begun to heal, but he could feel that she was struggling to walk with him. Derik kept a hand on her, keeping her from falling. Cara looked up at him, worry in those ice blue eyes of hers along with gratitude.

Once they were down to the ground floor, Derik released her elbow and slowed his pace, letting her take her time as they made their way back to the throne room.

Suddenly, the whole castle shook, and Derik was forced to grasp Cara and pull her to the side of the throne room. He shielded her with his body while the castle continued to shake. Nothing fell, nor did anything fall in. After several long moments, the shaking abruptly ceased, and Derik looked around.

"You get earthquakes often?" he asked her.

"No, and it wasn't an earthquake."

"What was it?"

A scream from the hallway answered him. Derik swore and secured Cara in the chains that hung still on the wall before he ran out.

Five mercenaries had fallen through the floor of the castle. Or at least they had partly fallen through. Derik looked in astonishment at the changed hallways. This wasn't the way they had been just moments before! Everything had changed, twisted themselves differently. And the floor had partly given out beneath these five mercenaries, only to reform around them before they fell completely through. Blood oozed from the trunks of the five now-dead mercenaries and Derik looked up as more of his brethren joined him.

"What caused that?" they asked each other, looking around themselves in astonishment.

"The castle, maybe. There's something strange about this place," Derik confessed, feeling uneasy suddenly as if the walls themselves would come alive to attack them next.

Derik slept uneasily now at night. Over the past several days, more accidents had happened. Only ten mercenaries, including himself, remained. The Captain of course was upset, trying to figure out what it was that causing things to change and kill his men.

At night, Derik kept dreaming of Cara, the way they had met. The way she had saved him.

By day, Derik guarded her in between sessions of torture. She was growing weaker and weaker and could no longer walk on her own. Now she had to be carried from place to place.

It made Derik sick to his stomach, seeing what Juktis was doing to her. Tonight, Derik paced in his chamber, unable to sleep. Next door, he could hear noises. Pressing his ear against the rock, he could hear Cara, groaning and pleading.

He could also hear Juktis laughing.

After an eternity, everything went quiet and Derik went to his own door. He slipped out into the hallway and hesitated outside of Juktis' chamber. He pressed his ear against the door and listened. He could hear Juktis breathing deeply, snoring.

And the sounds of a woman crying as quietly as she dared.

"This job isn't worth it," he murmured as he took out his lock picks and began to pick the lock. There weren't enough mercenaries left to patrol the hallways anymore. Since no one had come to the Castle to challenge Juktis, the mercenaries mostly worked and guarded by day and slept at night. Listening to the clicks as he picked the lock, he paused after a few moments and carefully tested the knob. It turned and he cracked the door open a little and listened again.

Then he pushed it open a little more and slipped inside before shutting it most of the way behind him. Creeping in, he paused to go to his hands and knees and crawled in a little further. There was a fire lit in the fireplace. In the bed, Juktis slept on top of the covers. He was nude as was Cara.

Cara lay beside the bed, not on it. She had pulled herself as far from the sorcerer as her chain leash allowed. She was hurt, naked and the smells in the air told him why she had been groaning and pleading.

Derik's blood ran cold and he crawled the rest of the way to her. She was a mess, bleeding from more cuts and scratches that Juktis had inflicted on her. Derik didn't waste time with the leash, but instead worked directly on the collar's locking mechanism. In no time, he had it off of the barely conscious woman. He hurriedly did the same to her manacles and shackles before lifting her up and carrying her out of the room.

He turned to close the door and noticed that the door closed itself silently behind him and relocked itself. He looked down at Cara, thinking perhaps she had done it.

No, she's too weak. I've got to get her out of here, Derik thought as he carried her back to his chamber. He slipped in and lay her down on the bed, then began to dress her wounds. Within a few moments, he had her wounds bound. Derik went and got warm water and a washcloth and began to clean her, trying to be gentle as he washed of her what he could.

"Derik?" Cara asked after a few long moments as he dried her.

"I'm going to get you out of here tonight," he told her softly. "Don't waste your strength. Juktis is right next door. I don't want him to know you're gone until morning." Derik went to his trunk and pulled out one of his tunics and a pair of his own breeches. They would be too big on her, but they would do for now. He returned to her and began to dress her.

"I can't leave. I'm bound to this place."

"Like chained?"

"No, magically bound. If you take me from here, I'll never recover. And Juktis will win," she told him, her voice shaking with the effort to speak.

"I have to get you away from him—"

"I have to defeat him. Here. Now."

"You're too weak to take him on—"

"Not too weak…to banish him. Need a distraction."

"Name it."

"We need to make him angry."

"Done. He's going to be pissed when he realizes you're gone."

"Then…you need to carry me back to him. In the throne room, preferably."

"He goes there every morning. That shouldn't be hard."

"You need to act…as if I ran away…on my own. You act....as if you…found me."

"Okay, done. Rest for now, Cara. I'm here. No one is going to lay another finger on you without going through me," he told her as he drew his sword and barred the door with a chair. He sat on the chair and leaned back. Cara sighed and curled up on the covers. Within moments, she was out.

::Well done, Derik.:; Derik startled as he heard a male voice in his head again. It was that same voice, the one he'd heard in the throne room.

Who are you? Derik thought back angrily as he looked around.

::I am the Spirit of the Council.::

What Council? Are you the reason why this Castle keeps killing the men I'm with?

::The Castle itself has been doing that, though I have assisted with it. My apologies, but we needed to get their numbers down if the two of you are to have a chance at winning.::

Why not just force Juktis and the others out? Why kill the men?

::The men we've killed are all killers themselves. To allow them to escape would be irresponsible. Justice must be served. There are only nine of them left and, from what I've seen in your memories, you're pretty handy with a sword,:: the voice replied, sounding almost cheerful at the news.

Yeah, the guild trained me fairly well in what I do. Picked up a few more tricks from these guys, though I can't stay with them anymore. I can't fight with them again, not after this. The Captain picked the wrong side. I told him I didn't think this was a good job, but he just...laughed and said to shut up, take the pay and this would all be over soon.

::Your Captain is no better than Juktis, but you are. Of course, swords will be of no use against Juktis. Tomorrow, make sure you get her close enough to Juktis that it looks as if you're about to hand her over to him. She'll banish Juktis. The Castle and I will do what we can to whittle down the mercenaries' numbers a bit more. You'll have to do the rest, I'm afraid.::

That's fine. I'm tired of watching these men just act as if she doesn't matter. No one should be treated as she's been. I wish...I could take it all back, stop them before they ever got in—

::They wouldn't have listened. Right now, all you can do is what you're doing now. Taking care of her, helping her to banish Juktis. Taking care of the last of the mercenaries. It's far better than I had begun to hope. Now, you should rest--::

Never could sleep before a big battle, Spirit.

::Ah. Well, if you'd like, I can bring you something to help you pass the time?::

Like what?

In answer, a book suddenly appeared in Derik's hands. Derik looked down at it and raised his brows in surprise.

It was a book of magic. Real magic. It almost tingled with power as he sat, cracked it open and began to read.

"WHERE IS SHE?!?" Juktis screamed as he stalked into the throne room. He had assembled the mercenaries, most of the those that were left. They had dropped to painfully few it seemed. The guard that was assigned to the Sorceress was also missing, he noted as he held the woman's head dress and choker as he paced back and forth before the steps that led to the dais above. He glared at them all, thinking about who might have helped her, who was most likely—

"My Lord! I found her. She must've gotten loose somehow," the guard said, carrying the wounded woman into the throne room. She was still nude, though no longer bleeding. Juktis snarled, seeing the Sorceress was barely awake, not fit to question.

"Bring her here! Now! I will chain her to that throne myself," Juktis commanded, his voice seething with rage as he glared down at his captive. How dare she think she could escape him?

The guard approached him, eager to get his reward. Juktis reached for the woman—

Her eyes suddenly snapped open and looked up at him—

"JUKTIS SEROS BANTHAMOS!" she cried! Blinding light hit Juktis as the castle began to shake. He dropped both of the items he'd been holding in his hands and screamed—

And found himself plunged through a gate into another dimension!

"NOOOOO!" he howled as he began to tumble through the timeless space.

There was a clatter as the items Juktis had been holding fell onto the solid floor. Somehow, Juktis was gone! Derik lay Cara down as her eyes rolled up into the back of her head. She had passed out again, and the Castle had shaken.

Derik turned, dreading what he might see, and almost gleeful for the price these mercenaries were about to reap.

Four more mercenaries had dropped through hidden traps onto spikes hidden beneath false tiles on the floor. Derik looked down at them, not feeling even a drop of remorse for them. They had chosen their path.

And he had finally found his. He looked to the remaining six mercenaries and wasted no time, using a two-handed pattern with his sword and dagger that they hadn't seen before. A dagger landed in the Captain's throat. Two more daggers were thrown as he parried and lunged with his sword, landing in the eye and throat of two more mercenaries that had begun to charge him. The last three he took out, bashing his elbow into one to knock him into one of the pits to his right while kicking one to his left to land into the other pit. The last went down as his sword plunged into the man's belly and jerked up, slicing him nearly in half. Derik turned, sheathed his sword and went back to Cara.

"Spirit, can you hear me?" he called out loud.

"Yes, Derik. I can hear you quite well."

"Is she all right?" he asked as he knelt over Cara and began to check her. Worry and dread filled him now. What if she died?

"She's immortal, Derik. She won't die. She will recover. The chamber Juktis took for himself is her chamber. Take her there, give her a bath. Put her to bed. Her clothes are in the closet. I'd suggest putting her in her night gown. She's gone into a deep sleep, a healing trance if you will. It'll be a few days before she wakes again, but she will wake. She'll need care when she does, but she will be all right."

"Thank the Gods. What about the bodies?"

"Those can wait until she's been tended to. I'm afraid that I won't be able to help you with the clean-up. Juktis drained too much power from us."

"Is he really gone?"

"For now. Unfortunately, where she sent him won't be able to hold him forever. We'll be lucky if it holds him for a few months," the invisible Spirit replied regretfully.

"Great," Derik muttered as he lifted Cara up again and turned to carry her away from the throne room. Something caught his eye and he leaned down, then picked up her jewelry from the floor. Juktis had dropped it. Maybe having it back would help her, somehow. “Let’s go get you cleaned up and to bed,” Derik said softly as he carried her away from the carnage.

Chapter Six

Ezra woke slowly, feeling her body still aching as it had when she had first been changed. But, the pain itself was far less than it had been when she last woke. She felt a warm blanket over her move as she shifted and looked up at her own ceiling in her chambers.

::Baelios?:: She called telepathically, not sure if it was safe to speak out loud yet.

::It's safe, Ezra. Juktis was banished and the mercenaries are gone. Derik cleared out the last of the mercenaries and he's been tending to you while you recover,:: Baelios replied as his ghostly image appeared next to her. She looked up at him, relieved to see that he looked like his usual self.

::I can see you are no worse for the wear. How are you feeling?:; she asked him, feeling worried that something Juktis had done would have hurt him.

::Better than I was. A little weak still, but nothing that time won't solve. Your wounds are nearly healed, but you may be weak yourself for a time. No magic for a few days, not until we're all feeling more like ourselves again,:: Baelios told her. Ezra gave a weak chuckle and nodded.

:;Don't worry about that. I feel like I did when I couldn't lift that vase one more time,:: she replied, remembering those early days. ::You said Derik has been tending to me?::

::Yes. I think he wants to atone for what he did. He's been exploring the Castle, which has gone back to normal. Well mostly. Juktis drained the power source down to the lowest it has been in centuries, but…he didn't get it all. The power is already beginning to replenish but the Castle feels like it feels like us; weak as infants,:; Baelios replied with a wink and a cheerful smile.

::You're rather cheerful, for a spirit that was nearly drained to nothingness.::

::Yes, well it's nice to have someone else around to talk to.::

::You're still talking to him?::

::Of course--::

::What have you told him, Baelios?::

::He calls me 'Spirit', for lack of a name. I haven't told him names or given him any information he wouldn't have gotten from one of the myths. Though I told him the Castle is responsible for whittling down the mercenaries…and that I helped it. That is all. Well that….and that you're immortal--::

::Baelios, you shouldn't have told him any of that!::

::If he's going to stay, he should know.::

::No, he's not going to stay. If he wants to atone, he can go to a temple—oh!:: Ezra tried to rise too soon and felt a flash of pain in her abdomen. She lay back, groaning softly in pain and silently cursing as she waited for it to subside.

::He's coming down to check on you now. No getting up! You're not ready to get up and walk just yet. Juktis--::

;:Juktis would have killed me if he could have. Yes…I'm well aware. He raped me too, as you're also aware I'm sure.:: She replied, snapping a bit at the Spirit.

::I'm sorry and yes…I know.;:

;:Thank goodness immortals can't have children.::

::What makes you say that? Immortals have been having children since the dawn of time.::

::Who told you that?::

::Bael knew a few immortals. Several of them had had quite large families.::

::Do I need to worry about getting pregnant, Baelios?::

::Maybe Derik should fetch a healer.::

Ezra began to bark at him telepathically again only to be interrupted when the door opened and Baelios vanished. She lay back again, feeling sullen at the Spirit's candid manner as Derik approached her with a tray.

"You're awake," he said, grinning at her with almost rogueish charm. He had bathed, his hair was braided neatly behind his head. His clothes were different, clean from the last set he'd worn. He had shaved off his beard and mustache as well and she found herself looking up at a very different face. "What's wrong?"

"Nothing. You're very handsome without the beard and mustache," she admitted, trying to remind herself that as soon as she was recovered, he would be leaving.

"I made broth. I've been spooning it into you while you slept. But, if you want something better, I made bread and stew."

"Broth is fine. I don't think I could handle anything richer right now. How long was I out for?" she asked as he put the tray across her lap. She reached for her spoon and began to eat, feeling the spoon shaking in her fingers.

"Let me. You've been out for about a week. The Spirit said you needed more time to heal than he had thought, but he said you'd wake up. I'm glad to see he was right," Derik grinned at her as he took the spoon and began to feed her. Ezra didn't argue and just let him baby her a little, suddenly glad that he had remained behind. In her state, she wouldn't have recovered if she'd just lay there on the cold marble. Baelios was weakened and wouldn't have been able to help her either until it was too late. She would've slept on, forever perhaps.

"So, what have you been doing while I've been asleep?" she asked after the broth was gone. She lay back, feeling weaker than she could ever remember being after a battle. But she was warm, dressed in her favorite nightgown and clean.

"Well, mostly I've been taking care of you. I also explored the Castle some more. Been reading quite a bit too. The Spirit gave me a book to read on Magic Basics. It's been…interesting," Derik admitted as he put the tray aside and returned to sit next to her on the bed.

"Has it? Well, I think I have some gold to pay you in one of the rooms. You can be on your way if you'd like—"

"Where would I go? You're in no condition to fight if anyone else comes up here anyway. I'd…like to stay, if you don't mind."

"Derik, you don't have to atone. You've done enough. I'll give you enough gold that you can retire as you wanted—"

"I…don't want to go, Cara," he admitted, looking rather sheepish.

"You don't know what you're asking. Most of the time, it's very quiet here. Boring most of the time. I can't leave. There's no one to pick up the burden that I put down and besides, I am magically bound to this place. I can't ask anyone else to subject themselves to the life I have to live—"

"Which means that you could use a friend. And what's the harm in having a warrior around in case someone else like Juktis shows up?"

"Derik, I—"

"I don't want to leave. Please, don't make me leave you. I feel bad enough about what that monster did to you as it is," Derik said, his tone suddenly both soothing and worried. Ezra felt the fight drain out of her as she looked into his sad eyes.

"Very well. You may stay for as long as you'd like," Ezra said after another moment or two and lay back against her pillows.

"Thank you. I'll make up to you everything that I did—"

"You have already done that, Derik. You kept him from subjecting me to a fate worse than death."

"I didn't stop him from raping you. Or from torturing you—"

"No, but you helped me to banish him and end his evil for now. He'll escape, sooner or later. But, for now, we have time. And that is a precious thing."

"Time for what?" Derik asked.

"To prepare for when he does return. Do you still wish to help me?"

"Of course."

"Good. I think we will manage to be a good team then," Ezra started to say, only to pause to yawn.

"You should get some rest," he said softly as he reached to pull a long strand of her hair out of her face.

"I've been asleep for days, but I feel like I just can't keep my eyes open," Ezra admitted.

"You've been through a lot. Go back to sleep. I'll be here when you wake up again, Cara."

"My name is Ezra, actually. Cara is the name I use…when I go out in disguise."

"Nice to meet you, Ezra," Derik said softly as he rose and picked up a book from her nightstand. He sat in a nearby chair and began to read. Ezra let her eyes close, content to retreat into a more restful sleep.

"Hey, you shouldn't be up so soon!" Derik said as he came in with another tray, only to find Ezra pushing herself, with real effort, out of bed. He put it down and rushed to her as she began to straighten up and grasped her elbow just as she sank back down again.

"Yes, I should. I need to see the rest of the Castle and make sure that everything is back to normal. I need to get to the library. I can't take another day of resting, Derik," she replied somewhat sourly, still feeling sore as she again pushed herself up and managed to stay up this time.

"You're shaking like a leaf, Ezra—"

"It will pass. I want to get dressed and to get around the Castle and check things," Ezra insisted as she took one trembling step after the other towards her closet. She managed it and grasped onto the edge and picked up one of her usual outfits, a tunic with leggings.

"I'll help you—"

"I can manage, Derik. But, thank you," she said, trying not to snap at him as she leaned against the edge of the closet and began to change into her chosen outfit. She managed to get the leggings on and drew off her night gown. Leaving that on the floor, she pulled on her tunic and turned back to him. "I'll have to make a new head dress—"

"No, Juktis dropped yours. Here, but…you don't have to wear it today. You could just go as you are," Derik offered as he picked up her throat guard and her head dress and brought both to her.

"Thank you," she said, relieved that she wouldn't have to re-forge something that had been a constant for the past thousand years of her life. She picked them up, one at a time and put them back on, and closed her eyes. It made her feel better, stronger inside just wearing them again. Granted, it wouldn't last for long, but Ezra needed familiarity today.

Of course, having Derik right there was the exact opposite of familiar, but she would adjust. Deep down, she knew he wouldn't leave. She was starting to want him to stay.

"I just want to see the rest of the Castle, Derik. After that, I'll rest. I'll read a book or nap, but I want to see the rest of the Castle. Please. I need to," Ezra explained, feeling calmer now that she knew she was protected again.

"All right. You should eat first—" Derik turned to pick up the tray, which had vanished. "Where'd it go?"

"It's probably in the library. It's where I usually take my meals. The Spirit moved it. He has his own way of doing things here," she explained, glad to see the first signs that Baelios was doing better.

::I knew you'd rather be up if only for an hour or two, Ezra. It's in the usual spot and I'm bringing something up for him. It'll keep until you've finished your inspection of the Castle, but keep it brief. We're all still very weak,:: Baelios sent wearily into her mind.

::Thank you, Baelios. We'll be along shortly,:: she replied before she offered her arm to Derik, who took it.

"All right, but brief. If you get tired, I'll carry you," Derik said as they began to walk.

"I'm glad to see that the Castle came through as well as it did. No wonder I still feel so tired, though. All of the magic I would be using to recover is going into repairing the Castle," Ezra said as they made their way up the stairs and into the library.

"The Castle moves and repairs itself?"

"It's alive, Derik. Of course, it does," she replied. "Just as our bodies move, just as our bodies repair the damage done to it, within reason. The Castle can do the same. It can't defend itself, which is why I'm needed here." Ezra lowered herself into her usual chair with real effort to keep from just falling into it and looked to her tray. There was a second tray, straight across from hers.

"What's this?" Derik asked as he looked to the second tray, curiosity and a bit of wonder on his face. Ezra chuckled, remembering how she had felt her first days here.

"The Spirit thinks you should join me. Sit down, enjoy," she replied as she picked through the books that were still on the table. A moment later, the one she had last been reading flew from the shelf to land beside her while the others lifted up and put themselves away. Derik sat, looking around himself again before he turned back to her. Ezra lifted her spoon, saluted him, and tucked in, reading quietly as she ate. She was already tired, having gone through as many rooms of the Castle as possible with Derik. Even so, she was glad she'd inspected as much as she had. The traces of the invasion were disappearing as were the traces of blood. The bodies had been disposed of in the moat. By Spring, only bones would be left. Derik took a book from off of the table that had a piece of red ribbon in it, opened it and began to read.

For a time, they just sat, eating and reading. Though Ezra noted he kept stealing glances at her from over the pages of his book. She of course was caught doing the same and they both chuckled after a little while.

"I hope you don't mind that I've been borrowing your library," Derik said sheepishly as he ran his fingers through his long red hair.

"Not at all. No knowledge is ever wasted. I'm rather glad to see that you share that same appreciation. Which book are you reading?" she asked as she put aside her own book. It was one Ezra had read before anyway.

"The Basics of Magic, Volume One," Derik said as he lifted the book so she could see the cover. Ezra chuckled.

"That was the first book of Magic I ever read. Why did you choose that one?"

"I wanted to understand more about you. About magic. About why this place is like it is."

"And now you know at least part of the answer," Ezra tilted her head to look at him. "What do you think about all of this?"

"I'm not sure yet. But I want to make up for my mistakes. I shouldn't have helped them."

"We all make mistakes, Derik. It's learning from those mistakes that's the hard part. Would you do it again, now that you know what the consequences would be?"

"Of course not!" Derik's voice was vehement, and Ezra found herself rather impressed with the change that had come over him.

"Peace, Derik. I only meant to point out that you have learned from this experience. What would you do differently?"

"I'd have helped to kill them."

"Well, you did that. What else?"

Derik took a moment and Ezra watched him, knowing he was puzzling out what he would have done differently. She could feel him thinking it over, looking at the problem from a new perspective.

"I would've cut Juktis' throat and thrown him in the moat. I would've killed the Captain and taken over so I could tell Juktis to leave you alone or risk facing all of us," he replied after a little while.

"Juktis is immortal. I sensed it the moment he touched me. He's easily more powerful than I am and, unfortunately, he's going to be back. Of that I'm sure. He would've killed you all if you'd gotten in his way or withdrawn and hired someone else. But I'm glad that you now see why I tried to get you to help me," she said gently to him, not wishing him to feel badly about his choices.

“I had a choice—”

“And you will again. And again, if you stay. Even if you go. There will always be choices and it’s learning how to be strong enough to do the right thing that is the tricky part of our lives,” Ezra told him, keeping her voice gentle.

“I will stay, as long as you’ll let me, Ezra.”

“You may stay as long as you wish, Derik. And if you wish to ever leave, just say so and I’ll see you off with my blessing.”

“What if I never want to leave?” Derik asked, a wry smile tugging at his lips.

“You will, one day. Until then, I’ll enjoy your company.”

He chuckled and leaned in closer.

“I have a feeling that I will enjoy yours. If you’re finished eating, I’d like to get you back to resting. Want me to bring some books down for you?”

Ezra had lifted her hand to stifle a yawn and shook her head.

“No, thank you. But, if you’d like to walk me back to my Chambers, I probably could use the help. I’m not as strong as I usually would be,” she said with a bit of frustration in her voice.

“You will be. Come on. I’ll clear the—hey!” He turned just in time to see the dishes whisk themselves back out of the room. He turned back to her and said, “Let me guess...the Spirit?”

Ezra was hard put to keep from laughing.

The sun was setting. Ezra stood on the parapet, having gone out for the first time since Juktis had been banished. It had been several days since she’d woke up and each day, Ezra felt stronger. Ezra held out a hand, a small scroll sitting within her palm. She whispered softly to the scroll, then smiled when it reformed into a dragon fly and took off, heading in the direction of Zethos. The construct would turn back into a simple scroll once it reached its destination.

“What’re you doing out here?” Derik asked as he came out to join her.

"Enjoying the sunset. Isn't it beautiful?" she asked him as she swept her hand out. Down below, the waste land was turning colors, the shadows were growing longer and longer. Up above, a pair of falcons circled high up in the sky, looking for prey. "I rarely see birds or any living creatures so close to the Castle. It's a rare treat for me," she explained as she watched the pair swoop and circle.

"I didn't think about that when I came here. How long have you been here?"

"Over a thousand years."

"Don't you get lonely?"

"Yes, but my responsibilities keep me busy. And I occasionally get visitors. Some more welcome than others," she explained, reflecting for a brief moment on her life. "The Spirit helps, though at times he…" her voice trailed off as she felt that grief touch her yet again.

"What's wrong?"

"I was married once, before I became the Sorceress here. He died," she explained, not giving further details. As much as she wanted to trust Derik, she didn't care trust him with all of her secrets. *He doesn't need to know,* she thought, realizing that unburdening herself might only burden another.

"I'm sorry for your loss."

"It was a very long time ago. But, thank you," she replied after a long moment.

"You should come inside and rest. You've been pushing yourself today."

"I'm just trying to get back into my routine," Ezra replied, chuckling softly.

"Training, reading, gardening? That's all in your routine?"

"I told you that my responsibilities keep me busy. If I don't train, my muscles will become weak. If I don't use magic, my mastery of it will waver when I need it. Reading gives me knowledge and keeps my mind sharp. And the garden is for two reasons: to eat and for herbs for spells. Now, any other questions about what I do in a day?"

"How do you do it all?" he asked with a smirk.

"The days are long when you're alone."

"You're not alone anymore. And I've been thinking. If Juktis comes back, he'll come back with an army. We should get more people to help keep this place safe. The more people, the less of a target you'll be."

"True, Derik, but I can't have just anyone here."

"So, we select the most honest ones."

"And how would we find them?"

"I was hoping you'd be able to help with that."

"I'll consider it, Derik. But I can't promise anything," she replied as they began to walk back inside.

Over the day, a new routine took shape. Ezra would rise and find that Derik had breakfast ready in the library for her. They would read until mid-morning, then would go downstairs. Once Ezra felt up to training, she'd taken it up again in her usual spot in one of the courtyards. To her surprise, Derik was already there. Now they had begun to train together daily and Ezra had been glad for it. Her fighting skills had begun to suffer over the centuries.

"Where did you learn to fight like that?" Derik asked, panting as they both put their weapons away.

"I was brought up as an orphan in a temple that was devoted to a Warrior Goddess. The priestesses there taught me."

"Which temple?"

"One that isn't there anymore. When I was twelve, we were attacked. I was the sole survivor and it was because one of the priestesses hid me before our attackers broke in. Once I was sure they were gone, I came out to find my friends, my teachers and the only parents I ever knew slaughtered," she replied stiffly, blinking back a few tears that had come to her eyes.

"Ezra, I'm…. I'm so sorry," Derik started. Ezra held up a hand and gave him a small smile.

"It was a very long time ago. There's no need to be sorry for something that happened long before you were ever born, Derik," Ezra reassured him with a small pat to his shoulder before they went back inside. "Tomorrow I have to go to see someone just beyond the forest. Would you like to go with me?" she offered, knowing that Cephra and her family should be back by now.

"I'd love to," Derik replied warmly as they headed back inside to get ready.

"Sorceress, thank the Gods you're safe!" Cephra exclaimed before Ezra could even knock on the farmhouse door. The walk from the Castle through the woods had been relatively uneventful. Derik had kept quiet during the walk and she just found she was beginning to enjoy his company. The plump woman threw herself on Ezra, giving her a bone-breaking hug that left Ezra breathless before turning to Derik. "And who be this?"

"Cephra, this is Derik. Derik, this is Cephra. Her family owns this farm," Ezra explained as Cephra studied Derik with her hands on her hips.

Derik bowed to the woman with a warm smile.

"My Lady, the pleasure is mine," he said while he was still deeply bowed. Ezra couldn't help but laugh, watching this attempt at courtly manners with a farmer!

"Tish! I'm no lady, just a farmer! Come along. I got your message and I think you'll be pleased, Sorceress," Cephra said as she came out and began to lead the way to the barn in the back. Ezra brightened and hurried her steps, eager to see Beauty and to see what Cephra had found for her. "I 'ad that nice Guild Master you sent us to help me to pick 'im out—"

"He's a good judge to go by, Cephra. I trust his judgement. So, you were well-treated by him and by the inn?"

"Very well treated, Sorceress, thank ye. We're glad to be back in our own beds all the same, o' course."

"Well of course you are. No place like home," Ezra agreed with Cephra as Cephra opened the barn door for them. Ezra stepped in and gasped at the sight of Beauty and a very handsome black stallion!"

"The stallion's name be "Dark Lightnin," Sorceress. He's been trained to carry, but not to fight," Cephra said as Ezra walked straight over to the Stallion's pen. Beauty neighed at the sight of her and reached out to nudge her arm with her nose.

"Easy, Beauty! I'll be right with you," Ezra giggled, pausing to scratch the mare between the eyes as the stallion turned to look at her with one intelligent eye. "Oh, Cephra, he's beautiful," Ezra breathed as she undid the gate and walked into the pen with the stallion. "I think he'll suit Derik quite handsomely, don't you?"

"Aye, M'lady! Quite handsomely."

"What? I don't know much about horses—" Derik started, clearly surprised at the sight of the pair of warhorses.

"I'll teach you, Derik. Don't worry," Ezra said as she began to put the stallion's tack on. Within a few moments, she had him saddled and ready and handed the reins to Cephra to lead out as she slipped in to give Beauty a few scratches before doing the same for her. Ezra led Beauty out herself and motioned Derik to come closer. "Come on, Beauty is as gentle as they come. She won't let you fall and all you have to do is hold the reins. I'm going to ride Dark Lightning so that I can see how much he knows and how much he'll need to learn."

"I'd rather not—"

"And I'd rather not take all evening to get home, Derik," Ezra replied a little sharply, and tried to rein in her own temper. "Now, up you come," she coaxed him, grasping his hand and putting one hand on the saddle horn. The other she put on the back of the saddle and then she leaned against him, making him bend a knee. Derik sighed and put his left foot into the stirrup and hauled himself up as he swung his leg over. "Very good. Here's the reins and just relax. Beauty will follow me home, don't worry," Ezra said as she slipped around to go to the stallion. She paused and slipped some extra coins to Cephra in thanks and gave the woman a hug. "I'm so glad you're all back safely," she murmured to the woman before she mounted the horse.

"We're all glad that you're safe, Sorceress! We'll see you in another moon or so!" Cephra called as the Ezra gently nudged the Stallion to get him moving.

"See you in another moon, Cephra! Let me know if you need anything," Ezra called back as she turned to wave before whistling.

Derik jumped a little in the saddle as Beauty began to move and Ezra couldn't help but laugh at the surprised look on his face.

"I can't do this!" he called, looking rather disgruntled.

"Of course, you can! You just haven't tried! Hold on with your knees and relax! We're just walking!" Ezra called as she turned her gaze forward and towards home.

Chapter Seven

Ezra looked back to Derik and slowed the stallion down, having him walk beside Beauty as they rode.

"There we go, much better. He takes a rider very well. When I'm done with you both, you'll be able to ride him and fight on him without losing your seat," Ezra told him, giving him one of those dazzling smiles that made his heart skip a beat.

"That's easy for you to say! I don't know anything about horses! I always wondered how skirmishers managed to stay on their horses and fight," Derik admitted. They were back in the forest, the living part of it and Derik still wasn't sure how she managed to sit such a big horse so lightly. "I feel like I'll fall off any moment."

"Beauty wouldn't let you. I promise. Relax. Look around. It's a beautiful day, the sun is shining. There's a nice light breeze. And animals are out," Ezra said as she nodded towards a pair of deer as they paused to drink from the stream. "Maybe we'll see more if we're quiet," she offered with a hint of mischief in her eyes.

"Why?"

"I hardly get to see anything, up at the Castle. The dead forest and wasteland are hardly the best places to have young, so the animals don't come up there much," Ezra replied, and Derik felt a surge of shame. Of course, she missed things like that!

"Can't you change it? Make it so that the wasteland can become like this again?"

"There is a spell to do that, but…what's the point? Better that those who come to steal my home think that I'm not there than knowing that I am. If it looks deserted, it makes my job easier to scare them off."

"I guess so, but what if the world knew you were there?"

"Then I might change it, just so that I might have a bit more beauty and visitors of a friendlier sort. But I've kept my presence here very quiet. I don't want them knowing that I really am here and alive."

"But the bad ones know that you are there."

"True. I'll think about it, Derik." Ezra grew quiet then and Derik silently berated himself as they rode, wondering if he'd stuck his foot in it.

Ezra's stomach was not feeling very well. She had felt off all day and as they rode, the silence stretched on. More animals did come out, which helped, and she put the stallion through a sedate set of paces for now. Ezra had no wish to scare Derik off from riding altogether.

Then she sensed something and tensed.

"What's wrong?" Derik asked, instantly alert.

"I'm not sure…I think someone's at the Castle. I'm going to pick up my pace, don't follow me at this pace. Tell Beauty "Sedate" and she'll stay at a walk—"

"Nope, I'll just hang on as best I can. Let's go!"

Ezra sighed, but urged the stallion forward into a fast walk, then into a gallop. Something was wrong, she felt it in every fiber of her being!

The source of that feeling she found on the closer side of the drawbridge. A woman lay crumpled on it and Ezra could sense, even from a distance, that she was wounded! Ezra leapt off of the stallion and threw the reins, ground-tethering him as she landed lightly beside the woman.

The woman had long, curly red hair and dark tanned skin. Ezra turned her over carefully and felt a surge of anger. The woman was obviously a warrior, and she had been left for dead.

There was a long cut from the pubic bone nearly up to her neck. She was alive, barely and Ezra began to immediately stabilize her with her magic. Anger boiled up as she recognized the mercenary's guild badge on the woman's arm.

Someone is going to pay for this, she thought vehemently as she managed to cut off most of the bleeding as Derik and Beauty stopped beside Dark Lightning.

"Want me to carry her?" Derik asked and Ezra shook her head.

"No, I'm taking us all inside. Hang onto their reins tightly, Derik. Lightning might spook after this and we'll need to make sure he doesn't hurt himself, or someone else," she warned as she gathered her energies and began to cast the spell.

"I've got him," Derik said as he swung stiffly down from the saddle and held the reins of both horses in his hands. Ezra could barely take an instant to nod before she finished the spell and teleported them all inside of Ammora.

::Baelios, we have an emergency. Can you settle the horses for me and show Derik how to groom them?:: She asked, desperate to get this woman out of the woods as quickly as she could.

::Of course, Ezra. I sense a mercenary company that's camped not a day's ride from here. They have a Healer,:: Baelios replied almost cheerfully into her mind as he allowed Derik to see him for the first time.

"Whoa!"

"Easy, Derik. I'm the Spirit of the Council. Ezra asked me to help you with the horses. May I?" Baelios asked somewhere behind her very politely. Ezra closed her eyes and used her telepathy, reaching out, losing her hold on the castle and seeking the beautiful green energy only a healer seemed to have.

And found it! Less than a day's ride, within a few hours at most. Ezra shut everything out and reached—

::Who are you?:: the question came immediately as soon as Ezra politely "knocked" with her telepathy.

::I'm the Sorceress of Ammora Castle. Is your company currently under contract?:: Ezra asked, knowing that the mercenary company might be on its way somewhere and prayed it was not.

::Not at the moment.::

::Good. I'd like to hire your company. I need a healer here at my Castle; A woman appeared on my doorstep very badly hurt and while I can heal injuries up to a point, I'm not as good at it as a true healer is,:: Ezra explained quickly, giving the woman images so she could see what Ezra was talking about.

::Let me talk to the Captain. Will you be hiring just me or the whole company?::

::If your company is honest and trust worthy, I'd like to hire you all for the foreseeable future,:: Ezra replied, realizing that when Juktis returned, this might be to her good fortune.

::How much are you offering?::

::What's your company's usual fee?::

::Captain says just to make an offer.::

::Very well. Gold and land for your company to settle on if you have need of it, as well as food and shelter until you build your own. Fair enough?::

There was a pause as she sensed the Healer relaying all of this to the captain of the company.

::We'll be there at dawn, Sorceress. Can you show me where you're located?::

::I'll send signals as you travel. Just follow them and I'll meet you at the drawbridge,:: Ezra replied with relief before the contact broke off. Ezra began a small series of spells, sending small psychic images of the land as she began to sense the company moving.

In the meantime, she kept a hand on the wounded woman and kept feeding a slow but steady trickle of energy into her, keeping her wounds stable while going into a trance, sending the signals necessary for the healer to sense while keeping the woman alive and warm.

Derik was more than surprised when suddenly, a man with Fiery orange eyes, blonde hair and amalgamation of features appeared next to him. Still fairly translucent, he found himself face to face with the resident Spirit.

"Ezra—"

"She's busy, Derik. I'm sorry, but she won't be able to heal wounds that extensive on that woman. She's sending for a healer as we speak. Let's leave her here for now and get the horses settled, okay?" the Spirit said soothingly and Derik couldn't help but give Ezra a worried glance.

"Are you sure she'll be all right?"

"Ezra is doing what she has to do; she's helping someone in need. We can help her best by getting the horses stabled and fed and then making her something to eat and drink. By morning, we'll have more guests. Invited ones this time," the Spirit said, sounding a little worried himself. Derik ran his fingers through his own long red hair and gave a nod.

"Okay, how can I help?"

"Lead Beauty. I'll take the stallion and we'll get them into the courtyard with the paddock," the Spirit said as he took Dark Lightning's reins from Derik's hand. Derik watched as the Spirit led the frightened horse away with ease, soothing him with soft gentle sounds as the pair walked. Derik led Beauty after them, giving a bit of distance between them in case Lightning decided to kick.

Vision of Darkness

Juktis floated in the alternate dimension he had been sent to. He had slowly begun to get a feel for where he was. It was dark here, cold, but he also sensed a current of power.

"That bitch! I'm going to get out of here and next time, she will be mine!" He hissed into the ether. Mostly he floated, there was no ground, nothing solid that he could truly grasp.

But he could still use his otherworldly sight to see outside of this dimension. He had spied on the woman for centuries before he had decided to finally go to Ammora to lay claim to it. Because he had not planned for the woman to gain an ally out of one of his own mercenaries, he had made a near-fatal mistake.

Of course, immortals could not die.

But worse could happen to them. Knowing that torment would never end with the sweet surrender of death was just a start.

"I need to see that Sorceress. She has weaknesses. I thought I knew them all, but she used those to her advantage. I must know MORE!" he roared into the emptiness.

He closed his eyes and watched, using those otherworldly senses to watch her….

Ezra reached without thinking and tapped into the Castle's power. She needed to replenish what she spent, and the Castle's reservoir was brimming with power, no longer depleted. Which was a very good thing as now the woman lay on a palette of blankets and cushions. It helped that Ezra had taken one cushion for herself and sat cross-legged upon it as she worked to keep herself comfortable.

She sensed the mercenaries were moving as quickly as they could, but it was hard to continue sending psychic signals to them that the Healer could sense. At the moment, they followed the Healer and those signals. It was just as well, as Ezra could send signals without thinking about it as she kept the woman stable.

All of her concentration was on her task, but she felt a chill, as if someone were watching her.

"Yes, use that power, Sorceress. Don't think," Juktis murmured into the ether as he watched, sensing that he might have an opportunity when she used her magic.

She was calling someone to her, but he might be able to use that like a beacon. With a smirk, he began to work on a spell of his own and began to follow that thread of power back to its origin.

Derik was impressed with the Spirit. For someone who was dead, he was excellent with horses! Both horses were in a paddock, brushed and groomed by the Spirit and fed with enough food to keep them sated without allowing them to founder themselves.

"How in the world did you do that without spooking them?" Derik asked and the Spirit chuckled.

"Beauty is used to my presence. As for Dark Lightning, he's following the mare's lead for now. And a little magic helped to keep him calm. Now he's got food and had a good scratch so…he's happy for the moment. Let's go make something to eat for you and Ezra. She's going to need something to help her last the night." The Spirit turned on his heel and began to walk through the corridors and Derik ended up having to break into a jog just to catch up with him.

"Do you have a name?"

"I do, but Ezra and I decided long ago that it should remain just between us. Names have power and we can't afford anyone learning mine and gaining power over me."

"What about Ezra?"

"She doesn't turn that knowledge to her advantage. Besides, we're a very good team. I help her, she in turn helps me to guard what we both protect here."

"Okay, well we've gone over that before. How come you never showed yourself to me before?"

"I only did so today because you aren't used to dealing with horses. I could have remained invisible to you, but I chose the most expedient route to help so that we can get back to Ezra quickly. She's using a very risky form of magic right now; she might be open to attack from the plane where she sent Juktis. I wish that we didn't need a healer so badly tonight, but we'll need one if that woman is to survive and heal properly."

"I hope she does. I'd like to find out what happened to her and maybe hunt down the person that hurt her."

"We all wish that. And the mercenaries that are coming with the healer should be able to help us for when Juktis returns. The darkness is coming, and we'll need others to help us if we're going to all survive this."

"Survive what?"

"The visions haven't shown exactly what, only a darkness covering our entire world...and the screams of every living creature as they die. We don't know who or what we're fighting except that it's evil and it brings darkness with it. A darkness that will eclipse everything if we don't defeat it. Go and stay with Ezra. I'll be there shortly with something for you both to eat."

The Spirit disappeared again, and Derik began to run back to the Entrance Hall where they'd left Ezra.

"Yes, there's the source! I see it!" Juktis roared into the ether as he got closer and closer to the source of the power that glowed like a beacon in the night. He raced towards it, using his magic to guide him through the darkness and that glowing thread of sheer power.

Ezra was deep in trance. Sending energy to two places, one greater than the other, wasn't easy. It was like a balancing act, trying not to drop while walking a tight rope across a vast chasm.

She didn't sense the danger. There was only the constant sending of signals to the Healer and the constant flow of energy to keep the woman before her from dying.

"Yes! Now!" Juktis roared in victory as he found the source and used his magic to open the portal back into Ammora Castle.

Derik had just gotten back to Ezra in the entrance hall. He sat down, prepared to wait until she broke her trance while the Spirit was busy in the kitchen.

"Derik, LOOK OUT!" The Spirit shouted as he appeared next to him—

And all hell broke loose! A portal opened just behind Ezra and Juktis burst out of it, glowing with power and fireballs in his hands.

Derik didn't think! He dove for Ezra even as the Spirit disappeared and knocked her onto the pallet with the wounded woman and covered them with his own body, acting like a shield.

"TRAITOR!" Juktis roared at Derik even as Ezra began to thrash beneath him.

"What the—"

"Juktis, the only traitor here is you!" Derik shouted back as he got back up and drew the sword he kept at his hip out of habit. Behind him, he could hear Ezra shifting and the click of her heels against the marble floor as she rose.

"Be gone, Juktis!" Ezra shouted behind him.

Juktis paused, then laughed and the fire disappeared from his hands.

"I'll be back, Sorceress," Juktis promised with a rather bizarre smirk on his face and then vanished.

"Where'd he go?"

"He's teleported himself out. He'll be going back to wherever it is he hides," Ezra replied as she sank back down to the stones. Derik turned to look at her and took another look.

"You don't look so good."

"I'm just tired, Derik. I have to get back to what I was doing. The Spirit will make sure that nothing else surprises us."

Ezra positioned herself again as she had been before and went back into trance even as the Spirit reappeared, this time with food.

"You'd better eat something before you do—"

"I'll eat when they get here. They're not that far away now. They'll be here in another hour or two. They're pushing their pace to get here for her sake. I have to make sure she's alive when they get here. Or it's all for nothing," Ezra replied before she closed her eyes. Derik sighed and looked to the Spirit, who handed him a plate.

"Don't worry, the Castle and I have recovered. We'll give her what she needs until they get here," the Spirit reassured him. Derik took his plate and sat down, feeling frustrated and angry.

"How did he get back from where she sent him?"

"Juktis sensed the amount of power she's using. She forgot to shield herself. I'm shielding her now so nothing else follows his example. Last thing we need is to add a demon to the mix."

"Tell me about it." Derik shook his head in disbelief and settled into eating.

Juktis returned to his home in triumph. He strode into his chambers and to his pool where he could scry for his prey. She appeared in the water, but he couldn't hear her, nor could he read her thoughts.

And he felt that familiar tingle of blood calling to blood.

"My plans are delayed, but they are still bearing fruit," Juktis said into the darkness of his Chambers.

"Good. See to it that you don't fail a second time. We must take that Castle and its power for our own if we're to succeed here," the sultry demonic timber echoed back.

"I won't. Next time, it will be different. She'll have something more precious than that castle to protect."

"And what could that possibly be?"

"You'll see soon enough. You will see," Juktis replied as he began to laugh. The laughter echoed through the dark halls of his fortress and inside, the warriors and servants that served him began to close their doors and hide.

Whatever it was that made him happy, they hoped it was enough to keep him satisfied at least for tonight.

It was with great relief that Derik saw Ezra gesture and the drawbridge lowered itself to reveal a whole mercenary company on the other side of the deep, dried moat. Derik rose, drawing his sword in case anyone meant them harm, but the Captain held up her hands, showing they were empty. Derik dropped his sword but kept his hand on the sword hilt as the Healer and Captain came across alone. The healer, a woman with dark curly hair and even darker skin, dropped with boneless grace down beside the wounded warrior and placed her hands on the woman. Ezra lifted hers away and accepted the plate of bread, cheese and fruit that the Spirit had brought for her earlier.

Outside, the sun had risen, and the early morning washed everything in gold.

"You did well, Sorceress. This woman was badly hurt, but you kept her stable. She'll be out of danger after this, but she'll need time to heal," the healer commented as she worked. The Captain came about and gasped.

"That's one of my scouts, Mara Krendo! How in the Gods' name did she end up here like this?" the Captain asked.

"I wish I knew. I found her on my doorstep, unconscious and wounded. Someone is sending me a message, I think. An enemy, but I wish I knew who," Ezra replied wearily as she picked up a bite of bread and put it down without eating it.

"Eat that, Sorceress. You used a lot of energy, you'll need to replace it," Derik scolded her as he came to rest a hand on her shoulder. "Captain, I can vouch for the Sorceress' story. We found your scout together on the other side of the drawbridge, wounded and unconscious. The Sorceress is why she isn't on the other side of the veil right now, making a report to someone else," Derik said after a moment or two. The Captain's lips settled into a thin line for a moment, then she gave a curt nod.

"I have no reason not to believe you and my Healer trusts you enough to have set up a contract with you. We're a registered company with the Guild. If you need fighters, we're one of the best," the Captain offered.

"Thank you, Captain—"

"Lita Faltha. And you are?"

"Derik."

"And of course, just call me by my title. Just Sorceress, not the full title," Ezra replied as she paused again mid-bite, then rose. "I'm very tired and not very well myself. Derik, could you show these people around and help them to set up sleeping rolls for now? I'm sure they're exhausted. Please, excuse me," Ezra said, looking quite green as she turned and began to nearly run back towards the hall that led to her chambers. Captain Lita looked after her and Derik felt torn between going after her and doing what she'd asked of him.

He ended up settling for doing what she'd asked of him for now.

"How many soldiers are in your company, Captain?"

"Three hundred and seventy-five, all told. I told everyone to go ahead and set up camp outside for now, though shelter was mentioned—"

"If she offered shelter, by all means, bring everyone inside. There's plenty of rooms and the dining hall is very large. I'm sure we can find a way to accommodate everyone. This *is* a castle. Do you have many horses or beasts?"

"No, we have sky chariots to move our people around. We have smaller sky chariots for battles and of course foot troops," Captain Lita replied with a smile.

"Okay, that's a relief. Well park the sky chariots out back behind the Castle and have everyone come inside. We'll see about getting food for everyone and sending you all to your bed rolls for some rest. I have a feeling we'll be seeing some action sooner than I'd like," Derik told her as he looked towards the drawbridge and felt a surge of hope chasing away the dread.

For now.

Chapter Eight

Eve checked in on her patient in one of the side chambers. Mara was still asleep, but her wounds were nearly completely healed. Eve turned, hearing the door open and motioned for the newcomer to be quiet.

"Any change?" Phyla, Eve's tent mate and partner, whispered as she eased herself in the room. Eve gave her a small smile, watching Phyla snake her way into the room with the ease of an assassin. Phyla wore her usual leather armor, which she preferred in between battles, boots, leggings and a few assortments of knives.

"Her wounds have nearly disappeared. I'll be waking her in a few hours, I think," Eve replied in a whisper of her own.

"Good. I'll tell the Captain. Um…is it me, or is the Sorceress spending a lot of time in her chambers?" Phyla asked her, keeping her voice down and looking worried.

"More like in her privy. Her room is on the other side of this one. I've heard someone getting sick to their stomach more times than I'd like. I'm going to go and check on her next, see if I can help."

"Good idea. Let me know if you need something gentle for her from the kitchen. Cook's having raptures over the kitchen—everything she's ever wanted is in it!"

"In a place like this, I'm sure there is! I'll send word if I need anything special for her. See you later tonight?"

"I'd better! I've missed my favorite bed warmer."

"I bet," Eve replied and kissed her with a soft giggle. Phyla waggled her brows at her in a way that was more humorous than amorous and slipped out the door again. Eve turned, checked Mara over one more time before following her out. She had another patient to check on.

Ezra was not feeling well at all. She hadn't hardly had any appetite at all these past several days, and she wasn't up to doing much. Baelios had been bringing her water and gentle things, but hardly anything was willing to stay down. She got up shakily for what seemed to be the fifth or sixth time in just the past two hours and washed out her mouth. She was just getting ready to lay down again when she heard a knock at the door.

"Who is it?" she called, unsure that she wanted any visitors.

"It's Eve, Sorceress. May I come in?" the Healer's warm voice called, muffled slightly by the wood of the door. Ezra sat on her bed and waved her hand, unlocking the door. It creaked open and Eve pushed it open as she entered and closed it behind her. "Sorceress, Mara is recovering very quickly. I should be able to wake her up in a few hours," Eve reported. Ezra gave a grave nod.

"That's wonderful news. Maybe now we can find out who hurt her—"

"I've also overheard…someone in here getting very ill, Sorceress. I'd like to help, if you'll let me."

That took Ezra by surprise. Ezra looked up at her and studied her and saw nothing but the need to help someone who needed it.

"I…. very well. I don't know what brought this on. I haven't been ill in a very long time," she admitted to Eve as Eve came closer to touch her shoulder.

"I understand, Sorceress. Lay down and we'll see what I can find. It's probably something with a simple solution," Eve reassured her as Ezra turned sideways and lay down on her back, wincing as a sore stomach muscle protested the movement. Eve held glowing hands over her, then lightly touched her as she began her examination.

Derik was worried. Ezra hadn't come out of her chambers in days, which in and of itself was unusual for the very active woman. He had continued on their usual routine, though now it included sparring with various members of the mercenary company that now dwelled here with them. When he wasn't sparring or cooking, he was out behind the castle, helping to build the beginnings of a new city for the mercenaries to settle in. Captain Lita was pleased so far with the progress they were all making, but she had expressed her concerns as well about the Sorceress.

"I would have thought that she would like to see what we're doing—"

"I'm not sure why she isn't. I'm going to go and check on her and see if she needs something. Hopefully I can get her to come out. She's been alone here for a very long time. Maybe she's a little overwhelmed with so many new people here," he explained. Captain Lita gave a nod and a brief smile.

"That's possible. Most people who have been alone for years tend to be overwhelmed easily. Let me know what I can do to help her out," Lita replied before she returned to helping with the building. Derik gave a salute and headed back inside, glad the Spirit was letting people in and out in Ezra's absence.

He headed to her chambers and knocked on the door.

"Hm. Well that's puzzling. I can't find anything wrong with you, Sorceress," Eve declared as she lifted her hands from Ezra's form at last. Ezra sat up, her eyes going wide.

"There must be something—"

"Oh, there's something but it's not something wrong. You're pregnant," Eve told her quickly and gave her shoulder a gentle pat. Ezra's eyes widened in shock and her jaw dropped. "You're going to be a mother in about 8 more months."

"That's...not possible!"

"It's very possible and I'm sure Derik will be overjoyed to hear that he'll be a father."

"You don't understand—" Ezra started but was startled when she heard the knock at her door. "Who is it?"

"Derik, Sorceress. May I come in?"

Eve brightened even as Ezra seemed to wilt. Granted, with Derik she had begun to feel something. He was a good friend, and while her heart ached to open again, she hadn't been quite willing to allow someone in yet. After all, a mortal would eventually die...and she would be all alone again.

I can't bear the thought of losing another husband, Ezra thought to herself, feeling guilty at even the thought of being married again. *Losing Bael nearly killed me the last time.* She rubbed her eyes and said in a whisper to Eve "Do not tell him anything. I will tell him when I feel it's time."

Eve looked at her in surprise but gave a simple nod. Ezra opened the door with a gesture, using her magic to unlock it so it creaked open again.

"Thank you for keeping me up to date on Mara's condition. If you'll allow it, I'd like to be there when you wake her," Ezra said to Eve who gave a brief nod.

"I'd like that, Sorceress. Captain Lita will want to be there too. I think we could all use some answers," Eve said as she headed out the door, surprising Deirk.

"Yes, I'm sure we all could. I'll see you later then," she said as Derik walked in. Ezra gestured again and the door closed. "What can I do for you, Derik?" Ezra asked as she rose, trying to look stronger than she really felt.

"Are you all right?" Derik asked bluntly. "Everyone's worried about you. Is it just the amount of people in the Castle, or is something wrong?"

"I'm fine. I'm just a little tired after keeping Mara stable overnight—"

"That was almost a week ago. And you had said that when the Castle recovered, you could use its energy to recover—"

"It's not as simple as it sounds—"

"But the Spirit said it is a simple as it sounds. So, what aren't you telling me?" Derik asked her directly, his eyes taking her garb—a nightgown—and her lack of headdress.

"I...."

"And why was Eve here? I'm sure that her briefing of Mara's condition didn't warrant a closed door."

"Derik—"

"And you look like hell. You're pale and the Spirit says you're not eating much. I'm not stupid and I'm not leaving until you tell me what's going on."

"Oh...damn you! I'm pregnant!" She snapped, losing her temper.

"Juktis?" he asked.

"Yes. We both know what he did to me."

"All too well. If that bastard wasn't immortal, I'd kill him."

"He is immortal...and I'd still like to kill him myself, Derik."

"So, what are you going to do?"

"I have to get up to the library and look up more information on immortal sorcerers. With two immortal parents, the baby—"

"Will be immortal," Baelios said as he suddenly appeared next to Derik and Ezra. Derik jumped back, reaching for a weapon he didn't have on him and looked at the translucent form of Baelios, surprise written in all over his face.

"By the Gods! Spirit, a little warning!" Derik exclaimed as he stepped back another step and took a breath to calm himself.

"My apologies, Derik, but since I've had my suspicions and the Healer has confirmed them—" Baelios started.

"Then I have no choice but to have the child," Ezra sighed, looking not very happy about the proposition. "And this baby will grow up without a father."

"Ezra, it doesn't have to be that way," Derik said gently then as he stepped closer and touched her cheek. "I care a great deal for you. More than just friendship—"

"It would never work, Derik—"

"How would you know if you never try?"

"Losing my first husband was hard enough, Derik. I couldn't bear that loss again."

"Don't you ever think about the times you did have with him? The happy times?" Derik asked as he dropped his hand with a sigh. "I think about lots of happy things I'd like to share with you every day. Maybe you should think about that," Derik said as he turned on his heel and stormed out.

Ezra rubbed her temples and resisted the urge to again run to the privy.

"Baelios, I'm making a mess of this—"

"Yes, you are. And he's right. Bael wouldn't want you to grieve forever for him. He'd want you to be happy."

"But, how could I ever really know that? It's not as if I can talk to him directly, Baelios. I…can't bear that loss again."

"Here, I brought you some ginger and a little bread. Get dressed. Get back out there into those halls. We will get through this together, Ezra. You need to tell the others why you've been ill. Let them assume it's Derik's…and reconcile with him. Talk with him. Tell him about your times with Bael. He'll understand."

Ezra took the minced ginger root and the bread with a weary sigh.

"I'll try, Baelios. I'll try." She began to nibble on both as she walked to her closet and began to take out her clothes for the day.

A short time later, she was dressed in her usual tunic and leggings and boots with her headdress on once more. She walked through the halls of Ammora, surprised at how many people were here. All of course bore the badge of Captain Lita's company, The Firefalcons. A good omen, at least in her thinking as Falcons were one of the few birds that ventured near Ammora from time to time.

Ezra noted that the fighters were all assigned to one of the various chambers within Ammora, that Eve had taken the chamber directly next to her own. Derik's chamber was on the opposite side of her chambers, but she also noted that he was sharing his space with four other mercenaries, just as Eve was.

In the courtyard, Dark Lightning and Beauty were both grazing peacefully and had been well looked after. She noted that the blacksmith with Lita's company was there, checking their hooves. Pleased, she gave the man a nod and a small smile as she continued on through the hallways into the dining hall.

Several cooks were laying out fresh things to eat on the buffet table, making sure that things remained hot or cold depending on which item it was. Hot things were at one end of the table, cold things on the other end. One peek into the kitchen and Ezra noted that the Head Cook, a rather handsome older woman with gray streaks going through her green hair, had things quite well in hand. There was enough food laid out for all of the fighters, and of course herself and anyone else with the company! Ezra took a peek into her food stores and was again impressed. It seems the cook took only what they absolutely needed but hadn't gone excessively into her stores!

I'll need to send word to Cephra that we're going to have people here and that we will likely need more of her harvest this time. Ezra sighed a little at the thought, but it was time. She needed people here. She was far more vulnerable with Juktis out there and knew he would be returning with far more force next time.

"I only borrowed a little, Sorceress—" the Head Cook started. Ezra raised a hand and smiled gently to her.

"Don't worry about it, Lady. I'm glad to share. There's a farmer nearby who brings our foodstuffs to us. I'll send word to her to send more if she can spare it. What's your name?"

"Gaela, Sorceress. Well met and I'm honored."

"We don't stand on much ceremony here, Gaela, and it's I who am honored that you would grace us with your cooking. Where is Captain Lita and Derik? I haven't seen them in the Castle."

"They're out behind the Castle, working on the plans for the city that Lita intends to build. Since you promised us land, the Captain wants to make sure that everyone will have a true home as part of their contract," Gaela explained with an excited look in her eye. "Though I doubt she could ever match this kitchen."

"Well if you'd like to remain the Castle as our permanent Head Cook, I would be honored, Gaela. And of course, if you'd still like to have a house in the city with your fellows, that can still be arranged so that you have a place of your own to go to on your days off."

"Thank you, Sorceress! I'd like that very much."

"Well I'll go out to see the Captain and Derik and see if there's anything I can do to help things along," Ezra replied with a chuckle as she turned and then teleported herself to just outside the Castle.

Before her, she saw the beginnings of a city. Sewers, with run offs to carry away waste, had already been taken care of under the ground. They were building rain towers, designed to collect rain to irrigate the city. But, in the wasteland, there would not be enough water for everyone for long.

I'm going to have to change the wasteland, if we're ever to grow enough food to support everyone. Cephra's farm is a small one, designed to support a family and a little more besides. But, there's at least three hundred people here now. I can't put that burden on her family and expect them to grow that much more this season!

Ezra spotted Derik and Captain Lita after a few more moments of watching and walked down the trail towards them to see what else their plans entailed.

Derik was bent over the plans with Captain Lita, looking over the plans for the next stage—building the buildings that would house everyone. Mostly houses with various designs, depending on each of the soldiers' requests. Some of the soldiers had paired up with people they wanted to spend their lives with within the company. Most hadn't. And everyone, depending on who and what they were had their ideas of what they needed.

Eve and Phyla, for instance. Eve, being the healer, wanted to build an infirmary and their living quarters right above it. Phyla, being a warrior and not needing much, had just asked for a decent sized kitchen behind the infirmary so their house would be fairly simple. Gaela, being the Company Cook, had requested for a large kitchen, but the amount of land would only go so far.

"I don't think she'll be able to have a kitchen as big as the one inside the Castle," Lita was saying when a bit of movement caught Derik's eye. He turned, startled.

"Sorceress!"

"I just spoke with Gaela and offered her the Castle's kitchen and position of Head Cook permanently. She'd still like a house, but I think that you can give her a normal sized kitchen so she can cook for herself on his days off. I'm going to let her keep on whatever staff she'd like so she can continue feeding everyone in the dining hall," Ezra offered, giving them both a much-needed solution.

"Oh, thank the Gods! We didn't know if you'd want to keep anyone on as staff inside the Castle, so we were trying to do what we could so everyone could take care of everything out here. That'll make it easy. Now, if we just had a way to get everyone into the Castle in cases of emergencies—" Lita started.

"I think I can help with that, too. There is a back door, but it's hidden and disguised and comes out in that cave over there. I've be-spelled the door so that it requires a password to get in and out. What I can do is I can change that spell and make it so only the Company, Derik and myself can come and go out of that door as we please. That should make it easier for everyone to come and go and save the drawbridge cables a little wear and tear," the Sorceress offered with a genuine smile.

"Thank you, Sorceress. That would be wonderful."

"I'll go and take care of that shortly then. So long as my stomach behaves, that is," Ezra said, pausing a moment to touch her mouth and looking a little green.

"Are you all right?"

"I'm...pregnant, Captain."

"Congratulations to you both then!" Lita exclaimed, giving Derik a light touch on the shoulder and looking very happy.

Derik gave Ezra an odd look.

::Derik, let her assume what she likes. Juktis may have fathered the child, but it doesn't mean that the child will be like him. The Spirit gave me a rather...large scolding after you left. I'm sorry about what I said earlier. I don't want to fight with you, your friendship means far too much to me,:: Ezra sent to him telepathically before he could say anything. Derik gave a nod and thought hard on his reply.

I understand, Ezra. I'd rather the child not grow up with the stigma of such a horrible father, either. And I don't like fighting with you, either. You've come to mean a great deal to me, too. Derik was graced with one of Ezra's rare, beautiful smiles and saw the relief in her eyes.

::Thank you, Derik.::

"We'll have a lot to do to get ready for the baby, but we still have a rather formidable enemy out there, Captain. One we could use your help with," Derik told Lita as they turned back to their plans.

"Oh? Well, I'd like a briefing on that tonight, after we're finished out here for the day."

"Of course, Captain Lita," Ezra agreed. "I'd like to work on a strategy to take care of that particular problem with you and Derik. I'm afraid that he will be back much sooner than I'd like."

"That's a plan then."

"I'll go change the spell on the door and send word if I can be of more help. I might be able to do something to help," Ezra offered before she disappeared.

"Wow, does she always come and go so quickly?"

"I'm still getting to know her, but I can tell you that she rarely sits still for long," Derik said with relief that he and Ezra were no longer at odds. "Now, let's move on to the next house. Who's moving here?"

That night, Ezra joined Lita and Eve in Eve's temporary infirmary in the chambers next to Ezra's. The mood was somber, and Ezra herself was struggling to remain calm. Whomever had hurt Mara would likely be back sooner or later and perhaps not alone.

Ezra watched as Eve began to bring Mara out of the healing trance she had been placed in and resisted the urge to pace the length of the room yet again. At long last, the redheaded woman's eyes began to flutter open and Eve and Lita both breathed a sigh of relief.

"Mara, this is the Sorceress of Ammora. She said she found you on her doorstep. Who hurt you?" Lita asked, getting straight down to business.

"Easy, Captain. She just woke up," Eve reminded Lita gently. "Mara, do you remember anything about the attack?"

Mara licked her lips and groaned softly, then began to sit up—

Vision of Darkness

"Whoa, there! Easy, Mara. You were nearly killed and if it wasn't for the Sorceress, we'd be at your funeral pyre right now. Take it slow," Eve reminded Mara quite sternly, but gently.

"I remember a woman. She was a mage. Hit me with a spell before I knew it. After that, I don't remember much," the redhead admitted, looking more than a little angry about it.

"Dark mages often use paralysis spells or restraining spells. Do you remember what she looked like?" Ezra asked very gently, opening her mind to the Mara's to try and catch a glimpse of what she had seen.

"Didn't get a good look. Only knew it was a woman from her voice. Too high pitched to be a man's. Sounded like she was enjoying what she did to me," Mara replied, leaving Ezra with nothing but a voice. Nothing more. Ezra gently sifted through Mara's memories, being as unintrusive as possible and once she caught the voice of Mara's tormentor, she withdrew her mind quickly again and left nothing of herself behind.

"All right, I'll begin looking into finding the woman who attacked you, Mara. Take it easy in the meantime. I'll let you all know when I've found something," Ezra said as she turned and headed back out into the hall. Anger boiled deep within her, but Ezra sent that energy into her private reserve. She might need it later.

:;Ezra, can I help?:: Baelios asked as she walked into her work room and closed the door behind her. He appeared right after and she turned to face him, looking over the table and her tools with a discerning eye.

"Of course, you can help, Baelios. A female Dark Mage is responsible for Mara's wounds. Juktis is on the loose again. We need information on both and as quickly as we can scry it out," Ezra replied, again wrestling with her own temper. "Whomever this Mage is, she obviously thinks she can challenge me if she can leave a victim on my door-step for all the world to see. So, we need to find her as quickly as we can and get as much information as we can about her," Ezra replied as she took her scrying bowl and put it in the center of her work bench. She poured water in and a generous amount of black ink. Not too much, but enough to darken the water enough to scry with. She took a moment and breathed, then got down to the business of pulling on that energy reserve and began seeking the Mage who had tormented Mara.

"Damn! Nothing! Not even a hint of a trace!" Ezra spat several hours later, soaked with sweat from her efforts and feeling weary. "Whomever that Dark Mage is…she's good. Better than Juktis even, I'd dare say," Ezra told Baelios as she sat heavily in an arm-chair she kept in there for spells that required her presence for more than a single hour.

"I didn't sense any magical traces on Mara either. I checked while you worked, Ezra. I'm afraid this is one enemy we'll have to wait to see what their next move will be," Baelios said regretfully and with anger flaring up in his orange eyes. "I'll watch for strange magical currents in the meantime. Sooner or later, she'll tip her hand."

"Hopefully before there's a dagger at our throats. Or a sword. By the Gods, I'm tired," Ezra said wearily as she rubbed her eyes.

"Do you wish to rest?"

"No. We need to find out where Juktis has retreated to. The sooner we find him, the sooner we can find a way to defend against him and, perhaps, be rid of him once and for all." Ezra shook off her weariness and sat back in her chair. She closed her eyes and began to slow her heart rate and breathing.

"But you've been searching for him for twenty years, Ezra. How will you find—"

"He left something behind, Baelios. The baby. I'll use it to track Him down if I have to."

"Good hunting. I'll make sure you're not disturbed," Baelios said as he again disappeared, leaving Ezra to her work. She continued to breathe, slowly, in and out and when she was ready, cast herself into the Astral plane.

On the Astral, she flared out angelic wings that sprouted from her back. She shook out her long loose hair and took a moment to study everything that was in the room with her. Various threads and shards hung in the space about her, and when she looked down at her body, she saw two threads. One that led to her and one that led from her belly out to somewhere else. Seeing how far it had stretched, she knew it would be a journey.

It figures that he wouldn't be close by. If he'd been anywhere near Ammora, I would've sensed him a long time ago, She thought as she gingerly touched that thread with one invisible finger and began to fly along it, holding it gently in one "hand." Ezra picked up her pace, flying through doors, walls and windows and finally out of Ammora altogether. Then she began to fly faster, racing over the wasteland and to the West.

She passed cities, lakes and streams. She went far into a wilderness she had never seen before but had only heard about. Ezra finally spied the place where the thread seemed to end and pulled up short just in time!

Before her was a large fortress, one that lay within reach of three small cities. It was big and formidable, built into the side of a mountain. Depictions of depravity, lust and greed were carved into the very walls and gave her a feeling of foreboding. Evil, red and thick, dripped down through the astral in streams that reminded her all too much of blood.

He's worse than I thought. He cares for nothing and no one but himself and his lust for power. He's not The Darkness, but he's embraced his own inner-evil, Ezra thought as she looked up at those forbidding gates and noted how many soldiers manned it above. *I better get back quickly, before he senses me.*

She turned and began to fly back to her body as fast as her wings could carry her.

Juktis stopped chanting mid-spell. He had been intending to try and see and hear past Ammora's walls, but then he felt something in the magical currents. He shifted his own awareness and reached.

And sensed that one beacon of light that glowed off in the distance outside his Fortress. Rushing into the Astral, he raced along and cut off the Sorceress' Astral form before she could escape.

::Leaving so soon, My dear?:: he asked smoothly, flexing talons of his own. His astral form was that of a dragon, a very large black and red dragon. Ironically, she looked like one of those feathered Fae he had heard about and chuckled. ::But, you haven't even had tea yet.::

::Juktis!:: She hissed, coiling back from him and glancing about for some other way to escape. He struck quickly, trying to trap her in his long tail and large draconic claws. She dodged and darted, twisted and jumped, giving him a fair chase of it.

::You can't dodge me forever, Sorceress,:: he chided her, beginning to enjoy the game she had given him as she continued to evade his grasp.

::Perhaps, or perhaps not. But, I'll never cease trying,:: she taunted him, throwing a blast of pure magical energy at him. It took him by surprise, making him coil back from her, blinded by the power she'd thrown at him.

He blinked the stars from his eyes and looked about.

And discovered she was already gone. He roared into the Astral once, making the trees about him shudder.

Ezra woke up, sweating, in her own body after having raced back even faster than she'd tracked Juktis to his lair.

:;Baelios, I found him!:: she sent quickly, feeling her heart racing as she rose, shaking with the effort.

::Good! I'm here. Let me help you back to your chamber. You should rest--::

::He sensed me in the Astral. He might be coming--::

Then Ezra heard it, a roar that came from very far away and yet seemed right next to her. She waited, counting heartbeats…and relaxed when a few minutes later, nothing else had happened.

::Maybe not. I'll raise the magical protections over the Castle. Let's get you to your bed. Tomorrow, we can make plans, Ezra,:: Baelios coaxed and Ezra at last let him help her back to her chamber.

Chapter Nine

"If only I could get a spy into Juktis' fortress," Ezra sighed with frustration as she looked over her map of Axrealia. The three cities that the foul Sorcerer's fortress was flanked by surrounded him in a neat triangle of power. "But, how to do it without them being seen or even suspected as being spies?" Ezra asked herself as she studied the map, using magic to highlight what was essentially Juktis' land and she didn't like it. The flow of power going into the fortress was being pulled from all three of those cities. That meant the populace was cowed and obedient to Juktis.

Which made it difficult for strangers to just walk into that land particularly if the farmers in the surrounding countryside had been told to report anything they saw.

It also made it damned difficult to come up with a viable strategy that didn't involve just using a portal or a dimensional gate to put fighters into place.

"He has more people than I do and most likely all of those fighting for him will be male and scum. I doubt he'll have any more mages on his side, so…since I'm not strong enough to counter him by myself…"

"Makes it all the more imperative that you recruit, Sorceress," Derik offered as he and Captain Lita appeared at the library door, where Ezra had taken her breakfast to study the largest map she could find. Captain Lita gave a sage nod.

"I do have several mages in my Company, but you really should get more. Probably more fighters. Is this the bastard that hurt Mara?" The Captain leaned over the table, which Ezra had cleared with a bit of magical aid and studied the magically lit map.

"Unfortunately, I couldn't tell who had hurt her. They left no traces. This is one that has eluded me, and justice, for the past twenty years. I found his stronghold at last, but…as you can see, getting to him is not going to be easy."

"Far from it, from the looks of that map. Is this why you hired us?" the Captain asked bluntly, and Ezra could only sigh and nod.

"Yes, but it's more to defend Ammora from him than to go after him. He isn't going to leave us alone and he is one of the foulest sorcerers I've ever met. If I remain on the defensive, he has the advantage in being able to take his time to come after me. That gives me time to recruit more fighters, but I'd also need mages to help me to fend him off. He's too powerful for me and the Castle to defend against without aid. The more dangerous path would be to go after him, but that could spark a war that could last years, even decades if it's not planned very carefully. I don't want to become a warlord, but—"

"You don't see any other choice anymore, do you?" Derik was the blunt one now, but he had a look in his eye. The one that showed that he would be one of the ones fighting, in the front lines.

And in immediate danger, once Juktis spotted him.

"There are always choices, Derik. It's a matter of weighing which is the lesser evil. But I can't leave him out there. He's hurting people. More, he's dangerous and he is determined to have Ammora's power for his own and if he gets it—"

"All of Axrealia would be doomed," Derik finished for her with a fierce, but sad look in his eyes.

"I'm afraid so. Besides, the later I get into my pregnancy, the more likely—"

"He'll come for you while you're vulnerable for you and the baby."

Lita looked between them for a moment, amazement written in every line of her face.

"How are you two doing that?"

"Doing what?" Ezra and Derik asked together, broken from their reverie.

"Finishing each other's sentences. It's like you know exactly what the other is going to say."

"I'm not sure. Derik has only been here for a short time, no more than a few weeks," Ezra pondered and shrugged.

"We have been getting to know each other fairly well in that time," Derik pointed out with a chuckle. "And we both have gotten to know Juktis a little too well."

"Ah, I see. Well, why would he want the baby?"

"Captain, this child is going to be born inside of Ammora Castle. Like me, it will have a tie, a small one mind you, but a tie to this place that will be fairly strong. He may see it as a way to get to the power he really wants deep within Ammora. And that power is not here for him. Its purpose is to defend all of Axrealia against a coming threat. A darkness that threatens to destroy all of Axrealia and its inhabitants. Ammora's power is the key to keeping that darkness at bay and perhaps even destroying it, root and branch," Ezra explained patiently. "It was foreseen long ago by the entire Wizard's Council. They're the reason why I'm here and why this Castle is the way it is."

"Alive, you mean?"

"Yes. How—"

"I've seen a few things move that shouldn't have all by themselves. Everyone's reported belongings being moved to a more convenient place or seeing a door or two open all on their own. We figured it had something to do with the magic our mages sensed here—"

"But your mages sensed something else?"

"Yes, they all said they felt a presence that wasn't you or anyone else here that's living. It was one of the things they asked me to ask you about, if you were willing to part with any information on this place."

"I can't share all of my secrets, but yes. The Castle is alive, in a sense. But it can't act on its own to defend itself, which is where I come in."

"So, keeper and ruler?"

"I'm not a ruler. I'm just a mage—"

"That was before you had people here, Sorceress," the Captain pointed out gently. "But, now—"

"Now, I'm an employer, not a ruler. There is a difference, Dear Captain. And now, there is more than one threat out there. One I can't find and another I can't seem to be rid of."

"Well, which strategies have you considered?"

"Many just over the past several hours. And far too many choices and lack of proper information is my main trouble," Ezra rused. "Keep in mind, ever since Juktis came, I've been considering what I can do, but without knowing how many men he has in that fortress, or even how many servants, how many people in the cities are loyal to him—"

"Puts a damper on your planning. Well, have you considered a spy?"

"I've been thinking of how I could have someone infiltrate his fortress to do just that. The problem is he's got these cities firmly under his control. And now that he knows that I know where he is, Juktis will likely have told all of his people to report anything or anyone out of the ordinary, Captain." Ezra rubbed her temples, trying to resist the urge to pull against her hair, having put aside her headdress for the moment. Her head ached, her neck ached, and the day was just starting.

Not to mention how much her stomach had begun to rebel.

"Well, I do have a couple of people that might be able to do just what you're asking. Mara and Aeryn. They're a couple. They could get in as a pair of servants seeking work."

"Going out all that way just to find work? No one would ever believe it. The nearest city outside of this trio is at least two weeks away by horse—"

"But, not by sky chariot."

"Servants wouldn't be able to afford sky chariots."

"Hm, I've seen a fair few manage to scrape the gold together for one. And a sky chariot would cover that amount of ground in less than an hour from this ring of cities at the outer perimeter to the fortress."

"Still, why would they seek work there?"

"Aeryn's a Master Blacksmith. He could easily choose his own place of employment, based on his skill level. And his credentials are under a name that was well known, but quite different from his current name. He uh…ran into some trouble with a bad crowd. Took a new name when he signed up with us," Lita explained with a smirk tugging at one corner of her mouth. "As for Mara, well…she could be his new wife and have a new name of her own."

"It's too dangerous and Juktis is likely to question any story they give."

"I've had them act as my spies before, on a difficult campaign. They've managed to weedle their way into a number of arrogant bastards' households. I'm sure they could do it again."

"If they get caught—"

"They know the risks and accept them."

"Are you so sure? Mara's still recovering."

"Eve said she's ready to get back into action and this would be the sort that wouldn't have a lot of fighting involved in it. Besides, Mara and Aeryn can both take care of themselves. Sorceress, you said you need information. How else are you going to get it?"

Ezra looked at Lita, very irritated at her all-too-logical reasoning. After a few minutes of trying to find another excuse, she sighed. This was war. People were going to get hurt.

More could get killed if she acted on the wrong information.

"All right. Ask them to come here and we'll see if they're willing to go into the viper's den."

"Yes, Sorceress. Right away," the Captain turned with military-briskness and hurried back out to go and fetch her charges.

Ezra turned back to Derik, who was giving her that penetrating gaze again.

"Ezra, you don't have to—"

"I know. I don't like it any more than you do. But, she's right. We need information, Derik. I can't get it magically; he sensed me the instant I tried last time. I don't think I have a choice. I just hope…that the cost isn't as dear as I think it might be."

"You don't like war, do you."

"No, I don't. Never have. But you're right. I don't see any other choice. Not anymore. I don't want to go to war, but if I don't, Juktis will continue to whittle away at my defenses until I have nothing left. He's not leaving me a choice. He'll be back. I can't keep waiting for him. It's…time I go after him. I don't like it, but I don't dare let him win."

Derik only nodded sagely and sat down next to her.

"How're you feeling?"

"Nauseous, sick and altogether tired."

"Do you want to talk about it?"

Ezra looked at him, amazed at how well he was reading her.

"Yes, no…. I'm not sure, really. Right now, the most important thing is making sure that we're all safe. But, being here…means we'll never be completely safe, Derik."

"I know. Maybe though, we can find a way to make it safe together."

"Maybe. But, for now—"

"I know, I know. Juktis has to take priority. What about Mara's attacker?"

"We'll have to wait for them to make the next move. Until I learn more about them, there's nothing I can do. They left nothing to point the way to them or showing who they were."

Derik frowned, looking rather unhappy at that news.

"How good are they?"

Ezra considered that question carefully and frowned.

"At least as good as Juktis. Maybe better. Juktis leaves traces. But Mara's attacker left nothing of themselves behind. Not even an energy signature. I've never seen that before. Usually those sorts of wounds are left by people willing to spill blood to raise as much energy as they can and stolen energy leaves a trace. But there was nothing, not on Mara's body, not anywhere in the vicinity where she was found. I just don't understand—"

"What if the attack was purely physical, nothing magical?"

Ezra looked at Derik with awe, having never considered that option.

"It's possible and…that wouldn't leave any traces behind except maybe emotional ones."

"Did you look for those?"

"No, I didn't."

"Maybe you should."

Ezra considered it, pondering how long such traces might last.

"I'll try again, but we still might not find anything."

"The you have nothing to lose," Derik offered as he offered her his hand. Ezra took it and began to walk with him, shaking her head at herself.

"Well, except a little time."

"I'll go with you. And by the by, everyone is congratulating me on the baby. So, are we going to talk about what they're assuming?"

"Let them talk. You're a good friend, Derik, and I don't expect you to be celibate, of course!"

"Well, that's what I am, and I don't mind it to be honest. I prefer a relationship to just sex. I like having a connection with the person I'm sharing pleasure with," he admitted to her as he paused and looked down into her eyes.

"Derik, I—"

"I really would like to court you, Ezra. If I may, that is."

Ezra sighed and shook her head.

"This isn't the time for it, Derik. Besides, why would you want to court me? My life isn't my own and my duties—"

"Come first before anything else. I know. Still, there isn't another woman I'd want to court here. Just you," he told her, turning away with a sigh to walk towards the entrance hall. Ezra shook her head and hurried her steps to catch up to him.

The search was uneventful and fruitless. After an hour of trying to sense any latent energies yet again, Ezra gave it up and they began to walk across the lowered drawbridge back towards the castle.

"Ho!" a strange voice called behind them. Derik and Ezra whirled to face the visitor. Derik's sword rang as he pulled it easily from its sheath. Ezra crouched, raising her energies in preparation for an attack and tensed when she recognized the face of the person standing on the other side of the drawbridge.

It looked like Juktis! But his eyes were different. Not as strange nor as crazy. He stood there, no mount or machine visible behind him. A simple pack was slung over one shoulder. His clothes looked clean, but some places had been hastily patched. Juktis had never approached in anything but black armor and underclothes.

This man's clothes were a faded red and blue. Ezra glanced out of the corner of her eye at Derik as she stood a little more at ease and continued to study the stranger but kept her energies ready for an attack if need be.

"Greetings, Stranger. How may we help you?" Ezra called back.

"I'm here to see the Sorceress of Ammora."

"Regarding what, Stranger?"

"It's about my twin brother, Juktis. I'm Jarod. I believe he's been giving her some trouble—"

"That is an understatement, Lord Jarod. Are you here to spy or declare war for him?"

"No. I've come to help her fight him. He's…changed. He wasn't always like he is now. I'd like to help her to stop him."

Ezra studied Jarod, continuing to note differences between him and Juktis.

"He could be telling the truth," she whispered to Derik.

"He could be here to lure you into a trap," Derik snarled softly back.

"I don't think so."

"Why not?"

"Look at him. Juktis is the epitome of evil. This man isn't. I think we should at least hear him out," she replied softly, releasing her energies with ease and relaxing. "Can you show us proof that you are who you say you are, Lord Jarod?" she asked. The man humbly held his hands out, his eyes radiating sadness and regret.

"What proof would you accept?"

"Allow me into your mind. A brief look through your memories should suffice."

"As you wish. Go ahead. I have nothing to hide, Sorceress," Jarod replied after a moment or two, closing his eyes as if he was expected a death blow.

Ezra reached out with her mind and dove into his as if she were diving into smooth, calm water. She went through his memories, looking for signs of victims, torture, something or anything evil. There was nothing. Nothing but regret, sorrow, false accusations and pain. She came out of his memories with a soft gasp.

"He's nothing like Juktis, Derik. He's been accused of all of Juktis' atrocities, but he's never hurt a soul," she murmured softly before she gestured for him to come forward. "Come, Lord Jarod. Let's go inside and you can tell us your tale," Ezra called as she turned to lead the two men back into the Castle.

Once they were all inside, Ezra raised the drawbridge. Food and drink were readily available in the Main Hall, with plenty of tables and benches to sit. Ezra sat in her chair, one she rarely used, at the end of the table that everyone insisted she use. Despite her protestations at not being a ruler, she had had the chair moved to the head of this particular table, but wouldn't allow it to sit at the center, as if it were a throne. She sipped at her water, wishing she could have wine today as Jarod revealed his tale.

"When we were young, Juktis and I were like peas in a pod. We loved magic, we loved doing things for our parents. But, as we grew older, he changed. He began to lust for power, and it was never enough. About a year ago, He returned to our family home. The next morning, our parents had vanished. I've been searching for them, but no one knows where they are. Juktis claimed he was ready to rule over the Fortress and he's changed it into…a horrible, dark place, Sorceress. I know he's done something to them, since they didn't just die. We're immortal, all four of us. And they wouldn't just leave the manor. They had people depending on them in all three cities at the base of the mountain. Gods know what he's done, but you can bet that it wasn't good… or gentle," Jarod said, running his fingers through his long dark hair in frustration. Ezra tilted her head as she watched him, continuing to monitor his thoughts. He was genuinely worried for them.

Poor man, he must be desperate, she thought quietly as she mused it all over in her mind. "Have you tried scrying for them, or using a spell to locate them?"

"Of course, I have, Sorceress, but the problem is I just can't find anything! Juktis did something to make them impossible to find!"

"Then you know that it may well be that even I couldn't ever locate them," she told him sadly, wishing she could help. "You said that you wish to stop him before he becomes unstoppable. Why is that?"

"He's after your Castle, isn't he? I sense a lot of what he does. Not everything, but enough to puzzle out that he's been lusting after the power that's contained here for centuries. He just wasn't ready to take you on until recently. I'm…. sorry for what he's done," Jarod said, dropping his voice. "I wish the babe weren't—"

"How did you—"

"Blood calls to blood in our family. I sensed it the instant I saw you. Something Juktis did made that blood call with our parents go silent. I haven't any clues as to what he's done, but I haven't sensed them anywhere on Axrealia," Jarod said, his expression showing his frustration and despair.

"He may have sent them into another realm altogether. Among all the possible worlds, it would be nearly impossible to locate them, Lord Jarod. I'm very sorry, but I'm afraid the search for them may have to wait until we've dealt with your brother. Have you any thoughts on how to deal with him?"

"You won't be able to take him on alone. He's getting more and more powerful by the day. Even I couldn't take him on and I'm his brother! You're going to need help, at least two more immortal mages at least."

"That is an idea. Of course, we'll need other help as I'm sure he's got plenty of soldiers—"

"All of the soldiers that served my parents were dismissed. He's replaced them with prison scum."

That sounded familiar and made Ezra raise her eyebrows in surprise before she composed herself. She coughed and got herself under control quickly, then went back to the task at hand.

"So, why two more 'immortal' mages? Why not just regular mages?" Ezra asked delicately, trying to feel him out some more. It could be prejudice; it could be something else. She had to know.

"Immortal mages don't die like regular mages do, even if they're drained of power. I'd rather have someone fighting beside us who won't die because they used up all of their resources, or worse because Juktis decided to toy with them. Juktis isn't going to be an easy target and you're going to need all the help you can get, Sorceress," Jarod replied, very passionately. His vehemence took her aback.

He really does care. He wants Juktis eliminated, and he feels tired and weary. Probably because they share the same face, he's faced with being accused of being just like his brother. Oh well. It seems I have more things on my "to recruit" list. But, how can I trust him. Unless... A new thought came to her and she had an idea.

"Well, the problem isn't just taking him down, it's containing him. I could turn him into a tree, or something equally immortal—" she started.

"Or you can contain him inside of something that'll be impossible for him to escape. I've been looking for an artifact that might do that and I think that I know which one would do the job. Problem is getting to it. I have no idea where the Orb of Eithal is," Jarod said, sounding frustrated. Ezra's lips quirked into a smile as she saw what she could have him do to prove himself.

"Well, I happen to know the location of that very Orb. I just don't have the time to go and get it. But, if you were willing to go and fetch it for me, then that would free me to up to find two more mages to go inside with us and give me to time to send for more soldiers to help with a distraction to keep Juktis' prison scum busy long enough for us to take your brother out," she replied, dangling that little "carrot" for him just enough that he might take the bait.

And take it he did.

"I'll get it for you, and I want in on helping with this. No if's, ands or buts. I want in," he replied coldly, his eyes showing that he wasn't going to be denied this.

Derik tensed next to her and she patted his hand, reassuring him.

"Of course. Let's go upstairs the library and I'll get you a map to its location. You can set out for it as early as tomorrow," she offered as she rose and led the way back to the staircase.

Once Jarod had the map, Ezra was able to show him to a room where he could spend the night. Most of the rooms were open again as the building of the new city behind Ammora was coming along fairly quickly.

It had helped that certain members of Lita's mercenary company had had stonemasons and carpenters for fathers. That early knowledge they had gained in their childhood had come in handy and while the city looked simple, Ezra suspected it wouldn't remain that way for long. A nice clean sewer system had been set up, the waste going to a pool where the dung would be collected and later removed to be composted along with any animal dung. Not that there were any animals yet, but Ezra knew that it wouldn't be long before people were sent out in search of animals for sale from Zethos or other nearby cities. Not that there were many of those, but she suspected they'd find a way to bring in animals sooner or later. Outside of where the city was being built, a new farm was being built as well, not that the soil was very fertile there yet. But, once building was over, Ezra was going to see about changing the soil around the Castle. She was tired of living in a wasteland.

It would be nice to see wild animals, as well as butterflies or birds again, she thought to herself and not for the first time. Grass would be welcome, too, along with flowers. She missed flowers and butterflies the most these days. *First things first. We need to get rid of Juktis and get things built. One step at a time,* Ezra reminded herself as she made her way outside and towards the city to have a word with Captain Lita.

Mara had recovered enough that she might be able to be sent out to the Fortress in the West. Lita was supposed to have talked with Mara and Aeryn, Mara's husband, about going out to spy for them.

Ezra hoped that Lita had truly spoken with them because Ezra intended to send them out right after Jarod left.

::Once Jarod is gone, you won't have a potential enemy reporting back to Juktis about our doings here. Good planning, considering that we're trying to get an idea of what we're up against,:: Baelios complimented her as she walked.

::We know he's an arrogant, blood-thirsty bastard who doesn't give a hangnail about our entire world. He'll do anything he can to destroy whatever he can't grab for himself. So, we're going to war. For that, we need three things: Soldiers, Spies and Strategy. We'll need supplies for the soldiers, if it drags out beyond one or two battles. Which it likely will. We just really need to know what his numbers are, what his supplies look like and if we can get the locals onto our side once we're out there. Right now, we need information. We need two spies inside, and more sent to feel out the locals. Let's start with seeing if we can get someone inside. After that, we'll worry about getting someone into the cities,:: Ezra replied, remembering one of those strategy books she'd read and memorized. It was going to be work. And it was going to be awhile before they could go out there.

Ezra paused just short of where the latest work crew was working and tried to get her sick stomach to obey her. It had gotten somewhat better since she'd found out she was pregnant a month ago, but it was still rebellious more often than not. *If only this would pass,* she thought for the fifteenth time today before she managed the last steps over to where Lita and the laborers were working.

"Captain, a word, please," she said gently, but loud enough so as to be heard above the noise.

"Sorceress! How do you like it so far?" Captain Lita asked, her eyes twinkling with excitement. Ezra looked about and gave an approving nod.

"It's coming along quite well. I'm sure it'll be beautiful when you're all done with it. A word, please. It'll only take a moment," she offered as she motioned for Lita to follow her. Lita did, thankfully enough, and without complaint after she handed over the scroll of plans they'd been looking over for the current project.

"What's wrong?"

"Nothing's wrong, but I'd like to send Mara and Aeryn out tomorrow if they're still willing to go. I can't manage to see inside of the Fortress with magic, so I need someone to be our eyes on the inside," Ezra explained, feeling unhappy about doing this. *It's not as if I have a choice..not anymore,* she reminded herself silently as she waited for Lita's response.

"I'll make sure they're in the Entrance hall waiting for your blessing before breakfast—"

"Lunch. We have that visitor that came to call on us. I want him long gone before I send them out, just in case. He seems harmless, but—"

"But we need to make sure he doesn't report them to his twin just in case," Lita finished for her. "I agree with that. He could be a spy, made to set up a trap."

"Exactly. I have him going out to do an errand for me. He should be gone right after breakfast. By the time they leave, he'll be long gone, and they should be able to make it to the Fortress before he could report anything back to Juktis. Assuming he is a spy, of course. If he's not, then the less he knows, the better until it comes time to attack."

"Less chance for leaks. I like it. Where're you gonna get the bodies you need to throw at this war machine?"

"I'm going to hire as many companies from Mercenary Guild for this one as I can. If I can find any other allies willing to toss their lot in with us, that might give us enough numbers to counter the amount of scum he has in that place. As soon as I have numbers, I can send messengers," Ezra replied, still feeling horrible. "I've never wanted to be a War leader."

"Then that makes you right for the job. Best war leaders are those who don't want the position. You'll do. Anything else you need for now?"

"Not unless you have Juktis' head in your satchel. I'll see you at dinner later," Ezra said as she turned to return to the Castle. "I set up the back door for everyone to use. After our visitor leaves, I'll show you all how to use it. Until then, mum's the word," she said with a wink to the Captain.

"Aye, and glad for that! C'mon you lazy blaggards, can't you get a simple wall up before I die of old age!" Ezra chuckled as Lita went back to asserting her authority over the laborers and Ezra hastened her own steps to go back to Ammora.

Chapter Ten

Dinner was uneventful, for which Derik was very grateful. Lord Jarod made his skin crawl and he disliked the man but had no idea why.

Something about him doesn't sit right. Like why he showed up here now and came willing to help go up against Juktis...not that anyone else knew that we were likely to do so other than maybe...Juktis. Maybe it's because he looks too much like that crazy mage, or maybe it's just the fact that Juktis hurt Ezra that makes me want to go and take him apart just to see how he's put together, Derik fumed silently and tried to tell that part of himself to take a long walk. A very long walk. After all, Jarod would be gone tomorrow and who knew if he'd ever come back?

Ezra had found a map with the Orb of Eithal's location. Both she and Jarod were studying it as they ate.

"It's in the mountains of Azroth, hidden in a cave there from the looks of this map. Mount Astaria in that range is where that cave seems to be located, but who knows what may have happened in the time since this map was drawn up. You'll be gone at least a month, maybe more, depending on what you find inside the cave. It mentions protections are set up around the Orb so it's not going to be easy to get," Ezra pointed out to Jarod as she pointed to various things on the map.

Meanwhile, Captain Lita's troops were all in the dining hall, helping themselves to food. Whatever was left at the end of each meal either went to lunch or breakfast the next morning or sent off by magic to children who had nothing to eat. Ezra had proclaimed quite clearly that there would be no waste tolerated in the food department. Derik found himself admiring her all the more for that.

::You know, Derik, Ezra really truly does admire you about as much,:: a familiar voice suddenly popped into Derik's head. Derik tried not to jump all the same but listened to the banter about him.

Yeah? And what would you know about that, Spirit? he thought back, taking another glance at Ezra while she was busy and didn't notice. His heart was wanting more than just to like her, but she was quite far out of his league. *She'd probably be happier with another immortal anyway. She'll outlive me...I'd hate to be the one to break her heart again. She's still so sad sometimes and she thinks I don't notice but...I do. I'd do anything to mend her heart, once and for all.*

::Oh, I know Ezra as well as she knows herself. We've been here for a very long time, you know. Besides, she needs someone she can be more than friends with. She needs someone to love, or she might lose her own footing on the path she's on,:: the spirit replied, sounding worried.

I doubt that. I don't know anyone else who's more devoted to her purpose—

::Yes, she easily could, Derik, without someone to help her keep her compass pointed to the right path. She has been tempted, more than once, but hasn't faltered yet. The day may yet come that she needs more than myself to keep her on the straight and narrow, as it were.::

Can't do anything about that myself. We're friends, but she's been avoiding me a lot lately.

::I'll try to get her to come and talk to you later. Mostly I think she's trying to push everything else aside in favor of taking Juktis down but…there's other priorities, not just him. I'll talk with her tonight,:: the Spirit sent one last time before he quieted again. Derik almost breathed a sigh of relief—talking with the Spirit was not something he could do easily, not being telepathic himself.

Derik glanced around at the soldiers, healers and other personnel of Lita's company. For mercenaries, they were quite humble though also careful. They joked with each other and acted more like a family than any other group of soldiers he'd seen. It also helped that some of them were nearing retirement age and talked excitedly about the trades they intended to set up within Ammora's budding city. The friendly banter eased Derik's tension. He would be glad to see Jarod's back in the morning.

Finally, Ezra rose and declared herself done for the evening and bid them all good night. Derik rose to follow her before Jarod could and escorted her through the hallways.

"I don't trust him, Ezra," Derik murmured as softly as he could as they walked.

"I'm not very sure of him myself, but it could be he's exactly as he seems. I'll be glad when he's gone tomorrow," Ezra admitted back just as softly. "Stay with me tonight, please. I…I really don't want to be alone."

That request took Derik by surprise, but pleasantly.

"I'd rather you not be alone, either." Derik paused as they came to her chambers and glanced up and down the hallway. "I'll be right there, Sorceress. Go inside, relax. I've just got to grab a few things before I join you," he murmured before he moved to his door like every other night. Inside, he picked up a few daggers he could hide on himself, even in his night clothes. He grabbed those as well, and the latest book he'd been reading on strategy. Only then did he pause and peek out into the hallway before going to her door, knocking on it twice and going in.

Once inside, he locked the door and moved to make himself a place to sleep.

"Derik, I don't mind sharing the bed tonight. It's...all right," she said almost shyly. Derik paused, considering that option for a moment, then shook his head.

"I don't want to do anything that'll make you uncomfortable, Ezra. So, no thank you, I think it'll be better if I sleep at the foot of the bed, within reach of the door. I want to make sure that no one else comes in." He turned and resumed making his bedroll down on the floor, between her bed and the door. He heard her sigh and then the rustle of fabric as she began to dress for bed. He stripped down to a tunic and night shorts, then lay down on his bedroll, his weapons laid next to him within easy reach. She clapped her hands and the light globes that lit this place dimmed so that they could both still see, but it wouldn't be fully dark. He closed his eyes, hearing her settle down in her bed and prepared to sleep as lightly as possible. *I'll sleep better once that bastard, Jarod, is gone.*

The next morning came without any incident in the night. Ezra rose early and saw Jarod off, giving him a copy of the map. She also gave him some supplies, saying simply "I wish you a safe journey and don't worry if you need to take extra time in seeking out the Orb. The legends say it's well protected. I'll begin seeking alliances and see if any other immortal mages are willing to help us."

"I'll be back as soon as I can, but you're right. I could be in that cavern for a week, maybe more. Be safe in the meantime. And if you find anything out about my parents—"

"I'll send word to you right away, don't worry. Be careful!" She called before he crossed the drawbridge to go to his sky chariot. As it raced away, she raised the drawbridge again and breathed a sigh of relief. *Now to make sure that Mara and Aeryn are provisioned and ready, she* thought as she turned to go to the kitchens.

"So, you two understand the risks you'll be taking for us as spies in Juktis' fortress? I won't be able to open a portal to whisk you away, though I'll do my best to help you if I can," Ezra asked yet again. She wanted to make sure they knew all of the risks and despite Captain Lita's assurances, she wanted to hear it from them.

"Of course. We've done this before, Ma'am. Our stories are we're seeking work and heard that he might need a blacksmith. With an army, he'll need people to make weapons for him," Aeryn replied, wielding a mace that looked like it had seen many battles, complete with dents and scars from various weapons all over its surface.

"Mara?"

"I'm fine. I'm his wife, I go where he goes. And I'm handy in the kitchen. Even better at cleaning. They'll find a place for me," she replied seriously, a hint of humor in her eyes.

"Are you sure you'll be able to handle anything, Mara?"

"Absolutely. I trust Aeryn with my life. Have many times before. I'll be all right. I promise, I'm okay, Sorceress. I want to do this. I want to do something to repay you for saving my life."

"I only helped to keep you alive for a little while, Mara. Eve is the one who truly saved you—"

"And if it wasn't for you, I wouldn't have been alive for Eve to save. Please, Sorceress. I can do this," Mara replied passionately, her eyes showing anything but fear. Ezra gave a solemn nod, then handed them both coin sacks.

"Be careful and don't take any unnecessary risks. In those coin sacks are rings, in addition to coin. Don't trade the rings. I'll use them to contact you, or you can use them to contact me. We need numbers and…beyond that, we'll see what else we need from you two. Now, time to get you out of here, before anyone might spot you," she told them as she lowered the drawbridge again to send them on their way. Outside, Lita waited with a sky chariot for them along with their fellow mercenaries. Ezra watched as they crossed the bridge, her heart feeling heavy as she watched them go.

"You don't have to send them, you know," Derik said as he came to stand beside her.

"I do. I need information about that fortress and about Juktis. Anything they can tell us will help us to fight him," she replied, feeling regretful already. What if they died or were discovered? That made the worry she had double as she watched them finally rise up and fly off, heading West.

"He hasn't attacked again yet, we've been lucky."

"No, he's just waiting until our guard is down. Something's coming. I can feel it, Derik."

"I hope you're wrong."

"I wish I were," she replied softly as Lita and her fellow soldiers came back in and raised the drawbridge.

Chapter Eleven

Mara glanced out of her eye at Aeryn as they approached the forbidding looking fortress. Where Ammora Castle was bright and beautiful, this was dark, foreboding and grim. Aeryn whistled very softly to himself.

They had landed outside of Sevabon, the southern-most city of the three that surrounded Juktis' fortress. From there, they had walked into the town, and then left it on foot and headed to the fortress. Word in Sevabon was Juktis was needing more soldiers, more blacksmiths and more servants. And that word had been hard to hear, whispered as it was in the inn where they had paused to take a meal.

"Look at the carvings," he murmured softly as Mara found herself staring at the walls and its carved guardians. Demons, imps and various other monsters were carved into the very walls of the fortress and Mara found herself impressed at how their eyes seemed to follow their every move.

"Horrid things. Where's the guards?" she asked softly as she looked up at the walls, studying them and trying to determine where guards might be lurking.

"Not a clue, but there's murder holes everywhere. I've got a bad feeling about this place."

"Then we're definitely in the right place," she murmured very softly back. Her eyes scanned over the walls and they moved up to the gate and waited. Aeryn rang the bell and moved up beside her.

"Who goes there?" A brusk, unfriendly voice called out.

"I'm Aeryn and this is my wife, Mara. We've come looking for work. I'm a black smith. Mara cooks and cleans," Aeryn offered. Mara was suddenly glad that she had pulled on peasant clothing on over her customary boiled leather armor and breeches. She had kept her usual on, not wanting to be caught unawares in case things did not go well today.

"Come in. We have room for two more servants and you two should do nicely," the guard captain replied as he motioned. The portcullis was raised, and the giant wooden doors were opened just enough to allow Aeryn and Mara to slip through. As soon as they were inside, the portcullis slammed down again.

They're on high alert. That's going to make things tougher, Mara observed silently as they were led over to the blacksmith's building. A small living quarters was over the forge and luckily there was enough space in there for them both. The kitchen was across the way, giving Mara an easy path to go each day to her work. The other blacksmiths, both single, slept in the barracks. They both seemed quiet, kept to their work. *At least they won't be here when we want to sleep, which means that will be the best time to report.* Mara took their rings and hid them quietly in the top drawer, which would allow them to report when they activated them. It was a low enough level of magic that Juktis wouldn't be able to detect it, or so the Sorceress of Ammora claimed.

Mara put away their clothes, pretending to be the dutiful wife and went downstairs to give Aeryn a quick kiss before she went across the way to the kitchen. *Baby steps,* she reminded herself as she went to introduce herself to her new superiors.

Juktis paced back and forth in his chambers. He had tried to continue to spy on the Sorceress, tried to hear what was being said in her Castle. But, of late, he couldn't even scry past the walls! She had blocked him out, just as he had blocked her.

"She's learning from her past mistakes," Juktis spat in frustration as he paced and considered his options.

"You need to think about this…advantage you keep claiming you have over her. Why not use it?"

"It's not big enough yet to use against her. It won't be able to hear half as well as I'd like. But," he paused as the idea hit him. "But I could use it in another way."

"How?"

Juktis looked at his partner and smirked as he went over the possibilities and found the idea to be more than sound. It would work.

"We need to wait until she's asleep. Then, I'll show you."

Ezra watched from the side of the courtyard as Derik worked with Dark Lightning. With very little else to do, other than wait, she had begun to investigate the kingdoms bordering Ammora as well as other mages. She had found two immortal mages that she was considering approaching, having looked up as much about them as they allowed to be found. Being immortal had both its advantages and disadvantages. Being mages made it very hard to fully disappear. So far, she hadn't approached anyone via a mirror spell. Yet.

And when she wasn't working on investigating, Ezra had begun to teach Derik how to handle a horse. Next, she intended to teach him how to fight on horseback, but for now, she had taught him enough that he was coming along to be an expert horseman at the very least.

At the moment, Derik was grooming Dark Lighting, having put the horse through his paces enough that he had been well exercised, but not pushed beyond his limit. Dark Lightning was leaning into the strokes of the brush against his sides, his eyes half-closed in pure pleasure. Derik no longer looked nervous but was completely content as he worked on removing every speck of dirt and sweat from the horse. Before he could see her, she turned and headed back inside, careful not to let her heels click against the floor as she moved.

::Ezra, how are you feeling?::

::The morning sickness has passed, Baelios, but I still feel as though the other shoe is going to drop any day now,:: she replied, pausing to put a hand against the small bump of her belly. Eight weeks had passed since Juktis had raped her and her belly, while it wasn't large yet, wasn't as flat as it had been before. While she couldn't feel the baby move yet, she still felt the hormone surges, the sudden hot flashes that hit or the sudden urge to cry over nothing. Ezra was trying not to let it show in front of others, but it was beginning to wear on her to not show a sign of weakness.

::You don't have to worry, Ezra. No one sees you as weak.::

::I know that, Baelios, but I don't want anyone to even begin thinking that either. I'm not a ruler, but they are looking to me as some sort of leader. I need to get them to understand that I'm not here to lead anyone. I'm just here to do a job, it's as simple as that.::

::They won't see it that way, Ezra. And you know it.::

::I can't declare myself a Queen! I won't. That's not who I am. I'm just a Sorceress.::

::Not just a sorceress. *The* Sorceress of Ammora. Other kingdoms are beginning to take notice that things are happening here.::

::Since when?::

::Since Juktis decided to take Ammora for his own. Other mages are sensing you are here, Ezra. That can be both good…and bad.::

::It can't be helped at this point, I suppose. Though, once this is over, I do want to pass into obscurity again.::

::I don't think that's likely to happen either, Ezra. You're going to have to accept that others will look up to you, or others will look at you as an enemy.::

::I accepted that a long time ago, Baelios. But I'll think about it. There has to be a solution, one that won't involve me taking power over people when I'm supposed to be guarding against the Darkness--::

The vision unfolded in front of her then. A wave of darkness, washing over the world, dimming out the light. A terrible laugh rose, echoing over the land as she heard the screams of men, women and children of all the races upon Axrealia as they all died. Then she saw a single light in the dark, glowing brighter, beating it back—

And it ended as abruptly as it started, leaving Ezra shaking in the corridor as it passed. She had heard what the Council had seen, but this was the first time that she had ever seen it for herself.

:;Ezra, are you all right?:: Baelios asked urgently as he appeared before her, worry showing in his glowing orange eyes.

::I'm…fine. It was a vision...a Vision of the Darkness to come, but I couldn't see who brought it.::

::That's because the vision doesn't show anything more than a single dark cloud growing over the surface, blotting out every bit of light--::

::Except for one single light…the Single Light in the Dark. Ammora.::

::They didn't see that in the original vision.::

::Because Ammora didn't exist back then. I…I'm at a loss as to what it means.::

::Perhaps that you and Ammora are the answer they didn't have back then.::

::Maybe. We won't know until it happens. I'm…tired, Baelios. I think I'll go lay down for a while.::

::Most wise, Ezra. I'll wake you if anyone needs you,:: Baelios promised as he vanished. Ezra hung her head for a moment, so weary she didn't feel she could take another step, then used her magic and teleported herself directly to her bed. Stretching out on the covers, she removed her headdress and closed her eyes, falling asleep almost instantly.

Vision of Darkness

Juktis finished his preliminary spell and was surprised.

"She's asleep! Now, let's see what you are hiding from me, Sorceress," he growled as he sat on his own throne and allowed his eyes to close.

The dream started simply enough. Ezra found herself back in her old traveling leathers, walking into the main hall, where the wizard council was chanting. She had dreamed of this moment from her past fairly often, so she wasn't alarmed. Not at first.

She pled with Bael to come with her, but he only looked at her sadly before continuing to chant.

"Well, well, well...." A cold and all too familiar voice rang out. Ezra turned.

"Juktis!" She gasped as she saw the tall, muscular dark-haired sorcerer standing there in the center of the room. He was looking around almost with glee.

"Yes, Sorceress."

"You can't be here!" She gasped and reached for power that she didn't yet have to cast him out.

Juktis laughed.

"How quaint. You weren't born a sorceress and, in this moment, you don't have the power to do anything to me," Juktis replied with a smirk as he approached her. "Now, what are you hiding from me," he murmured as he reached for her. Ezra dodged him and grasped her quarterstaff and drew her sword, bringing both to bear on Him. "Impressive. A warrior," he murmured as he drew a sword of his own and attacked.

In the dream, he was formidable! Ezra dodged and parried, thrust and lunged only to roll barely out of range of his sword as he arched it down towards her. After an eternity of fighting, all while the wizard's council chanted, he disarmed her. The blast filled the room and threw her back into the wall—

The dream changed and she found herself chained down to an altar in a room she had never seen. Juktis stood over her, smirking as his fingers ran over her, leaving fire in their wake.

"No, this isn't possible," she gasped as she struggled against her chains, trying to raise power in her sleep.

"All things are possible with magic, Sorceress. Particularly when a child is involved. It provides a perfect conduit, allowing me to look even into your mind." He continued to rake his fingers over her, as Ezra screamed—

She sat up in her own bed, screaming as she forced herself to wake!

"He knows…he knows about the baby!" she cried, unable to keep from shouting it out loud. Baelios appeared next to her, but Ezra couldn't stop shaking. A few moments later, Derik was pounding on the door and Ezra waved a hand, unlocking it for him. Baelios disappeared as Eve followed, hard on Derik's heels along with her partner, Phyla. Phyla looked around, sheathed her blade and sat next to Eve as Derik sat down on the edge of Ezra's bed.

"Sorceress, what are you talking about?" Derik asked her gently.

"Juktis broke into my dream," she whispered, feeling tears falling down her cheeks.

"Impossible. It was just a dream. You've been concentrating so hard on defeating him—"

"He broke into my dream, Derik. With magic…just about anything is possible. He was in my dreams and used the baby to do it!"

"How can that be? The baby is Derik's—"

"The baby isn't mine, at least not…biologically. Juktis…raped her," Derik said gently, and touched Ezra's hands, trying to soothe her. "We don't want that being spread around right now. She doesn't want what that bastard's done being held against the baby. It's not the baby's fault that it's father is a horrible, demented, sadistic asshole," he explained. Ezra hung her head, feeling foolish that she could hide this forever. "Not that I hold anything against the child. It's not the baby's fault. It isn't the Sorceress' fault. And…I will be this child's father as it grows…if you'll let me, Sorceress," he said softly. Ezra lifted her gaze to his, seeing that his words were nothing but sincere truth.

"You don't know what you're asking, Derik. I am the Sorceress of Ammora, first and foremost. Everything else comes after that—"

"I know. I've been here long enough to know that. You were willing to suffer while I made up my mind about helping you. You were willing to sacrifice yourself to beat Juktis and if I hadn't been here, you'd still be recovering. I know that I can't replace the husband you lost. All I'm asking is for you to let me love you, be here with you, as a husband to you and a father to your baby. I love you," he said as tears made his own eyes shine. Ezra felt her walls crumbling, her loneliness crushing them as her heart yearned for the love he was offering.

::He means it, Ezra. Bael would want you to be happy,:: Baelios whispered into her mind. Ezra began to sob and leaned into Derik's arms, unable to hold her own emotions at bay any longer.

He wrapped his arms around her and soothed her, whispering softly to her like a litany. "I love you; I won't ever leave you." Neither of them noticed as Eve and Phyla eased themselves out of the room, giving them both some much-needed privacy.

Juktis came out of his trance with a smile.

"Well?" his dark partner asked impatiently.

"It worked. I was able to go into her dream and see some of her memories. She was there the night the Wizard's Council disappeared. They sacrificed themselves…and made Ammora what it is. Made her what she is. But I didn't catch her name. Not yet. In time, I'll learn all of her secrets."

"Good. In the meantime, it's time I left another gift."

Mara shivered as she finished cleaning one of the officer's rooms in the Fortress. Everything here felt tainted, sick. Even the servants looked ill and pale. She and Aeryn had done what they could, taken supplements and drank and ate from their own dwindling stores rather than eat or drink anything out of the kitchen. Mara was assigned to clean upstairs until lunchtime, then prepare soup and porridge for the evening and next morning down in the kitchens. Which was a very good thing.

I could poison a lot of these scum easily if I needed to. I'll settle for making them sick the night before we take off though. This whole place gives me the creeps! she thought as she left the room with a shudder. Someone had been used in there, she could tell from the smell. That same someone had bled a lot. She wondered if they were even still alive. *Sadistic, evil bastards. I hope we can give the Sorceress what she needs and get out of here soon.*

With a sigh, she went downstairs to begin her work in the kitchen, shivering as she heard Juktis, or "M'lord" beginning to laugh again.

That can't be good. Mara hurried her steps and got to her work, listening to the quiet murmur of gossip that seemed to be ubiquitous in every kitchen. Not that there was much of it allowed, but the little she'd gleaned had given her a clear picture.

Juktis meant to make war on Ammora and then on the rest of Axrealia. He wouldn't stop either, until everything and everyone was firmly under his thumb. Mara and Aeryn were waiting to report until they had enough information to make it worth the Sorceress' while. But they both knew they were against the clock. Every day, more soldiers poured into the Fortress. Or left it, but those that left went to the cities around the mountain to take more arms, more women, more slaves and more food. As it was, they had enough food here to outlast a siege, if need be.

Today there wasn't much gossip to be had, so Mara kept her head down and hurried through her work. Once she was dismissed for the evening, she fled to the forge and went up to the small room she shared with Aeryn. Bathing herself from the pitcher in their room, she changed her clothes and combed her hair and waited for Aeryn to finish for the day. Tonight, they had decided it was time to report.

Jarod approached the cave cautiously, having found the cave after a week of searching Mount Astaria. Even with the map, it hadn't been easy. He'd had to abandon his sky chariot in order to get close. Now he stood at the cave's mouth, and watched it for a moment, reaching out with his mage senses even as he pulled out a scanner.

Good thing that I keep up with technology, even if the Sorceress of Ammora doesn't. Once I have it, I can take the easy way back. I'll get the sky chariot another day, if I have to, he thought as he began to walk forward, slowly. *She said it was well protected. Well, here goes nothing.*

He lit an orb and sent it ahead and took out a small scanner from his belt. It detected movement just seconds before a trap was sprung and he leapt out of its way, rolled and came back up to his feet.

"That was a little too close for comfort. Whew. Okay, let's find that Orb." Jarod reached out with his senses again, seeking it. "They should've masked it's energy. I can feel it coming from the tunnel on the left." Turning to that direction, he hurried through the cave, picking his way through as carefully as he dared.

A prickle of warning was all he got from his magical senses as he rounded the corner. Jarod ducked as a magical trap came to life, sending fireballs raining down on him from the ceiling. Unlike the physical traps, the magical traps didn't trip his sensor. His magical senses, however, were sharp enough to feel them as they went off. He made a shield and deflected the fireballs that rained down on him, then made a mad dash to the tunnel beyond. "I must be getting closer! Any mortal would've been dead by now," he said to himself as he paused again to check his sensor. He waved his hands, casting a spell to reveal any more magic to his sight and breathed a sigh of relief. "That must've been the last one. Well, here goes," he said as he stepped at last into a large chamber. In the center of the room stood a pedestal with a single large globe upon it. He approached and touched it. "Rosar Morlesa," he murmured and lifted the orb smoothly from the pedestal.

"Let's get out of here," he murmured as he teleported back out of the chamber. The protections on the place wouldn't allow magic in, but it had no problem letting magic out. After all of his exertion, he didn't quite have the strength to teleport himself further than the sky chariot. "So much for teleporting back to Ammora Castle, then. Let's get to an inn. I need a bath and a hot meal followed by a real bed for a change." Using magic to disguise himself, he set off for the nearest town between Mount Astaria and Ammora.

Chapter Twelve

It was late, past midnight easily. Mara and Aeryn took out their rings and touched them and waited in the darkness. The other blacksmiths had long since left the building. They had extinguished the candles. Most of the soldiers had long since sought their own beds.

Even the fortress was quiet. It was the perfect time for a quick report.

::Yes, Mara and Aeryn?:: came the telepathic reply, the Sorceress' voice tinged with weariness. Mara touched the stone of her ring and opened her mind to the Sorceress.

We're in the fortress. There's six-hundred and seventy-five soldiers. Fifty officers, at least another hundred and fifty servants. That's the count I've gotten so far from working as a maid and as a soup girl, Mara thought, keeping her mind focused on the facts.

This place gives me the creeps, Sorceress. I'm one of five blacksmiths and we're all working on weapons. They want a thousand swords, easily as many shields, knives and spears. Everyone here is scum, the men look at every woman with an eye at rape. Only thing keeping Mara safe is that I told anyone I caught looking at her that I'll personally hand him his own balls if he even touches my woman. Mara almost jumped as she could hear Aeryn's report and saw the small nod as she looked at him. He had heard hers as well. She relaxed, glad that they would know what the other was saying.

::Well done, you two. Have either of you overheard any plans that they're making?::

Not in detail. He means to take Ammora, then put all of Axrealia under his thumb. I'm being assigned to clean Juktis' chambers tomorrow. I'll let you know tomorrow night if I see or hear anything, Mara promised.

::Be careful, you two. Once we figure out a plan, I'll let you know what our next move will be,:: Ezra promised before the rings ceased to glow, breaking the connection for the night. Mara and Aeryn put them away in their top drawer and lay down in the darkness together.

"Let's get some rest," Aeryn whispered very softly to her as he held her in the dark. Mara gave a nod and tried to rest, hoping that tonight the nightmares wouldn't come.

Vision of Darkness

Ezra sagged as she broke the connection with Mara and Aeryn, dismayed at the news. Juktis was preparing to return, but how and when? She rubbed her eyes, feeling so tired. Ever since the nightmare where Juktis had broken into her dreams, she hadn't dared to sleep for very long or often. But she was at the end of her resources and she felt so tired, she could barely think.

:;Ezra, you need sleep,:: Baelios urged silently. Derik stirred next to her, snoring softly from where he slept beside her. She hadn't allowed herself to be alone at night since the nightmare, but she couldn't bring herself to sleep. She no longer trusted that Juktis wouldn't find a way in again.

::Baelios, you know why I can't--::

::Use your second headdress. The soft one. It should keep him out--::

::What if it doesn't?:: Ezra asked him, bluntly.

;:If it doesn't, then we'll work on something else, something that will block anything from entering your mind while you rest. Please…just try,:: Baelios pled with her as he handed her the brown headdress, the one from her disguise pack. Ezra sighed, but pulled off her silver one, then put on the brown and lay down.

::If I have another nightmare about him, Baelios--::

::Then I'll help you if you do. We'll find a solution. Rest.::

Ezra sighed again and closed her eyes, allowing herself to drift off.

Derik was down with Captain Lita and the builders behind the Castle. The city was complete, but there was room to grow. Torches, candles and fires illuminated the city, giving light to every building, which had been erected so quickly, Derik wondered if the mages Lita employed had helped to speed things along.

Or Ezra, maybe. I wouldn't be surprised. She seems so worn out lately, he thought as he watched the final stone being placed on what was to be, according to Ezra, the Council Chamber. The rest of the mercenaries stood there with him and cheers erupted from them as they regarded what had become their City.

"Speech! Speech!" the crowd demanded as Captain Lita went to stand on the steps and regard her company.

"Quiet now, quiet! All right. We are all very grateful for our new homes. The Sorceress of Ammora has been the most generous employer we have ever had! But, with everything, there is a price. This City is our pay. And our contract is not yet complete! So, this is home, but we're here to do a job. Those who are close to retirement, you'll be here to help guard and defend. The rest of us, we all know that the Sorceress has enemies. One, in particular, has been cruel enough to hurt one of our own. That one, we will find. But we also know of the other, Juktis, the Dark Sorcerer of the West. That one, we will bring to justice. So, my people, are you ready to prepare to go to War?"

The answering cry of defiance pleased even Derik.

We're going to need more people than this, though. Where will we find them all? Even the Guild doesn't have more than three or four companies at a time who aren't already in a contract, Derik realized and sighed. In order to take on Juktis, they would need more.

But, where to find them all?

Ezra woke with a start as she pushed her way back out of another nightmare. She sighed and rubbed her eyes and rose, wearily trying to think through the fog of fatigue.

::Baelios, this isn't working. We need a solution and we need it now. Even the headdress doesn't keep him away.::

::I've looked through every memory of the Wizard's Council, Ezra. There's no knowledge there of how to keep someone out of a dream if they have a biological component of themselves within your body.::

::You mean the baby,:: she sighed. ::It's immortal--::

::Yes, but there may be a way to…::

::No. I'm not going to experiment on it. It's not the child's fault that her father is--::

::What did you say, Ezra?::

::I was saying that it's not it's fault--::

::You said "her."::

::So?::

::How do you know it's a girl?::

::It's just a feeling I have. I could be wrong.::

;:Intuitive feelings such as that are rarely wrong, Ezra.:::

::There's plenty of mothers out there who think they're carrying boys and they end up having girls. I doubt I'm any more accurate.::

::I would trust your feelings in this case. You're a mage, one who can see things most others can't.::

::If that's true, then why can't I see how we're going to beat Juktis? Or find Mara's attacker?::

::Because you are so tired that you can barely use magic. You need to fight back against him, Ezra.::

::How? In the dream, he takes me to a time when I'm not the Sorceress.::

::So wrench control back and use your powers on him. You can do it, Ezra. Your will is greater than his if you believe in yourself.::

::I've never been able to control a dream.;:

::You have, in the past, when you refused to allow yourself to go to see Bael in your dreams. This is the same thing--::

::How did you know about that?::

::I could sense it and sometimes, I watch your dreams. It's not often.::

::After this, make sure you don't do that anymore.::

::As you wish. I'm sorry, Ezra.::

Ezra rubbed her eyes and lay down again.

::If you can watch, then you can help. Go in with me this time. Help me fight him. Let Bael…help me one last time, please.;:

::Very well. Close your eyes, I'll be right behind you.::

It started off as it usually did, within that single night when Ezra had been changed and Ammora itself given life. Ezra burst into the throne room, saw what the Council was doing and turned to Bael—

The Council itself was gone. Baelios stood in its place and he offered her his hand with a comforting look. She took it and turned—

"Sorceress, I…who is that!" Juktis exclaimed.

"Now!" Baelios cried and Ezra took that moment of surprise to seize control of the Dream even as Baelios' power joined with hers, bringing her past this moment—

And into the present. Ezra's appearance changed to that of the form she had held since, with long white hair, white and silver clothing and headdress. Ezra's hand squeezed Baelios', which was as real as hers in the dream, and she brought up a spell and sent it straight at Juktis—

Who disappeared as if he were mist.

"Is he gone?" she asked softly as she looked around.

"I think so. I'll remain with you tonight, but I think it's safe to say that you can rest. If he comes back, we'll face him again."

"Thank you."

"Don't thank me yet. We don't know for sure that he's gone. Rest."

Ezra released control of the dream to Baelios and allowed herself to drift into the first restful sleep she'd had.

Something was wrong. Ezra sat up in the darkness, her heart pounding like a drum in her chest. All of her magical senses were going off, every protection she'd ever put into place vibrating like a spider's web with a fly caught in the strands. Without thinking, Ezra rose from her bed and began to run through the halls in her bare feet. Her clothes from earlier in the day were wrinkled, but at least it wasn't a sleeping gown. She ran straight to the Entrance Hall and lowered the drawbridge without thinking, running towards the alarms rather than away from them.

The sky was still dark with just a hint of false dawn on the horizon. Ezra started at that, realizing she must have slept through the night.

Vision of Darkness

On the opposite side of the bridge, a bundle of cloth lay on a rock like an offering. As Ezra continued to walk, she sensed that the trouble lay there. She knelt beside it, using both her eyes and her magic to look about her.

No one was nearby, but the bundle glowed red to her inner eye with recent dark magic. Dreading the worst, Ezra opened the bundle.

And out fell a falcon. Not just any falcon. One of the pair that flew over the Castle now and then looking for food. Ezra knew that the pair had nested long ago in the forest, as their parents had done before them. There was no blood, no broken bones. The look on the falcon's face was that of sheer terror.

Bitter tears began to roll down her cheeks as Ezra gathered it into her arms like a broken doll and turned to carry it back into the castle. While her heart wailed in agony, her mind began to work, testing the magical traces that were so strong they caused the bundle to glow like a light in the darkness.

The traces didn't belong to Juktis. They were decidedly more devious and left a very dark stain, one that Ezra had never detected anywhere on Axrealia.

Inside the Castle, Ezra took the bundle to her work room.

:;Baelios, can I—::

::Ezra, that sort of thing is necromancy. You can't bring it's spirit back from the dead, not without the help of a God. Only they can undo what's been done,:: came the sorrowful and solemn reply.

::Then it's time to call upon them. This poor bird didn't deserve to die like this. Perhaps they can undo this horrible sacrifice.::

Ezra lay the bundle upon her altar and unwrapped the bird. Summoning herbs from her garden, she lay flowers from each of the stems about the bird, for life. Berries were also summoned, to show fertility. Last, but not least, she took dead leaves, crumpled and dried for future use, and sprinkled these as well about the bird in a circle.

"Sulos tiravan lumya farr. Sulos tiravan lumya farr. Sulos tiravan lumya farr. SULOS TIRAVAN LUMYA FARR!" Ezra chanted, growing every louder with each repetition. She closed her eyes, swaying as she began to pour energy into the spell, calling for the Goddess with every fiber of her being. After the thirteenth cry, Ezra went quiet and opened her eyes, prepared to wait for an answer.

And discovered that the answer had already arrived. A woman, young to the eye with eyes that held no traces of iris or pupil and skin as dark as the darkest shadow. Long white hair fell in a waterfall down to the woman's knees. She was clad in a simple tunic and breeches, as Ezra was. No crown or any symbol of rank adorned her, yet she held herself with the ease of one whose was used to others doing her bidding.

"You have called, Sorceress of Ammora. You seek to intervene in fate," the Goddess' echoing voice observed dryly as the Goddess held her gaze.

"I seek to ask for this foul deed to be undone. The falcon is innocent and was used to send me a message. It's only fault was to be one of a pair that flies over my Castle seeking food. The mage who did this did this only to hurt me and to show what may happen to others who stand with me. Please, Goddess. I cannot bring her back, but I ask for you to give her mercy and undo this. Give her life again, please."

"There is a price for such a favor."

"I will pay it."

"Even if I seek to destroy this castle and make you mortal again? Even if I allow this world to fall to the Darkness?"

"I will pay any price you require, Lady. There is no one to take up the burden I lay down. If it is your will that our world die…then I would gladly ask that you take me instead."

"You would sacrifice yourself and leave this world unguarded?"

"I would, if it were your will that we all die. I'm tired of waiting, Lady. I'm tired of pushing myself to get stronger and better and to stop the evil that seems to sprout everywhere. I'm tired..so tired, Lady. I ask you to spare this bird and our world…and just take me instead. Take me and Ammora if you must…but let our world and this bird live."

The Goddess seemed to look right through her.

"No. The Darkness is too big a threat and it must be stopped here. But because you were willing to sacrifice yourself…I will do as you ask. The price is paid." The Goddess touched the falcon, which drew a great shuddering breath and began to flutter its wings. Soon, the falcon had hopped onto the Goddess' arm, looking as calm and serene as if it had never died.

"Thank you, Lady."

"This bird will return to you in your darkest hour. Remember that in that hour…you are not alone. You may be the flame in the darkness…but that doesn't mean you are the only one."

Before Ezra could puzzle out what she meant, the Goddess and the falcon disappeared. Outside, she heard a single raptorial cry of triumph.

::Ezra, Lord Jarod has returned. He's approaching the drawbridge,:: Baelios reported and Ezra hung her head for a moment.

::Let him in, please. I'll meet him at the entrance hall,:: she sent back as she turned to leave her work room. ::It seems that it's time to begin preparing.::

::For what?::

::For war, Baelios. If he has the Orb, then it's time to go and take the fight to Juktis.::

Derik entered a chamber he'd never gone into before and paused. It was round, with a circle table in the center. He had come at the Sorceress' summons, just as Captain Lita was. Eve, the healer was here as well, along with the blacksmith, Ren.

The only unexpected person that was there was Jarod.

"Derik, Captain Lita, please come in. Welcome to the War room. We have much to go over," Ezra announced as she waved her hand over the circular table. A map of Axrealia appeared and highlighted in red was Juktis' fortress.

Derik took a seat next to Ezra, giving Jarod a dark look as he settled down.

"Lord Jarod, thank you for coming back and bringing the Orb of Eithal with you. We now have the means to trap Juktis, but we will need more mages. Some to help the fighters. Others to help myself and Lord Jarod to imprison Juktis within the orb. So, here is what we have so far from Mara and Aeryn."

It wasn't good. Juktis had six hundred fighters. Captain Lita had two hundred and twenty.

They were going to need more.

"Have you contacted the Guild, Sorceress?" Captain Lita asked.

"Not yet. In this time of year, they don't have as many companies that haven't already taken up contracts. We might get another one, maybe two. Any suggestions for allies?" the Sorceress asked, looking worried.

"The Desert Tribes might be willing to help. They like a good fight and they are honorable. They might help," Lord Jarod offered.

"A good suggestion, but how willing are they usually to leave their desert? Not usually, if I recall. I am going to reach out to Queen Durala of Surzika. She usually helps her allies and Surzika is only a little further than Zethos," Ezra replied, though Derik saw more worry flash in her eyes.

"We should try the Desert Tribes anyway and…I would reach out to Zethos. The rulers there—"

"Don't get involved with their neighbor's troubles, Derik. I have been watching them for a very long time. They stay within their own borders and never leave it."

"Have you tried the Elves?" Eve asked.

"Not yet. The surface Elves have been fighting with the Elves of the Caves. I'll ask, but I'm not expecting a reply."

"We might not have enough then to counter him, Sorceress," Captain Lita observed dryly, looking worried.

"If we can't take him on in a direct fight…then we need to cause him trouble. I'll go see to arranging for that. Lita, please send three couriers out with these messages. One to the Elves, one to the Desert Tribes. The last to Surzika. And this message…I'd like you to take it yourself, Derik."

Derik took the scroll and looked up to Ezra.

"Where am I going?"

"To the Guild in Zethos. Take Dark Lightning with you. You're ready to take him out." She winked to him, then turned to the others. "Eve, please begin preparing healers to go out with the soldiers. Ren, please begin making whatever weapons you deem are necessary for our soldiers. We're going to need them. Particularly if they come for us before we're ready to go to them."

Everyone rose to go about their business. Derik turned to talk with Ezra and found her leaving with Jarod, already deep in conversation about mages that they might recruit. He sighed and went to his quarters to begin packing.

Chapter Thirteen

"You haven't found any other immortals yet?" Jarod asked, astonished. Ezra sighed and looked back to him.

"I have found two that I'm considering asking for help, but I wanted your thoughts on them first. I just haven't asked if they're willing yet. I've been doing some research and we've been busy while you've been gone."

"Busy how? I saw the city was done, but—"

"We've had a gift left to us on our doorstep. Not from Juktis, but someone like him. A woman. She left magical traces this time and I felt a similar trace the last time I tried to use the astral to investigate Juktis' fortress. I think your brother has a partner. One who has even less morals than he does."

"That's hard to believe."

"They also like to torture their victims nearly to death. Or to death. We're going to have to be very careful in how we proceed."

"We knew that already. Who are you thinking of contacting?"

"Lady Reanalia and Lord Faorir. Lord Faorir seems to have all but dropped out of sight and all signs point to 'Leave me alone.' But, Lady Reanalia helps sometimes if the cause is worthy enough. Or if she has an interest in it."

"Juktis tried to steal her power about fifty years ago," Jarod offered.

"Then she'll be interested in it. I'll have to find a way to convince Lord Faorir to help, but I think if he knows just how dangerous Juktis and his partner are—"

"But we don't even know who the partner is."

"No, only that she's a woman. And her magic is unlike any I've seen before. But I'm going to find out. It'll be easier with four of us, particularly since our balance should outweigh theirs. We'll be just enough to counter them, I hope."

"All right, in the meantime, what do you need me to do?"

"Rest for now and be ready for when they come. The four of us will be putting in some long nights in the War Room."

Ezra left him at his chambers and went to Derik's next. She paused outside his door, having seen the flash of hurt in his eyes as she'd gone to consult with Jarod. But she needed to see him before he left.

She tapped on the door and waited.

Derik was busy packing for his trip to Zethos. He looked at his closet, considering just packing it all and leaving it behind. All that stopped him was his promise to Ezra. A promise to not leave her alone again. A promise to atone.

Was this part of that? He had begun to feel more than just friendship towards her from the very beginning. But, did she feel any of that in return? He sighed and rubbed his temples.

"A copper for your thoughts, Derik?" the Spirit of Ammora asked as he appeared before him.

"You know Ezra better than anyone. Does she...feel...anything for me at all?"

There was a knock at the door then and Derik sighed. The Spirit simply bowed.

"You will have to ask her to find out. I can tell you it would be a mistake for you to leave us behind. We need you. We all do," the Spirit said softly before he disappeared. Derik kicked the bed in frustration.

"Who is it?"

"It's me," Ezra's voice replied, muffled by the door. "May I come in?"

"Wouldn't you prefer the company of Lord Jarod?" he replied back bitterly.

"If I preferred him, I would say so. Derik, please...I want to talk before you go."

Derik glared at the door, but moved to it and opened it to let her in.

Ezra stood there, in her usual everyday tunic and leggings. Her headdress was in her hand and she stepped inside, then closed the door behind her. He realized that she seemed shorter than usual, then saw that her feet were bare.

"If you weren't immortal, you'd catch your death, running around in bare feet," he said as she moved closer to him.

In answer, she swooped in and kissed him. A long, deep kiss, the sort that made his heart soar.

After that, there were no words, not for a long, long while.

Vision of Darkness

Derik left on Dark Lightning later that afternoon. Ezra watched him go with a heavy heart, not knowing how long he might be away. The message he was to deliver would need time for a response and she knew it could easily be a month or two before he returned.

Once she lost sight of him, she raised the drawbridge and went to her throne. Everywhere in the Castle, mercenaries were either working or training. The cook had managed to get a couple of people to be her assistants. Others were busy cleaning in various places. Out in the city, more mercenaries trained and prepared. The black smith was putting one of the new forges to use and making weapons and armor for any who needed it.

The noise was both soothing in a way and welcome, but it had begun to wear on her as well.

I'm not used to having so many people around anymore. When this is over, I'm hoping they'll stay more in the city than in the castle, Ezra thought wearily as she sat down on her throne, the one room where no one else was or would disturb her.

Well except for her work room, which she had locked magically.

::Faint hope, Ezra. You were very generous, but the price of that is that they intend to stay and help you from now on,:: Baelios chimed in, practically cheerful with so many new faces around.

::It's fine, so long as I get a little peace now and again,:: Ezra replied telepathically. ::I'm going to need a bit of quiet to get this done anyway. It's time to talk to Lord Faorir and Lady Reanalia. Who should I try first?::

::Lady Reanalia is more open to others. I would try her first. She might be able to help you to convince Lord Faorir::

::Good idea. Well, here goes. Watch my back for me.::

::Anytime, Ezra. Anytime.::

Ezra closed her eyes and began to relax herself. Slowly but surely, she pulled her astral form out of her body and spread her angelic wings. It took time and quiet...but so long as no one disturbed her, Ezra knew that her body would be all right. She jumped into the air and began to fly, searching over Axrealia. Leaving Ammora, letting her magical senses guide her towards Lady Reanalia's location first.

Lady Reanalia lived in a tower that was built on the top of Mount Dearoth in the Floating Mountain range. A place that very few could go, but in her astral form, Ezra sped towards it. She pulled up just meters away from the place and reached out, knocking magically so that Reanalia would know that she had a visitor.

::Who are you?:: came the suspicious reply.

::The Sorceress of Ammora. Greetings, Lady Reanalia. May my astral form enter and we can speak, face to face?:: Ezra asked politely.

:;Very well. I haven't had a visitor in decades. Come on in, Sorceress. I see your astral form. You'll come to no harm here, so long as you don't intend it yourself.::

::Thank you, Lady.:: Ezra flew inside and landed lightly on the stone floor and used magic to make herself look more solid, though it was only her spirit that stood there.

Lady Reanalia was seated at a table, much like Ezra's library table. It was covered in scrolls and books. The Lady herself regarded her, toying with a quill while regarding Ezra with soft brown eyes. Long red hair was bound up in a long braid that hung down her back. The lady's dress was a deep burgundy velvet and trimmed with gold ribbon.

::I've heard much about you, Sorceress. Though I have to admit, I thought you were a myth,:: Reanalia started.

::I spread many false rumors to try to keep tongues from wagging too much and also to make others think as much. I imagine you've done the same as it wasn't easy to find you.::

::True. Well, why have you come to see me?::

::Juktis has tried to take my Castle and my power. I defeated him, barely, but he's going to come back. Before he does, I'd rather take the fight to him. He's too dangerous to leave loose and he is intent on destroying our world. Innocents will die if he wins. I have a plan to defeat him once and for all, but…I'm going to need help. Please, Lady, I need the help of others if he's to be dealt with permanently.::

::What's your plan? You can't kill him.::

::No, but he can be imprisoned. I have the Orb of Eithal, which should serve that purpose. Please, will you help us?:: Ezra asked, swallowing her pride and asking with all that she was.

Lady Reanalia chuckled a wonderful warm chuckle and rose.

::Of course I'll help you. Juktis has it coming after what he tried to pull with me five decades ago. It's time for him to have a bit of his own medicine. I'll set out for Ammora at once. Expect me at dawn.::

::Oh, Thank you! I'll see you at dawn, Lady Reanalia. May the Gods bless you and protect you on your journey.::

::And may the Gods help us all, if we fail. Go. See you tomorrow.::

Ezra flew back out, allowing her form to return to its invisible state and began seeking for the next mage. Lord Faorir was more reclusive. She knew that that journey would be a much longer one.

* * *

After what felt like days, Ezra finally found the right path to Faorir's hut. He had receded so far into the wilderness, that he was nearly impossible to find. Layer after layer of protection surrounded his home and Ezra almost felt sorry for the hermit.

Finally, she landed just outside of his protections and sent a single little whisper of magic through them, seeking him.

::GO AWAY!:: was the bellowed telepathic response.

:;Lord Faorir, I've come a very long way. Please, I must speak with you. For the welfare of all of Axrealia, please listen to what I have to say,:: Ezra sent back, using another small bit of magic to make herself visible to his eyes.

::NOT INTERESTED!::

::All of Axrealia will die if I fail. Please, My Lord!::

::I'VE DONE MY BIT FOR AXREALIA! GO AWAY!::

Ezra pursed her lips in irritation and crossed her arms.

::I'm not leaving until you hear what I have to say. I'm fighting a man named Juktis. A dark mage who is intent on killing every man, woman and child of every species of our world. Even the insect-peoples. Please, My Lord. I need three other mages to help me to trap him into the Orb of Eithal. I'd rather that those who stand with me to be with honor, compassion and understands the balance that we all try to preserve. Please, My Lord. I need your help.::

She sensed a mental sigh, then the immortal emerged. He was old, very very old and ancient, but he looked as young as she did. But she sensed his weariness just as he likely sensed hers.

"Astral projection. I need to make myself more invisible. How'd you find me, woman? And who are you?"

::I'm the Sorceress of Ammora Castle. I found you through persistence and patience and remembering the lore I've read of you, My Lord. Will you come to Ammora? Please?::

Faorir sighed, then said finally "Fine! I'll come, but you have to tell me who you really are when this is all done…and allow me to write down your tale for my Chronicles."

Ezra tilted her head with a hint of a smile.

::Chronicles of what?::

"The Chronicles of Axrealia, of course! I'm old, I've done my bit for Axrealia. But, I keep track of others. Those who are important to Axrealia. I'll come, but you have to tell me all of your tale. Agreed?"

Ezra could see no other way but gave a solemn nod.

:;Very well. I agree. When should we expect you?::

"With the dawn, youngling. Now, go home! I've got to pack!" Faorir went back inside with a chuckle of his own and Ezra shook her head and spread her invisible wings. As she faded back into the color of wind, she sped back to her body with a lighter heart.

They had the power they would need to defeat Juktis and his partner. But, would it be enough?

"I'm sorry, Derik. But I don't have any companies that are currently available to join your cause right now," the Guildmaster, a large well-muscled man named Rowland, replied. He had replaced the old Guildmaster about ten years ago, but he and Derik had trained together when they were growing up. Both had been orphans and on Ezra's generosity, both had been saved.

"What about pairs of soldiers then? Solitary men, people who aren't in a company. Men and women both. We need help, Rowland. Juktis is dangerous and he'll overrun Axrealia and destroy all of it. Everything we ever knew and loved…will die if we don't stop him," Derik said softly, not wanting to start a panic.

"I can send word around. I know of a couple of companies that might be at the end of their current contracts. And well...I know some solitary soldiers that are good honest folks. I do have a pair of friends that are with the guild. Have been for a long time. You might remember them," Rowland said with a smirk. "And, lucky for you, they're in town."

"Who?" Derik asked, a smile breaking over his face.

Rowland nodded and Derik turned around.

In the doorway stood a pair of warriors. One man, one woman. Both had blonde hair and tanned skin. Both looked as young as thirty-year olds and hadn't aged a day from when Derik first met them.

And both were smiling at him.

"Been a long time, Brah. Need a pair of Hunters?" Wahya, a tall, muscular warrior whose blonde hair was down to his shoulders asked as he extended his hand. Derik rose and took his forearm and shook it, gladly.

"More than you know, Wahya! More than you know."

"I'll send word out to the kids and our tribes. How many you need, Brah?"

"As many fighters, hunters, warriors you can get me. We have a big problem—"

"We've heard. Ammora's going to war. Hey, Rowland. You got a spare contract lying around? We're signing up right now. C'mon, Tala. Let's have a drink with our old friends," Wahya said as he made his way to a bench to sit. Tala chuckled. She was tall, buxom and as ready for a fight as Wahya. Long blonde hair was loose and curly, kept back only by a clip at the back of her head. She poured ale for all of them as Derik began to explain the situation.

"Sounds like this Sorceress needs more allies and friends. From all of Axrealia if all of this is really at stake, Brah," Tala said as she slid the ale across to Derik and Rowland.

"She knows, but she's stubborn. She's only recruiting now because he's already beaten her once. She doesn't want to chance it happening a second time."

"If he beat her, then how is it that we're not already under siege?" Tala asked, her eyes worried.

"I helped her. She banished him after I tricked him. Then, I…let's just say between what I did and what that Castle did…the rest of the warriors were either dead or running for their lives."

"Okay, so we've got the case of a very powerful immortal mage, one whose so dangerous he'll never give up. The case of another immortal mage, one who's here just to take care of people like him and keep our world from being destroyed. Pretty clear whose side we all need to choose. Rowland, send my name out to these three companies. I saw them at the Eastern Sea campaign a couple of months ago. They were almost ready to head for home. By now, they should be there. From what I recall, they weren't too happy with their last contract. Maybe this'll help them to make up the difference. In the meantime, I'm sending word to my tribe tonight," Wayha said as he wrote down the names of three companies on a piece of palimpsest and handed that over to Rowland. He looked to Tala, who was still looking worried.

"How are you getting information on Juktis?"

"I'll tell you, once we're back in Ammora. Rowland, any chances there's more soldiers around that'll be willing to come and help?"

"Oh yeah. I've got another dozen scattered between here and the next three towns. I'll send messengers out right now. They should be at Ammora in the next couple of weeks."

"I'll take it. Thanks, Rowland."

"My pleasure. Excuse me, Brothers and Sister. I'm going to get to it," Rowland grunted as he rose and headed out to do just that.

Derik turned back to Wahya and Tala.

"Any ideas on who else might be willing to help?"

"Oh, I've more more than a few ideas, Brah," Wahya replied and he began to laugh. Tala shook her head and looked back to Derik.

"You're gonna wonder what got you into this mess when he has half of Axrealia show up at your doorstep, Brah," she said with a hint of exasperation.

"I've been wondering that ever since I fell in love with the Sorceress."

"In love, are we? That's a first. What's so special about her?"

"You'll see when we get there."

Tala laughed and gently punched Derik in the arm.

"Tale, Brah! C'mon, I'm itching for a good hunt and a good fight. I need something to take my mind off of it."

"All right. It all began when I signed up with that one company. The one you told me not to take."

"Mmhmm. Learned your lesson, didn't ya, Brah?"

"More than you can imagine."

"I can imagine a lot, Brah."

"Well this is what happened...."

Chapter Fourteen

Mara had been sent to clean in Juktis' chambers. He was out, slithering about his own war council room, which suited her just fine. She dusted quickly on the few shelves that were there. His chambers were mostly sparse. Only a large bed, a pool of water that glowed with a foul purplish light that made the shadows dance eerily on the stone walls. A throne in the next room, that served as a smaller audience chamber. His main throne room was in the other end of the fortress and held more foul things.

Here, she was able to spy a little more easily, without any guards to see what she did. Mara went to change the sheets on the bed and froze.

In the bed, asleep, was a woman. A lithe, pretty little thing with long black hair and strange tattoos on her arms, legs and torso. This was of no surprise, really. Juktis sometimes took servants to bed, or so Mara had been told.

But this woman was no servant. Mara's eyes grew wide and she left the chamber as quickly and quietly as she could.

I remember that woman! She...she was the one! Mara thought frantically as she closed the door to the chamber. She took a moment and calmed herself and hurried on to another room. She would have to be more careful! *If she sees me, she'll know who I am! I need to tell the Sorceress!* Mara's heart pounded as she went about the rest of her chores. She glanced over her shoulder often and did her best to keep out of everyone's sight. Once the final room was done, she went down to the kitchens to tend the soup pots. It was agony, waiting as the hours slowly passed before she was finally allowed to go back to the forge and to Aeryn.

Aeryn took one look at her pale face and nodded her straight upstairs. Mara went up the stairs and shut the door and took out the rings. She hid them both in the pocket of her tunic as she lay down on the bed. After what felt like hours, Aeryn joined her, bringing two rations packs with him. She turned into him, clinging to him as she struggled with her fear.

"We need to report to the Sorceress..tonight!" Mara pleaded with him. Aeryn stroked her hair gently and pulled out his mace.

"We will. Soon as it's dark."

Ezra felt the pull of a summons and rubbed her eyes.

"Excuse me for a few moments, please," she told the War Council and went outside of the War Chamber. The War Council now consisted of eleven members, minus of course Derik. Derik hadn't returned yet, but she hoped he would be back as soon as possible.

Ezra closed the chamber door and leaned against the wall and reached out towards Juktis' fortress.

And seized upon Mara's connection as soon as she saw it was her.

::Yes, Mara and Aeryn?::

::Sorceress, she's here! The woman who tortured me! She's in Juktis' chamber! She's got black hair and strange tattoos all over her body. Please, Sorceress! If she sees me—::

::Shh. Very well. Can the two of you get out?::

::Not easily, Sorceress,:: Aeryn replied. ::Not without blowing our cover.::

::Then Mara needs to be reassigned just to the kitchens. Find a reason—say you can't walk far or you've sprained something that'll make it difficult for you to clean,:: Ezra suggested. ::I need you both to please hang on a little longer.::

::What if Mara just covered her face? I've established that women in my part of the world cover their faces as part of our beliefs. Mara could pretend to convert. No one would recognize her with a veil on.::

::That is an excellent idea. And it would be easier for you to clean and move about if no one could recognize you,:: Ezra sent back, grateful for Aeryn's quick thinking.

::I…think I could do it. Aeryn's told me enough about his religion that I could fake it. I do have veils with me, just in case. I just hope I don't run into her. At least she was asleep this time.::

::Next time, don't take a chance. Take the veil, pretend you and Aeryn are having trouble and you're trying to please him. They'll understand that. Anything else?::

::Juktis is getting more impatient. He's wanting to move against you soon.::

::We're doing our best to get more numbers. I'll let you know as soon as we're on the move.::

::Thank you, Sorceress. Good luck.::

::You, too. Stay safe!:: she sent as she closed the connection, then turned to go back into the War Council.

Please, Gods, watch over them, Ezra pled silently as she took her seat and went back to the business at hand.

Lord Faorir and Lady Reanalia had both arrived, to Ezra's immense relief. Both had arrived later than she had thought they would, but they were both waiting across the moat when she woke and went to check on that all-too familiar feeling of a visitor's arrival. She lowered the drawbridge and waited as they crossed and sent both of their sky chariots to be hidden within the city behind Ammora.

"I don't remember that city behind this place. When did that happen, Sorceress?" Lord Faorir asked grumpily, leaning on his walking staff with a look of mischief twinkling in his eyes as he studied Ezra.

"Oh, that is new. I've hired a mercenary company to help me with keeping this place safe from Juktis and others who might misuse its power. Captain Lita and her company didn't have a place to rest or recover. Now they do," she explained quickly.

"Most mages in your position wouldn't want the uncertainty of mercenaries—" Faorir began.

"Most mages are not me, My Lord. Shall we get you both settled and then I can brief you over some refreshments in the library?"

"That would be lovely. Thank you, Sorceress. I'm very sorry for my delay, but I was waylaid by some bad weather. I could've sworn it was sent, the way it suddenly sprang up," Lady Reanalia stated as Ezra began to lead the way to the chambers she'd had prepared for each of them.

"I was stalled by bad storms as well. Felt dark and evil, and definitely smelled of magic. I didn't do anything to expel it, but I wouldn't be surprised if it hits your Castle in another day or so," Faorir added. Ezra winced, having felt a headache building for days.

"It's probably been sent by Juktis. I'll send a messenger to Captain Lita and warn her that we'll be putting up a shield later. I'd rather not take a chance that his storm does anything to this place. He's getting impatient."

"Upstarts like him usually does, Sorceress. They take as many shortcuts as they can in their race to gain more power," Faorir counseled as Ezra led them through the ever-changing maze of hallways. These days, the Castle sometimes changed daily, though it hadn't killed anyone since Juktis' last bold invasion. Even so, Ezra was having to remind it that people didn't enjoy being lost within its halls.

"This place is different. It feels alive!" Reanalia gasped as she touched a wall while they walked.

"It is alive. I'll explain when I brief you. These rooms are yours. I'll come and get you in an hour. Feel free to relax until then," Ezra said as she waved her hand and two doors opened, just a few doors down from the main hallway. "If you ever get lost, just call my name and I'll send an orb to guide you to me," she offered.

"Living Castle? What next? Moving walls?" Faorir grumbled as he closed his door. Reanalia chuckled as she closed hers and Ezra moved to go to the kitchen to ensure that refreshments would be ready on time with a chuckle of her own.

"Oh, this is going to be fun," she grinned.

* * *

Jarod studied the map on the table in the library, which was bathed in both red and blue colors. Blue was for Ammora and its forces. Red was for anything that belonged to Juktis, including the three cities that formed a triangle at the base of the Mountain where his fortress rested. Faorir and Reanalia studied it as well and Ezra was watching all of their faces carefully.

"This doesn't look good. He's got a hell of a strategic advantage," Faorir said dryly, noting the magical markers with a look that spoke volumes. Ezra felt horrible at having to request his help, but she knew there was few other choices that she could've made. His reputation was second to none and she was grateful he'd come.

"Yes, he does, and he has quite the advantage when it comes to numbers. Our job, in addition to imprisoning Juktis, is to make it possible to take away that advantage. We're the only mages powerful enough to send all of our soldiers in through portals to surprise all of them. We can drop them at the base of the mountain, or we can position them anywhere that we can break through his shields. The problem is, he's shielded most of that mountain. So, we need to come up with spells to break through his shields and send our soldiers in. That, or we need to distract everyone from inside so that our soldiers can move in undetected and then let them in once they're ready. It's...a problem and it's part of the reason why I asked for your help," Ezra explained as they looked it over.

"Juktis is arrogant and such arrogance also comes with a bit of recklessness. So, you mentioned distracting from the inside. How can we do that if we're locked out via his shields?" Reanalia asked.

"Shields often have weak spots. We should be able to locate one. I also do have a couple of little birds inside. That's how we've gotten all of our information is through them. Now, I'm going to have them stall Juktis and delay him with a bit of subtle misfortune. If they do their jobs well enough, they should have a nice distraction in place for the soldiers inside the fortress. Then we can begin keeping Juktis busy while they let our soldiers in. It's not going to be easy. It may take more than one battle and more than one distraction to get everything in place so we can win. Our problem, at this point is numbers. Derik is working on that for us as we speak—"

"Sorceress, please forgive the interruption!" Captain Lita called suddenly from the doorway. Ezra turned, worried.

"Yes, Captain?"

"There are some people out front across the moat. Tribesmen from…well…all over, Sorceress."

"Have they said what they want?"

"They said they wish to speak with you, Sorceress."

"Very well. Please excuse me, it seems my duties call again," Ezra said as she stepped up the ladder that led to her favorite parapet.

Looking down below across the moat, she blinked at what she saw. Legions of Tribesmen, all of which had all of their belongings with them, as was traditional for their people.

"Who speaks for you all, Tribesmen?" she called, worried for what this might mean.

Down below, figures shuffled and moved until three people came forth. Two blondes, a man and a woman with deeply tanned skin came up front and before them was a very familiar face.

"Sorceress, I hope this is enough," Derik called up to her. Ezra chuckled and relaxed.

"You could have sent word!" she teased as she lowered the drawbridge with a flick of her fingers and teleported herself without a second thought to land directly in the middle of it as it came to rest so they could enter. Derik ran to her and scooped her up, kissing her and Ezra kissed him back passionately, having missed him more than she could ever admit. As they finally broke apart, she turned to see the two hunters she had once known long before she had become the Sorceress.

"We wondered what happened to you! You've got a lot to explain to us, Sista!" Tala greeted her with a hug and a kiss to her cheek. Ezra looked at her, then at Wahya.

"It seems we'll have to have a small meeting of our own later. Don't tell them what my name is, please. Names have power—"

"You're preaching to the choir, Sista," Wahya replied with an amazed look of his own. "Bael—"

"Gave his life, along with the rest of the Wizard's Council…and changed me the same night. Listen, I'll explain all later, but we have to get everyone inside. A magical storm is coming tonight, one sent by Juktis. We have to get everything under shields before then," Ezra replied quickly.

"We can bivouac inside if you have room."

"We have room. Everyone, please come inside! Quickly," she called loudly before she turned with the other four to go inside, amazed as Derik led Dark Lightning and Wahya and Tala across the drawbridge.

:;Baelios--::

::It seems that the Gods have answered our mutual prayers, Ezra. Have them all go to the throne room and the dining room. Between the two, there should be enough room from there through the hallways for tonight. Tomorrow, we can have them bivouac behind Ammora.::

::Good idea,:: she replied telepathically, glad for his foresight. She looked around amazed.

:;The odds just tipped into our favor, I'd say.::

::You're right…now we just need to survive the night.::

Once everyone was settled, Ezra had returned to the Mage Council in the library. Over the hours, they poured over possibilities and plans before going outside to raise the shields that would protect Ammora and the city from the magical storm. Between the four of them, they raised enough power and raised the shields, tying it to Ammora's power to feed it so nothing could knock it down.

Even so, it was barely enough. That night, lightning and thunder, then hot unnatural flames rained down in a seemingly never-ending stream from the skies. Ezra stood with Derik in the library, watching from just inside as it kept coming down. Just behind them, Jarod, Faorir, Reanalia, Wahya and Tala waited as they waited to see if their shields would hold.

They did, but there were one or two loud booms in the night that made even Ezra jump and go pale.

Finally, everything went quiet and they all breathed a collective sigh of relief.

"I think it's safe for everyone to go to bed now," Ezra said with a smile that hid just how close that last boom had come to breaking through.

"I'm for that. Reanalia, shall we continue our discussion in the morning on your tale?" Faorir asked as he offered Reanalia his arm. Reanalia took it and walked out with him.

"Yes, I'd like that."

"As would I."

Jarod just gave a bow and headed out, trailing after them. At that point, Ezra closed the door to the library and locked it behind them for privacy. She shoved a bit of cloth into the keyhole, to keep anyone from listening. Then and only then did she relax.

"Okay, who's first? How are you two still alive?" she asked.

"We got cursed with immortality two decades before we met you, Ezra. Now, sista, how are you still alive?" Tala asked with a playful smirk on her lips.

"It's a bit of a tale."

"We've got the time to hear it. Start at the beginning."

"In that case…" Ezra started, but Baelios appeared before them all, beating her to it.

"How about if I explain?" he offered with a smirk of his own.

"Bael?"

"My name is Baelios. I'm…what is left of the Wizard's Council after the End of Days spell they cast."

"How did Ezra—"

"Bael changed the spell when she came and refused to leave. As a result, she is the Guardian and Protector of our home, Ammora. And I am her helper and the Castle is alive. It's all come out to be a rather strong arrangement," Baelios replied with a bow. Ezra bowed back and sat, feeling the baby squirming inside of her for the first time. Her belly was just starting to round. Ezra touched it gently, feeling it kick inside as they began a conversation that would last long into the night.

::Mara?:: The call made Mara sit straight up and touch her ring. She shook Aeryn and handed him his ring and she focused on the call from the Sorceress of Ammora.

"Yes, Sorceress?" she whispered softly to the stone in the ring.

::Oh good, I'm sorry to call so late. But we have a plan. I need you to start making things very inconvenient for Juktis and his partner. The worse, the better. Start small. Maybe make his soldiers sick, or find a way to eliminate his supply base,:; the Sorceress sent to them both. Aeryn smirked grimly and touched Mara's hand.

"Not a problem, Sorceress. We both have some ideas. How much time are we buying?" Aeryn whispered.

:;As much as possible. I'll let you know what your part is in our plan before it happens. Be careful and do not get caught.::

"We'll start tomorrow then. Be safe," Aeryn replied. Mara lay back down again, worried but ready to do something to strike back. "Still have soup duty?" He whispered softly into the darkness.

"Yes. I already know what to do. Let's get some sleep."

"Yes, it's going to be a busy day. I'm already making sure everything I'm making is weaker than a newborn kitten. One strike, it'll break," he murmured softly. "Am keeping all of it until it's time."

"Hopefully, it discourages a long war," Mara whispered back in agreement and snuggled into him before she closed her eyes. Sleep was long in coming, but she knew that it would be worth it in the end.

"How is this possible!?!" Juktis raged loudly as he paced his large private chamber. "Those shields withstood everything I threw at them! Worse, she's made them reflect back at me every time I try to peek the Castle!"

"Patience, Juktis. Patience. She's clearly up to something if she doesn't want you to see what she's doing. Have you tried going into her dreams again?"

"She manages to avoid me in them."

"So cast a spell. Make her your prisoner."

"It's hard to catch her asleep these days."

"Think. If she's not sleeping much, and she won't let you see in…what's she hiding?"

Juktis ran his fingers through his long black curls and looked into the orb that showed him nothing.

"She's getting ready for a fight. She's coming here."

"Yes…and you should let her. Once she's here, she'll be weaker. Easier to take and control. She's stubborn, so she won't come with others. She'll be alone and vulnerable. More so since your child is in her belly," his female partner crooned, running one slender hand over his shoulder as she came to look into the orb with him.

"I'm ready for her. My troops are ready for her. But, the traitor—"

"Will doom himself, insisting on coming with her. Even if he comes along, what can he do against all of your soldiers? He'll be dead at last…and you will have your prize. Her Castle will be yours for the taking."

"Too bad our troops are sick tonight. Stomach troubles plague the men. They need something to distract them from drinking and wenching soon. Otherwise, I'd strike her tonight, before she's ready."

"Why? Why go to where she's strongest? Let her come. Here, she is no threat. Here, you will not only win, you'll be able to imprison her and keep her vulnerable. With the child, you can finally cross into Ammora and take its power and it's secrets for yourself…without the burden of the mother to distract you."

"And what is your reward in all of this, my Pretty?"

"My reward…will be had after you've won. My darkness will spread over Axrealia…through you."

Juktis thought on that and smirked, then grasped her by the hair and led her back to his bed.

"Then let's celebrate getting our rewards."

The sounds that echoed down the corridors made the servants relax. For tonight, at least, their Master was distracted with more interesting prey.

Chapter Fifteen

Mara and Aeryn were once again plotting. Both of their daily duties had been completed and they were eating their supper alone in their tiny apartment above the forge.

"Their wagons have all needed new axles. I've been taking my time fixing them, too. The Guard Captain says I'd better hurry on it tomorrow though, or else there'll be trouble from Juktis," Aeryn said softly in between bites.

"Every time I'm in Juktis' chamber to clean and he's not in it, I make sure to throw every potion he's brewed out. And most of the ingredients to make them and to spoil whatever he does have brewing by throwing sneezing powder in it," Mara replied. "Can't do that too many more times, though. As it is, I've managed not to get caught. But, sooner or later someone's going to catch me at it."

"Then don't do it again, Mara. Try setting his spell book on fire by 'accident' next time," he suggested with a wink.

"Tried. He's got it protected by magic."

"Damn. Well, lay low for a few times, then start up again."

"Got it. What're we doing tonight?"

"I'm tired of being rushed by these assholes. Let's burn something tonight, hm?"

Ezra rubbed her eyes, feeling more and more tired as she sat through yet another planning session with just the mages that she intended to have fighting by her side. They had created new spells together, gone over the plans of the fortress and of course gone over as many likely scenarios as possible to plan for the war ahead.

. "He's obsessed with capturing Ammora. Our coming to him is going to take him off-guard," Jarod said thoughtfully as they looked over their latest plans.

"We hope. He might know what we're up to," Reanalia pointed out as they studied the diagram that Jarod had sketched out. Being as it had been his family's home, Jarod had been happy to help.

"How do we know he hasn't changed the layout of the fortress?" Faorir asked, a worried look on his face.

"My grandfather built it so it could never be changed. Stones are magically fused together. Jarod, as powerful as he is, couldn't counteract Grandfather's power," Jarod replied, a worried tone to his voice.

"What happened to your grandfather?" Ezra asked, curious.

"No one knows. He just left one day, told Mother and Father they could handle the fortress without him. He was immortal too, so…he's still out there somewhere."

"Why didn't you send for him?" Ezra asked.

"I tried. I couldn't find him. Jarod left the same year I did. I went out to learn new magic and learn other skills and to see Axrealia. He…he changed. Next time I saw him, he was more powerful and darker than I ever remember him being. He…I think he went in search of power."

"And found it…in the darkness," Ezra sighed before a Vision grasped her.

She was in a cave. There was a sound of steadily dripping water. The air was heavy, damp…and foul. At a first glance, there was nothing in the cave except a fire pit. As she watched a fire sprang up before her and on the opposite side of the fire stood Juktis.

"At last, I have found you," he murmured, holding his hand out to the strange red and black flames. He reached in and pulled…

Out came a hand, followed by a woman's body. The woman looked like a dark mirror of Ezra, complete with purple eyes and black hair. Odd tattoos laced and intertwined over the woman's skin, making an odd tapestry on her flesh.

"We must destroy Ammora before we can take Axrealia for our own," the woman told Juktis, her voice smooth as silk, seductive and venomous all at once.

"And we shall. Together," Juktis replied, his eyes glowing with greed as he reached for the nude woman, kissing her—

Ezra came back to herself all at once, the Vision releasing her as quickly as it had grasped her.

"He sought the Darkness willingly. It has chosen a form…and it's more dangerous than he could ever realize. She's the one who hurt Mara…and the falcon," Ezra stated, knowing at once why the woman's aura was familiar. Mara hadn't had a trace of magic, but there had been a strange aura about her for a day or two until she was healed of her wounds. The falcon had both a magical signature and an aura.

The woman was a match to both.

"How do you know this?" Faorir asked, looking at her with worry.

"A vision," Ezra replied. "A vision of their first meeting. He found her in a fire within a cave. It was dark, foul and rotten to its core."

"A forbidden place, perhaps?" Reanalia asked.

"Yes, but I haven't read of any such place—"

"I have, Young Sorceress. We can match Juktis, but the Darkness? She's been released from the Cave of Sorrow under the Serpent Sea," Faorir sighed, rubbing his temples. "If she thinks he's going to lose, she'll run."

"Does she have a name, My Lord?" Ezra asked, hopeful.

"None that has been recorded. Not even by me," Faorir replied sadly.

"Damn. Without a name, we can't bind her."

"Not yet anyway. Our goal is to stop Juktis. If she retreats, that's fine. I know her face now. I can prepare for her properly, now that I know who I'm really fighting. Let's focus on that. Tomorrow, we're sending our troops by portal to the three cities. Tribesmen will attack Sevabon. Wahya's tribe is going to attack Fasioth while Captain Lita and her company will attack Perab. Simultaneous attacks, we should have control of those cities by tomorrow night. After the way Juktis has been treating the people there, they may just surrender and if that's the case….they will be under our protection until this is all over," Ezra explained as she thought over the plan that They and the War Council had come up with. Reiterating it didn't hurt, but it also gave them a chance to think of anything and everything that could go wrong.

"After that, Juktis is probably going to retaliate," Jarod pointed out.

"Which is why there's mortal mages with each group…and they all have a charm. They'll activate the charms and I'll augment their power from here," Ezra replied.

"A good plan, Sorceress. So far, I can't see any way that Juktis can get around that. The tricky part will be the next day."

"That's where our little birds inside will come in handy. They'll have a distraction ready."

Mara crept along the alley in the darkness. Luckily there was no moon tonight, but that only made it harder to see. She stayed back as she saw a pair of guards coming with a lantern. Hiding in the shadows, she waited for them to pass before creeping out into the main walkway that led to the Guard's food stores. Her veil only added to her disguise of black breeches with black suede boots and a black tunic. Her target was the food stores that would be used for the march on Castle Ammora, though the word around the Fortress of late was that everyone was staying put. The soldiers were getting bored, reckless and as a result, they were beginning to wreak havok on the local towns. A grim smile on her face as she began to pour a bit of oil around her half of the building, taking her time as she walked and moved. Whenever she saw anyone coming near, Mara paused and hid, then started as soon as they were out of sight. Aeryn met her halfway around and they made a small trail that led into a different alley than they intended to take. Aeryn lit a match and dropped it on the oil and the two of them ran like hell into their escape, heading quickly for the blacksmiths. By the time they got there, the whole building was ablaze, and everyone was distracted with putting the fire out. Aeryn and Mara then joined the crowd as the mercenaries descended upon the blaze to organize a bucket brigade.

It was a beautiful sight. Nothing inside would survive the blaze and even as they both passed bucket after bucket of water, nothing seemed to do anything more than to keep the blaze confined to the one building.

By morning, nothing was left but cinders. Mara and Aeryn went wearily to their duties feeling an odd sense of satisfaction in their night's work.

Ezra woke early the next morning and dressed herself with a feeling of dread. She hated going into battle, it made it difficult to rest. Even as a mercenary, she'd never really slept very long or well the day before a campaign started. Throughout each war she'd been in, she'd never really rested well until it was all over.

She hurried out, dressed in her usual tunic and leggings, but she had added white boiled leather armor over it. Derik had wanted her to have real armor. Ezra had refused, not wanting to be weighed down by anything heavy. Her fighting style preferred to strike and retreat quickly rather than hack and bash. Ezra pulled her hair up, braiding it that long braid she normally wore. Today however, she pulled that up and began to coil it over her head, making it harder to seize. Braids could be a disadvantage on the field of battle, and she wanted every advantage that she could get.

In the Entrance Hall, Ezra was pleasantly surprised to see that all three immortal mages were there, waiting for her with the rest of the mortal mages. Faorir and Reanalia had been teaching the mortal mages spells that would be within each of their range of talents to add to their arsenal. Being long-lived had its advantages.

Ezra couldn't help but feel proud of the group she'd assembled to take on Juktis. Watching them, she could sense how much power they all had gained just by working with her.

Though, she felt a sense of dread every time she looked at Lord Jarod. He had lightened up and relaxed considerably. But, whenever he looked at her, she saw the desire that was growing in his eyes and it made her shudder.

He was too much like his brother in looks and while he wasn't evil, he certainly wasn't completely innocent either. Ezra sensed that much in his thoughts whenever she lowered her shields enough to read him.

"Can I have a word with you, Sorceress?" Jarod asked, having asked this same question several times since his return. Ezra sighed and shook her head.

"This really isn't the time—"

"You've said that every time I've asked. Please. It'll only take a few moments."

"Very well," she replied, then turned to the other mages, who had noticed this conversation. "We'll be right back. Please excuse us," she said before turning to lead him out to the hallway and an alcove there where they could talk. "What is it, Jarod?"

His response was to kiss her, deeply and firmly. She was taken by surprise, but quickly broke it by pushing him away.

"Lord Jarod—"

"Please, Sorceress. When this is over, I want us to be together—"

"You barely know me!"

"We have all of eternity to get to know each other. I want to help you guard this place—"

"I have plenty of people here now to help me with that."

"Together, we wouldn't need anyone else."

"I have made promises—"

"They can keep their city and we can help protect them. But you wouldn't need anyone else here. I've watched you. You're uncomfortable with so many others around. You often seek places to be alone. And at night—"

"At night, what I do is none of your business! I appreciate your offer, but—"

"Derik couldn't possibly make you happy. He's a mortal—"

"Again, that is none of your business! My relationship with him is between me and him!"

"He'll die someday, and you'll be alone again!"

"Yes, he'll die…someday. Years from now, decades from now—"

"A blink of the eye to one such as us!" Jarod insisted vehemently.

"Maybe. But, it's my choice, Jarod. Not yours. Now, we are going to go back in there and get our people on their way to battle. I suggest you get your mind on that and off of who I choose to spend my life with!" Ezra hissed, irritated that he had assumed that she would want Him, after all of this? She pulled away and walked back to the Entrance Hall, smoothing her hair as she walked and putting her own mind on the business at hand.

Derik paused to touch her elbow as she entered.

"You okay?" he asked softly. Ezra gave a nod and a smile.

"I'm fine. Never better. Are you ready?"

"I've been ready. Let's go save the world." They turned together, fingers lacing as they walked to where the mercenaries and the tribes had gathered.

::Ezra, there's more people outside,:: Baelios chimed in suddenly.

::Who, Baelios?::

::Orcs, The Hive Peoples, Gargoyles, Giants. Take a look for yourself.::

"Excuse me, we have some unexpected guests," Ezra announced before she turned and lowered the drawbridge. As she walked out, she blinked at how many people had gathered before her Castle and all were flying a single flag.

The flag of Ammora. It could be nothing else as it held the symbol that hung on every banner that had hung here for thousands of years. It was of a single ball of light, surrounded by dark material. The symbol of why this place still stood here.

Her symbol, Ezra realized as she watched.

"Sorceress, we have come to help you fight!" A single warrior announced before she heard the sound of swords, banging on shields, the sound of quarterstaffs hitting the ground in time to a single rhythm.

The drum of war.

"How did you know that I intend to fight today?" she called over the din.

At that, Baelios suddenly appeared beside her, standing and completely solid for once.

"I sent for them, Sorceress. On behalf of the Wizard's Council," he said before he called out loudly. "For the Wizard's Council!"

"FOR THE WIZARD'S COUNCIL!" the mass cried back before they all went silent.

::Baelios, how did you--::

::The Wizard's Council decided, after the spell was cast, that if the need was great enough, they'd send for all of the peoples of Axrealia that could come here. Every member of the council is represented here, as is every person of Axrealia..minus the mermaids, of course. And the dragons. Sadly enough, the Dragons are very few and are less and less inclined to fight these days,:: he replied as he touched her shoulder.

::If Juktis is watching, our surprise will be blown.::

::I know. But, his lack of action indicates he might already know what we're up to. Or at least, he thinks he knows.::

::Well, let's not keep him waiting.:: Out loud Ezra cried "Today, we will free people who are enslaved to Juktis' will. Tomorrow, we will all strike to fight the Darkness and to stop a dangerous man from destroying our world. We fight, not just for Ammora. We fight for ALL OF AXREALIA!" She shouted and the warriors, outside and inside, all began their battle cries. "Commanders, come to me now, and we will show you our plan so that we may all strike AS ONE!"

The commanders of each of the peoples outside rushed to heed her orders and Baelios disappeared. Derik, having heard, came back to the Entrance Hall with the bespelled map so that she could show them all what to do.

The portals were open. Before them, three hordes of mixed soldiers, mages, healers and commanders all flew or ran through. Sky chariots raced through as well. These particular portals were large, much larger than the normal ones that Ezra made. They would all take multiple people through at a time.

"Remember the plan. One of you must each be in the towns to protect them tonight, in case Juktis tries to retake them. I'll remain here for now, to protect the Castle. He may try to strike here if he thinks Ammora is empty," Ezra reminded Reanalia, Faorir and Jarod. The three gave solemn nods.

"We'll put them all under shields once we're there. Those people have been mistreated so badly, they'll likely surrender without much of a fight," Faorir said with certainty. Ezra gave them all a look of what she hoped was reassurance.

"I'll see you all at first light," she said before they all turned and raced for their own portals. Reanalia was going with Wahya's tribe and a third of the new arrivals to Fasioth. Faorir was going to Sevabon with the rest of the tribesman and another third of Axrealian soldiers. The last third was going with Jarod and Captain Lita to Perab. The look that Jarod gave her before he went through chilled her to the bone. It was full of resentment, hate and jealousy.

::I hope I haven't made an enemy of him, Baelios,:: Ezra said, knowing that her response had been blunt, but at least it was honest.

::You might have, but he hates his brother more. For now, at least he's an ally.::

::And afterwards?:;

::Worry about that later. Concentrate on today,:: Baelios advised and Ezra couldn't help but agree. Once the last of the warriors were through, Ezra closed the portals and began the work of raising her own shield over Ammora. She moved to her throne, where it was quiet, and she could sit. It was directly above Ammora's power source and made it easier to tap into it while concentrating on what she had to do.

She closed her eyes and began her work, chanting softly as she reached for the power she required.

Derik had run through the same portal as Captain Lita's troops.

::Keep an eye on Lord Jarod, please, Derik. After what he said to Ezra, I don't trust him,:: Baelios had sent to him telepathically as the portals had been opened.

Neither do I. I'll keep an eye on him, Spirit. Just watch Ezra's back for me, Derik thought carefully back.

::Good luck, Derik!:: Baelios replied just before Derik ran through. As they emerged into the battlefield, Derik kept Jarod in sight while they fought the few men that Juktis had stationed here. In less than an hour, they had captured or killed all of men loyal to Juktis and the town had willingly surrendered to them.

"One down, two to go," Derik murmured to Captain Lita as they began the task of securing the town while Jarod began the task of raising the shields to keep them all safe.

"Let's just hope our defenses hold through tonight. Tomorrow, we'll take it to the Fortress," she agreed as she sent the healers out to help the wounded and the sick.

Wahya and Tala was surprised at how few soldiers were here to defend the town. It was almost as if Juktis didn't care about it. Which surprised them both. Already the people of Fasioth had brought the soldiers to them and surrendered. Most of them were sick, or starving.

While Lady Reanalia began to set up the dome to protect them all from Jutkis' wrath, Wahya and Tala went with the healers to help the sick and wounded.

"Here you go, Brother. Some water will help while we wait for your turn with the healer. Now, Brah, you gotta look at this as a blessing in disguise. The Gods brought us here into your life to help you see the way, Brah. Here, want a smoke? That's it, we're not going to hurt you. You can't want to be mean like this, Brah. Sure, you might get rewarded, but no woman will ever love ya," Wahya told a soldier with a rather mild flesh wound. He took some gauze and pressed it over the wound, putting pressure on and handed a rolled smoke-stick to the man and lit it for him with a match. The soldier listened and began to share his sad tale. His mother had died young, his father had beat him until he'd run away. The rest, Wahya had heard many times before.

Nearby, Tala was doing the same with another soldier, encouraging him to change his life.

"This is your second chance, Brah. I used to be bad like you, once. It took someone cursing me to live forever before I turned my life around. Now, it's your turn, Brah. Don't take a genius to see that you're not happy with your life. What's your dream, what do you want out of life, Brah?" Tala asked as she tended to the man's wounds. Wahya gave her a wink and they continued on with their work, talking to each of the enemy soldiers in turn, encouraging them all to change.

It was, after all, what they had decided to do to help others avoid their fate.

Nearby, Reanalia finished raising the dome and turned the task of helping others that needed more help to stay alive before a healer might be able to reach them.

Faorir cursed as he saw the populace. Nearly everyone here was sick, drained magically to the dregs. He used a mirror spell and told the Sorceress, Jarod and Reanalia.

"We'll all be sick too if we don't do something about it," Faorir pointed out.

"Agreed. You three keep up the domes but keep the mirror spell active. I'll take care of it," the Sorceress told them all. Faorir gave a nod and watched as the mirror began to glow. In the distance, he could see two pillars of light hovering over the other two towns. "Where darkness feeds, light will cleanse. This illness now comes to an end!" the Sorceress chanted in a language lost to all but to the mages of old. The light from the mirror grew brighter and brighter until it flared out, washing everything around it in a white light. When his vision cleared, the mirror was back to normal and the sick red flow of energy had stopped all around them.

"Sorceress, you did it!"

"Here too!" Reanalia reported.

"And here!" Jarod agreed.

"The people will recover with time, though the healers may be able to help speed the process. Remind them not to wear themselves out before tomorrow," the Sorceress told them all before the mirror spell was closed.

"Wish I had that much power to waste," Faorir chuckled as he went to go and tell the healers that their jobs should be much easier now.

Chapter Sixteen

The night was quiet. Far too quiet and things were going far too well for Captain Lita to be able to trust herself to rest tonight. At her insistence, they had camped within the city limits, but within their own tents. Thus far, the shields had held, and the healers had made great progress with helping the population here. But she had expected something. For Juktis to *do* something! And so far, there was nothing.

Captain Lita stepped out, wrapping her cloak tightly about herself as she walked to check the camp again. She always took a turn at sentry duty during a war and it was why the people she had followed her. They knew she wouldn't assign any task that she herself wouldn't be willing to perform. From armor repair, to managing animals, even to guarding prisoners or peeling vegetables for the evening meal. Lita always did chores with her fellows, and they respected her for it. She gave a nod to a soldier who was also uneasy and out to check things.

"It's too quiet, Cap'n. I'd have expected the bastard to strike back by now," Ren told her softly as he blew on his hands.

"I did as well. It's got me unsettled."

"If you're unsettled, there's a reason. Yer guts better than any magic that I've seen."

"Except maybe the Sorceress," she reminded him.

"Aye. She helped with the building. Put spells on the materials to help them dry faster once walls were finished. Never saw mortar set so quickly."

"She's a good lady. Let's hope that we'll get through this and back home."

"Aye," Ren agreed as he began to walk with her as they began to check on things again.

Ezra couldn't sleep. The child was large enough that she was able to feel it kick or squirm at random times throughout the day and night. But it wasn't the child that was keeping her awake tonight.

It was a feeling of foreboding. Ezra gave up any pretense of rest and began to check the camps of the Tribes and the Mercenaries in the three towns they had liberated from Juktis' control.

What she found chilled her to the bone.

Wahya was restless. He and Tala were both doing quiet things in their tent to prepare for the next day. While they had checked on things and had set sentries, Wahya just couldn't shake the feeling that something bad was going to happen.

::Wahya, enemies are at the Northern border! Rouse your brethren!:: Ezra's mind suddenly snapped him back to fully consciousness. Tala's head jerked an instant later and they both scrambled out of the tent to rouse everyone from their rest.

It seemed Juktis had sent soldiers under the cover of darkness, but Ezra had warned them just in time.

Derik wasn't asleep either. He was pacing, missing Ezra so badly his heart hurt in his chest and just unable to settle down. He had done everything he needed to do for the next morning but sleep just wasn't coming as usual.

::DERIK! Eastern border, enemies are preparing for an attack!:: Ezra's voice jerked him back to consciousness and that sent Derik scrambling.

"Got it, Sorceress! Warn the others!" he shouted as he ran out to report to Captain Lita.

She wasn't surprised but gave a quick whistle. Out of the tents, soldiers boiled out along with Orcs and Hive people, all of whom had come with them.

"We have visitors. They may try to sneak through the shield. Let's not keep them waiting," Lita said just loudly enough to get everyone moving silently through the streets and the gate to go and give those soldiers the surprise of their lives.

Reanalia was awake. Magic was vibrating in the air, giving her just the beginning of the warning—

::Enemies at the West edge! Rouse the warriors!:; the Sorceress' mind shouted into hers. Reanalia got up and gave the signal she'd arranged for earlier in case of attack. A single red orb that flitted from tent to tent, giving the message to each of the warriors.

Tribesmen, Elves, halflings and various other warriors including Ogres boiled out of their tents and went on their way to the smallest of breaches where the enemy was trying to come through.

Ezra watched on pins and needles with her telepathy and her mirrors, watching as the battles took place. Within an hour, everything was quiet again and the men who had come to slay the Warriors of Axrealia were either captured or no more.

Ezra breathed a sigh.

"That was close," she said softly as she relaxed back onto her throne.

"Very close, but you saw it in time. I'll keep watch and send warnings if I see anything else. Go rest, Ezra," Baelios urged her. "If not for your sake, for the baby. You've used up a lot of your energy today."

"True, but I've been saving everything I could for months, Baelios. Very well. Wake me if there's any trouble," she told him as she rose and went to her bed, setting an alarm spell to wake her at dawn.

She lay down, closed her eyes and drifted off as soon as her head hit the pillow.

Mara hadn't gone to the kitchen today, claiming she felt ill. It wasn't quite a lie as she felt tense and ill-at-ease. Soldiers had gone out in the night to attack the villages that had somehow risen up against Juktis' rule. They hadn't returned. Mara was suddenly grateful for her veil that Aeryn had insisted she bring and wear. It kept her face hidden and hid the fear she felt deep in the pit of her stomach.

Instead, she had prepared the weapons she and Aeryn had brought up in their chambers while Aeryn continued to work in the forge, like always. They had a diversion planned and these days, they wore the rings that the Sorceress had given them.

Suddenly, Mara glanced down at her ring in time to see it glow.

::Mara, it's time!:: Mara heard the Sorceress' voice in her head just before the glow vanished. Mara armed herself quickly and took Aeryn's down to Him, making sure that she hid her own weapons under her tunic and detachable skirt. She passed Aeryn's to him with a grim look in her eye. He gave a curt nod and a meaningful look down at her ring.

"I'm still not feeling well, my Love," she simpered, trying to sound sicker than she truly was.

"Let's go for a little walk. I'll be back shortly," Aeryn told the other blacksmiths before they slipped away, his arm wrapped protectively about her shoulders. They made their way back towards the latrines and Mara ditched the veil quickly, as they both dropped down behind a set of barrels.

This bit of sabotage they had come up with as a quick diversion so they could open the gates. They'd set it up in the nights and made sure they'd hidden the fuses. Aeryn dug the long fuse out and Mara took out her fire-lighting kit from her boot. A quick strike with the switch and they had a small flame, which Mara used to light the candle. She blew out the kindling, stowed the fire making kit back in her boot and they both walked away, Aeryn appearing to help her along as if she were very weak after a stomach purge. Suddenly, the barrels blew up just as they came close to the gates!

Soldiers took up arms and went running and Aeryn and Mara quickly ran to the wheels that would raise the portcullis. Working quickly, they got it up just in time for the warriors of Axrealia to come boiling through it!

"Captain!" Mara called to Captain Lita, who made her way to Aeryn and Mara's side.

"Good work you two! Mara, lead the way! The Sorceress is coming!" Lita told them both.

Ezra was not having as good a luck. She sent the message to Mara and Aeryn, but now she was trying to open a portal directly into the courtyard where they were.

And as soon as the explosion went up, a magical shield dropped over the entire fortress.

Ezra swore inwardly and looked over the fortress with her scrying spell and finally picked up the Orb of Eithal and began to use it to amplify her power.

An explosion in the courtyard shook the walls! Juktis raised his hands and brought up his power to block the spell coming from Ammora Castle. A grim look on his face as he turned to his partner.

"She's coming. I feel her," Alvra told him as she shook out her long black hair and ran her hands over her body. Black tattoos darkened on her pale flesh and swirled as she created a dark blue tunic and black leggings with blue boots out of thin air.

"Let's give her a very warm reception, shall we, Alvra?" he offered as he turned to her.

"I'll boost your powers from the shadows," Alvra promised with a wicked grin before she disappeared, becoming nothing but shadow herself for now.

Juktis felt her boosting his power and he thickened the magical shield. If the Sorceress wished to enter, she'd have to come through the front gate.

The shield over the fortress resisted Ezra's efforts at first. Little by little, Ezra drew on more power from the castle before she realized what he was doing.

He was stalling.

::Faorir, Jarod, Reanalia, meet me at the front gates!:: she went, seeing that as the only weakness in the spell.

She heard their wordless replies of agreement and began to build the portal, spinning it as quickly as she dared.

"Ezra, be careful. It could be a trap—"

"It's definitely a trap, but one that must be sprung and dealt with, Baelios. Guard the Castle!" Ezra replied a little sharply before she took up her quarterstaff, hid the orb in a sack on her back and went through.

She came out swinging at the first enemy soldier that dared to confront her. A quick hit to the man's neck with her quarterstaff downed him and a quick stab of her dagger finished him. She pulled it loose and looked about herself at the chaos that had become the courtyard.

The soldiers had been surprised, but they were still so many! She realized that without all of the people that Wahya and Tala had recruited for her, they would have been overwhelmed.

Tala popped up on her right, using her bow to take down another foe just over Ezra's shoulder. Ezra gave her friend a quick nod of thanks and hurried, seeking the four auras that shone brightly to her magical senses.

"Fighting through will take too much time!" Reanalia shouted over the din as she magically appeared by Ezra's side.

"Agreed! Let's see if we can make a quick shortcut!" Ezra called back as she reached out with her magic into a small empty space beside an alcove that had seen better days. She spun the portal quickly, just as Faorir and Jarod managed to teleport themselves to her. It broke through easily, giving Ezra a sense of dread.

"This is definitely a trap. Be ready," she reminded them all. Jarod went through first, followed by Reanalia and Faorir. Ezra went through last, bringing out the orb as she walked into the heart of the foul place.

Derik was busy out in the courtyard. He dodged and parried, lunged and dodged again. Arrows and lasers flew through the courtyard as the warriors of Axrealia battled the scum of the fortress.

"Where did those come from?" he asked over the din. Aeryn laughed.

"I forged those for our company years ago. I just made sure there's nothing like that here! Oh, and their weapons are weak at the hilt!" Aeryn yelled back as he swung his mace with deadly precision. Mara had her sword out and her own laser pistol and she was taking out archers in between slitting throats of anyone that came at her on the ground.

"That's great! I want one!" Derik called back to Aeryn.

Wahya clapped Derik on the shoulder.

"Welcome to the right side, Brah! Now let's clear out this trash so we can catch up to the mages!" Wahya crowed as their side charged at the lazy scum who had thought that this world would be so easily conquered. Blood ran in rivers over the stones of the courtyard as Derik looked around.

"Where's the mages?"

"They took a portal somewhere else. Probably went after the bastard directly!" Captain Lita called back over her shoulder.

"I need to get to them. The Sorceress—"

"Can take care of herself!" Lita called back. "We need everyone here!"

"C'mon, Brah! Let's finish giving these punks their lesson!" Tala called to Derik as she and Wahya waded back into battle.

The ground shook, a loud roar came from inside the main part of the fortress and filled Derik with dread.

"For Axrealia!" Someone cried. The other soldiers took it up around him until all of their side was screaming.

Derik joined in, praying that Ezra was all right!

It was very dark inside of Juktis' private chamber. Only a few sputtering candles and a fire under a large cauldron provided any light. In the center of the room was a macabre altar, stained with blood and various other fluids. At the top of a narrow staircase, a strange dark twin of Ezra's throne stood.

And on that throne sat Juktis.

"You shouldn't have left your Castle today, Sorceress," Juktis taunted her in a smooth dark baritone. "And you shouldn't have allied yourself with my brother and these other…insignificants."

"I'll show you who's insignificant—" Reanalia started, but Ezra gave her a look and motioned her to be quiet.

"Your reign is at an end, Juktis. Surrender and we'll allow you to keep a fraction of your power—" Ezra started.

"Surrender? I think not! None of you have enough power to beat me and your precious allies are dying outside at the hands of my troops—"

"Look again, Juktis. I saw your own soldiers abandoning and fleeing your fortress, those that are smart enough to know that our allies are far better than yours," Faorir replied in a huff. "You aren't half as smart as you think you are, Whelp!"

"Regardless, your reign is at an end, Brother. Surrender. Be honorable and tell me what you did with Mother and Father—" Jarod started.

"Those weaklings were dealt with. You'll never find them, Jarod."

"What do you mean 'Dealt with?'" Jarod asked in a growl.

"I absorbed their power, along with them," Juktis replied with a taunting laugh.

"No! They were immortal—"

"And far weaker than I was. Their power added to my own and now even the Sorceress of Ammora trembles in anticipation of the punishment I intend to mete out to her."

"The only one trembling here is you, Juktis. If you won't surrender, then we will deal with you right now. You have a choice—" Ezra replied with annoyance at his arrogance.

"Yes, I do, Sorceress. But, with such juicy flies caught in my web, I don't intend to let any of you go." A fireball appeared in Juktis' hand and he casually tossed it at the four Mages.

::Scatter!:: Ezra sent as she teleported herself out of the way. She reappeared behind the cauldron and released a lightning spell at Juktis, hearing the air crackle and the stone break as it hit his suddenly empty throne.

He reappeared, teleporting behind the altar at the center of the room. Faorir, Reanalia and Jarod all appeared in different points of the room, forming an odd sort of circle around the center.

::Are you sure that thing can contain him?:: Faorir asked as the four mages began to chant at Ezra's signal.

::If it can't, then we're all in trouble!:: Ezra sent back as they began to close the circle, each of them randomly shooting off spells at Juktis in an attempt to keep him busy. ::We have to drain him down as far as we can before we pull him into the Orb!:: Ezra sent back to all three of them.

::Use the Orb, Sorceress. Boost your power!:: Jarod sent back as he dodged a whirlwind from Juktis. Ezra ducked under a volley of lightning sent by Juktis and returned fire with a spell that had vines sprout from the floor and begin to twine around Juktis' legs.

"Is this all you have, Sorceress?" Juktis taunted as he sent the vines on fire with a wave of his hand. Ezra pulled the Orb out of the sack on her back and put away her quarterstaff, pushing the button to retract it so she could put it back on her belt. She dodged again, teleporting herself to stand on the staircase to Juktis' ruined throne.

"Not quite, Juktis!" she replied before she returned to chanting. A fragile shield began to grow over Juktis, which he smashed with a spell. The other mages teleported themselves out of the way of a whirlwind, joining Ezra where she stood and she pulled them in, using the Orb to augment all of their magical energies.

The shield grew again, then was shattered by another spell. Each time, they continued the spell, using it as a distraction, keeping Juktis' attention focused on it until he smashed it with another spell, one so powerful it sent a shockwave, making them all have to scatter again.

"RISE! DRAGOS SEALIAUM FORIS!" he screamed in anger as Ezra and the others reappeared in various points of the room.

Juktis rose on a whirlwind of air as the stone floor shattered in the center of the room. From the ruins, rose the remains of a Dragon. It was mostly bone with only a bit of rotting flesh clinging to its frame. Juktis rose on his turret of wind as the ground parted and a large bony wing pushed up and through the floor. Another wing followed, then a very large skull rose up out of the pit it had created and stared down at them with glowing red eyes.

"A Dragon!" Ezra gasped as she stared up at the undead creature. ::You didn't say he had a dragon!:: She sent as her head snapped to look at Jarod, who was across the room to her left. Jarod shook his head.

::I didn't know, I swear!::

"As I said, Sorceress of Ammora, you should not have left your Castle today," Juktis taunted as his feet came to rest on the large bony shoulder of the undead dragon. "I am flattered that you sought out other immortal sorcerers to try and get rid of me. But as you can see…I am not just any immortal. This dragon was once the most powerful creature in all the land and once her egg finally hatches, it will only add to my arsenal."

Ezra looked below and sure enough, there was an egg. A very large, scaled Dragon's egg! She felt for the poor thing, knowing that Dragons only hatched when they were ready, but how would it ever be ready there, in a cold dark dungeon? Ezra waved her hand, using a portal to send it to Ammora Castle. Baelios would look after it until she arrived.

"No!" Juktis bellowed suddenly.

"That Dragon's egg is precious, and it will never hatch here, Juktis. Let's finish this, Juktis. Winner takes all," she called back as she turned her attention back to Juktis and his creature.

::Everyone, listen to me. We must send that poor creature back to the depths. It has lived it's life and Dragons hate humans who try to enslave them. We need to undo his spell, send it back to its rest. If we're lucky, we'll manage to survive this.:: Ezra sent telepathically to the other three.

::I have just the spell, Sorceress. 'Dragos Featorum Sanos.' I've dealt with necromancers who tried this trick before in my youth. The Dragon will be grateful to go back to the Underworld,:: Faorir sent to them.

::I haven't seen any sign of his partner, either,:: Ezra sent as she held up the Orb, readying herself to cast the spell to send the Necromanced Dragon back to the land of the dead.

::I think she's watching and waiting,:: Reanalia added. ::I feel something in the shadows, but it's not letting me see what it is::

::Let's give her a show then. Ready?::

::READY!:: the three voices echoed in her head.

Outside, Derik and the rest of the combined Axrealian forces were having a hell of a time fighting the scum that Juktis had hired. Those who hadn't fled were tenacious, brutal and enjoyed inflicting pain. Arrows had begun to rain down on Lita's company from behind them, where archers had taken up positions on the walls that surrounded this place.

"TAKE DOWN THOSE ARCHERS! EVERYONE ELSE, KEEP GOING FORWARD!" Captain Lita yelled from somewhere in front of Derik. Masses of bodies moved as one as Wahya's tribe turned and began to take down the archers with their own bows and arrows.

"Derik, what's the plan?" Wahya asked him from his left as Tala materialized suddenly on Derik's right.

"We have our jobs. Take down this scum first, then we'll break in and help the mages. Follow orders," Derik replied before he ran to join the fray.

Inside, spells flew one after another. All of the mages were doing their best to distract Juktis even as they all teleported from one place to another, trying to avoid the Dark Sorcerer's spells and the balls of fire from the undead dragon.

::NOW! Start chanting!:: Ezra sent as she began to chant the spell to send the Dragon back to the Underworld.

"DRAGOS FEATORUM SANOS!" the mages cried over and over together, continuing to rain other spells they had already prepared at both Juktis and the Undead Dragon. Ezra could sense something, someone, watching them from the shadows, but she couldn't locate where! It was frustrating and annoying, but her main concern was to stop Juktis and this Necromanced beast here and now!

"FOOLS! You can't undo my spells!" Juktis laughed as he continued to rain fireballs and lightnings down around all of them. Ezra hastily raised a mage shield, deflecting it all away from herself, and glanced around at the others. With relief, she noted the others had done the same.

::Sorceress, use the Orb to magnify your spells!:: Jarod sent to her telepathically as Ezra remembered that she was still holding it.

::I am! All of you get over to me, let's all amplify our spells together!:: She sent to the group as she raised the orb.

"DRAGOS FEATORUM SANOS! DRAGOS FEATORUM SANOS!" Ezra chanted as she sensed the other mages had teleported next to her shield. She hastily expanded it, bringing them all in and brought the orb down so they could all touch it. Power poured through the Orb, and she saw a beam suddenly fly out and strike the Undead Dragon—

Only to hear it screech as the light reduced it to ash before their eyes! Juktis fell to the altar beneath him and looked at the pile of ash with fury. The ground shook furiously beneath their feet and the four of them grabbed whatever they could to keep their balance.

"NOOOO! You will pay for that!" Juktis barked as he whirled to face them.

::We have to pull him into the—:: Ezra had just started to say when the next horror hit!

Demonic creatures with large venomous fangs whirled out from Juktis's outstretched hands and flew at them with a shrieks of joy and anger! Joy at the sight of prey, anger as Ezra thickened her shield, keeping them at bay, for now.

::What ARE those things?:: Jarod asked them all as their view was obscured by the flying whirlwind of terror.

Derik looked about and the whole battle paused as the ground suddenly shook. Everyone scrambled for balance and his gaze met Lita's just as a loud roar echoed up from the Fortress.

"DERIK, GO!" Lita motioned at the Fortress and motioned to one of her lieutenants. That lieutenant hurried over with a small iron battering ram. Derik took it and motioned to Mara and Aeryn.

"FOR AMMORA!" He cried as he led the charge towards the door. "Mara, what's in there?"

"That's the kitchen. Be ready to fight. Kitchen Master has a mean temper!" Mara reported as the three of them grasped the battering ram and swung. Three swings of that ram and the door caved open. By this time, the rest of the Ammoran recruits had lined up behind them and they all charged in. Aeryn picked up the battering ram and rested it up on his shoulder as if it weighed nothing.

Ezra watched the whirlwind of unholy terror that Juktis had unleashed upon them and studied them. They seemed familiar, but she wasn't quite sure what they were.

::They're Vaksari. A demonic form of bat. They'll keep whirling around us and eventually crush our shield!:: Reanalia sent to them as they stood, back to back, trying to weigh their options.

::Are they afraid of anything?:: Faorir asked, his mental voice tinged with more annoyance than fear.

::Fire, fireballs. Not much else, though,:: Reanalia replied.

::Spread out! Bring up your shields and let's coat them all in fire. That should render them fairly useless for now,:: Ezra replied.

::RIGHT!:: the other three echoed in her head as they all suddenly disappeared. Ezra shrank her shield, then brought a flame spell to ripple over its surface. The demonic bats shrieked and flew around the room, seeking a target—

And finding only Juktis. With annoyance, Juktis opened a portal and sent them back to their own plane of existence.

::Now! Get him off balance! We need to weaken him as much as we can before we pull him in!:: Ezra held up the orb, sending more power through it as she sent lightning spells hurtling at Juktis. Faorir sent fireballs. Reanalia sent a cyclone at him to keep him contained while Jarod rained hail the size of fists down onto Jutkis.

Juktis swept his hands down and to his sides, sending their spells back at them. Ezra hastily reflected it back again, doubling all of the spells with the Orb.

We have to do this. We have to contain him! Ezra focused on that thought, knowing that failure was not an option!

The battering ram had worked. The Kitchen Master had given a good fight, but he was dead. The servants had fled. Derik, Wayha, Tala, Mara and Aeryn marched through the hallways. More soldiers came out into the halls, but they took them down quickly. Mara led the way, walking towards Juktis' chambers.

"Mara, what's in there? Other than the foulest evil mage we've ever met?" Derik asked softly as they walked along.

"A bed, a throne sits in front of that. Looks a little like the one in Ammora, but evil. And an altar, things to make potions with, that sort of thing," Mara replied. "It's more open than not, but who knows what he might have in there that we won't be able to see?

Somewhere up ahead, there was the sounds of battle. No screams, but explosions and the sounds of thunder and lightning.

"The Mages got in, at least," Wahya noted as they all paused.

"Then they're gonna need back-up. Let's go," Derik growled as he took up his sword and began to run down the hallways. The others followed suit as they came upon more soldiers and the deadly dance began again.

Ezra deflected another spell, and glared up at Juktis as she studied him, trying to guess his next move.

"This is Child's play, Juktis! Do you really think I'm so uneducated as to not know how to defend myself against that?!?" She cried, taunting him as he began to prepare another spell, one that would call forth an elemental spirit, one aligned with air. She was growing tired, despite the Orb, but Juktis seemed as strong as ever.

::On this next spell, begin the chant. Let's contain him as quickly as we can. Wherever his partner is, if she's going to jump in, it'll be then. Be ready!:: she sent as Juktis paused and began to laugh at her.

"I'm just warming up, Sorceress!"

"That Dragon was your ace in the hole, Juktis. You're stalling!" Ezra taunted him again and flung a spell at him.

Chains appeared, snaking around his wrists and ankles as manacles and shackles snapped shut about the Dark Sorcerer's limbs. He cried out in anger as Jarod began to strengthen her spell, giving her support even as Reanalis and Faoris added another spell, a shielding spell, one that would contain him. Ezra brought the orb in front of her as the other mages walked back around towards her, beginning the chant—

Just as the door into the chamber caved in. One of the mercenary soldiers lay there, groaning as Derik led the charge into the room. Distracted, Ezra hesitated for an instant—

And in that Instant, Juktis got a hand free and sent a spell right at Derik's chest.

"TRAITOR!" Juktis roared as his spell flung Derik back into a wall—

Where he fell and didn't rise. Ezra stared for an instant. She looked back to Juktis—

In time to see his smirk, that taunting look that said he had won. Ezra stared…then screamed in fury as she poured her power into her spell, pulling Juktis in with a cyclone that tripled and quadrupled the instant the other mages hands touched!

A flash of light encompassed the Dark Sorcerer, who shrank as the Orb pulled him in. When Ezra's eyes adjusted, the light was gone. So was the cyclone and Juktis with it. She looked down—

And saw Juktis, shrunk to the size of a small doll, glaring up at her from within the Orb. Contained. Helpless. Ezra felt tears spill down her cheeks as she broke from the other mages, Orb and all and ran to where Derik lay.

He was alive, but only just! Blood ran down from his mouth and nose. More blood ran down from a cut on the back of his scalp. His breathing was ragged, and he looked dazed as she fell to her knees next to him and lay her hands on him.

"Derik, no! No! Stay with me! Stay with me!" she gasped as she pushed Tala and Wahya out of the way and poured power into him, trying to stabilize him as she had Mara. "Get a healer!" she snapped to everyone else as she closed her eyes, concentrating on just keeping him alive.

Inside, she sensed the mess that the spell had made of Derik's organs. He was bleeding in far too many places! She felt his hand touch hers, felt another brush her cheek, making her open her eyes to look at him.

"Sorcer—"

"Don't talk, Derik. Save your strength. You're going to be fine—"

"No. I'm finished. Don't…save your power for one who…. deserves it," Derik said weakly.

"You do deserve it! Everything you've done since you came to Ammora, Derik! You saved me! Saved Ammora! You aren't going to die here—"

"Love…. you." Derik's eyes closed and she felt his body shudder, sensed that he was fading, despite the energy she was feeding into him.

"I love you, Derik! Don't you DARE die on me!" Ezra cried, shutting everything and everyone out, sending all of her energy into him and using the orb, using it to help replace his blood even as it tried to seep out of him. She poured everything she had, all of it, feeling dizzy with the amount of power flowing out of her and feeling her body ache in response. "I won't… let... You…."

She sensed two others suddenly sit next to her and across from her, hands brushed hers, touching hers and more power ran through her, this time laced with the serene green of healing. Ezra added her energy to theirs, feeding it all into all of the places that needed that energy the most—making wounds and lacerations inside close even as she sent blood racing back into his veins and reducing swelling, sending the excess fluid into the places of Derik's body where he needed it most.

She felt a great long breath of air going into Derik, sensed him moving and opened her eyes in time to see his open again—

And fell back as her head swam and her body collapsed. Arms caught and lowered her as Ezra succumbed to exhaustion and the darkness that promised sleep and rest.

Alyra watched as the battle progressed. She stayed in the shadows, giving Juktis a boost in his power, but little else. She sensed the mages looking for her with subtle glances with their mage powers. Cloaking herself in shadow, she watched as first the dragon she'd helped to resurrect was destroyed, then as Juktis sent spell after spell at the mages, with little results.

Fool. I should leave you here, she thought.

Then others arrived, mortals. A smirk crossed her dark lips as Juktis sent a spell right at the one mortal she sensed meant more to the Sorceress than anyone else.

Time to go. I'll have another chance, she thought as she studied the mages one last time—

And felt a pull towards the twin brother…Jarod. His face was a mask of jealousy as he watched the Sorceress fussing over the dying insect of a mortal.

He covets her! That's something I can work with, Alyra thought as she teleported herself back to her cave, to leave the Sorceress to her sorrow and the mortal to his death.

Or so she thought.

Chapter Seventeen

Tala and Wahya caught the unconscious Sorceress as she slumped back and lowered her down to the ground.

"Gods! She's drained herself to practically nothing," Eve swore softly as she checked the unconscious mage before looking to the other three. "You all have nearly nothing left. We won the battle outside. I suggest you all get something to eat and get some rest! I've got enough work without adding three more casualties," she scolded them as she picked up the orb that had been curled in the Sorceress' arm and handed it over to Wahya. Wahya looked at it and slid it into a bag and put it next to the unconscious woman while Eve finished with Derik and began making arrangements for the pair to be taken to the infirmary in the main hall of the Fortress.

The three mages looked at each other rather wearily and went off to find themselves a place to rest. Eve let them and worked with Wahya and Tala to get the Sorceress and Derik onto stretchers. She sighed and moved on to the next patient outside. No time to rest. Her job was to save what was left of those caught in the War Machine.

Once the Sorceress and Derik had been moved, Tala and Wahya went out to help those who still needed help. They took water, prayed with those who were not long for this world to have mercy in the next and talked to those who would recover from the other side.

"Brah, you can't live your life on the wrong side of the stick. This is your wake-up call to do better. You have a second chance, Brah. Don't waste it," Wahya told a mercenary that had a broken leg from when he'd slipped and fallen down the stairs in his haste to fight the Axrealian forces.

"Here you go, some food and water, Brah," Tala said off somewhere behind Wahya, doing her own work to help their enemies realize where their paths were going.

There was more dead than wounded, but it was enough to overwhelm the healers, none the less. Wahya and Tala did what they did best, talking and feeding and giving water to those who would survive. Those who were dying, they prayed with. It took hours to get all of the surviving wounded into bedrolls and to treat their wounds. By the time it was over with, Wahya and Tala were on the last dregs of their energy. Before they went to seek their own beds, they stopped by to check on Ezra and Derik.

Derik was awake and watching Ezra's every move. Ezra was still unconscious, but she wasn't as pale as she had been.

Wahya breathed a sigh of relief as his hand sought Tala's. His wife was his own rock, his foundation. His friend when he needed it, his lover and love all wrapped into one package. He knew how he felt whenever she was wounded.

He saw that same feeling reflected into Derik's eyes.

"Feeling any better, Brah? Next time let me lead the charge," Wahya chided him with a wink as they paused to give Derik a little support.

"She shouldn't have saved me," Derik started.

"Why not? She loves you, Brah. I'd do anything to save Wahya if he were dying. Just because she's a woman, doesn't mean that you get to do all the saving, Brah," Tala reminded him soberly, concern for his well-being reflected in every line of her body.

"I don't deserve it—"

"Just because you made one mistake. Derik, we've both made mistakes. Hell, she's made mistakes too! She's forgiven you for what you did. Don't you think it's time to forgive yourself?"

Derik reached over to touch Ezra's hand with trembling fingers. "I'm trying."

"Don't try. Do! And you'd better hurry because Captain Lita's already talkin' about the wedding you two are gonna have when we all get back to Ammora."

"Wedding? What wedding?"

"Yours and hers. That's if you want a wedding. I'm betting she would...if you asked," Tala said as she tugged on Wahya's arm. "C'mon, Big Daddy. Let's go get something to eat, I'm starved!"

"See you in the morning, Brah. Remember what we said," Wahya told Derik as Tala dragged him from the room towards the kitchen to get their own meals.

At the door, Wahya looked back again and smiled as Derik pulled Ezra's bedroll closer and curled up with her in his arms, protecting her.

"They'll be okay. Let's go...I want something to eat and then I'm aiming to find us some privacy so I can give you your reward," Tala whispered with promise into Wahya's ear.

Vision of Darkness

"Ha ha ha!" Wahya laughed as he scooped her up and threw her over his shoulder and carried her off for a little time alone…together.

::Ezra…:: Someone called in the darkness. Ezra had been floating in this darkness, too tired to even move. She wanted just to float like this forever…

::Ezra…:: that voice called again, like a Siren in the night. She couldn't see, it was all so dark… ::Ezra!:: the voice insisted, forcing her to focus on it. Ezra opened her weary eyes, unable to think or remember how she had gotten here. ::That's it! Focus, Ezra.:: The voice was female, and vaguely familiar.

::Who?:: Ezra wearily replied, still floating in the darkness, too tired to say more than that.

In answer, there was a flare of light that seemed to blind her, and she heard the cry of a falcon…then she saw a familiar silhouette.

::Goddess?:: Ezra sent wearily, unable to move as the Goddess came to stand over her.

::Yes, Ezra. I said I would be with you in your darkest hour. Didn't you think I would be with you before then?:: the voice of the Goddess said rather cheerfully into her mind.

::Derik? Is he--?::

::He'll be fine. You kept him together long enough for Eve to heal his wounds. He'll be sore, and he'll have to take it slow…but he'll live.:: Relief flooded through Ezra, briefly.

::Juktis' partner…she's the Darkness the Wizard's Council fore-saw, isn't she?:: Ezra asked rather bluntly.

::Yes, she is one of the causes of the Disaster that the Council saw in their Vision. But, Darkness is a rather vague description of something so Evil, isn't it?::

::How can I stop her if she won't even face me, Goddess? I…I can't fight if I don't know what I'm dealing with.::

::She is studying you first before she takes you on, I suspect. She is a product of my darker half. The Destruction God has given her the power she wields. Just as I gave you yours.::

::Wait…what? I thought--::

::Bael changed the spell, but I was the one who allowed it to succeed. He could have let you die, but he loved you more than anything. Just as you loved him. Such love and such sacrifice all at once required my attention. When I saw what you could become, I granted the spell my Blessing. Just as my darker half gave his blessing to your new foe.::

Ezra wished she could swear in that instant as she heard that.

::How could I ever beat her if she's blessed by the Destruction God?::

::You can. You have all of the power within you and within Ammora. And with that new Orb…you can increase both. As I promised, in your Darkest Hour, the Falcon will return. When she does, you'll know that I'm with you. You may be the Light in the Darkness, but you are not the only one. Rest now, Child. Derik is beginning to fret over your condition. Let's not prolong his recovery, hm?:: The Goddess chuckled into Ezra's mind once more and the light faded…

And Ezra opened her eyes to look up into Derik's worried face.

"Derik?" she whispered, feeling as drained as she'd felt when she was floating in the darkness.

"Eve, she's awake!" Derik called, causing several others to turn.

"Oh, Thank the Goddess! I was beginning to think you wouldn't wake at all," Eve said as she came to kneel down next to Ezra. Wahya and Tala suddenly came and dropped down as well and Ezra saw worry in all of their faces.

"The baby?" Ezra asked softly.

"The baby seems fine—I've been checking, and the child's heartbeat is strong. How do you feel?" Eve asked brusquely.

"Weak…tired," Ezra admitted.

"You drained yourself to nearly nothing, Ezra. I'm prescribing more rest and some soup for you along with liquids. I want you to rest—"

"Ammora…I need to get back."

"You spent three days unconscious. I'll have a mage send you back when you won't need constant care. No magic for the next two weeks, at least! I catch you doing anything magical and I'll give you a tincture that'll make you sleep for a solid month. Got it?"

Ezra gave a solemn nod, feeling so drained that even the small movement was exhausting.

"Got it. Promise," Ezra replied.

"I'll get the soup and water," Tula offered before anyone else could. Eve patted Ezra's cheek and went on to another patient.

Wahya chuckled and patted Derik's shoulder.

"Ask her quick before someone else tells her, Brah," Wahya said as he rose and stepped over to help an injured warrior while Derik looked after him in shock.

"Ask me what? Tell me what?" she just asked, unsure of what Wahya was talking about.

"There's a rumor that Captain Lita is planning our wedding," Derik said with a shake of his head as he pulled her pallet closer to his. Derik pulled her close, letting her rest her head against his chest. Ezra cuddled into him, finding his presence soothing even as she chuckled.

"Why?"

"We had a lot of witnesses to you saving my life. Apparently, you said some things that showed how much you care. That and they've assumed the baby's mine. Not that I mind. I just wish it was."

"There's more to being a father than just putting it in a woman," she replied softly, soothed by the sound of his heart. Too close, she sensed that he could have easily died even with her intervention. ::Thank you, Goddess…for letting him stay with me,:: she sent silently, hoping the Goddess heard her.

"True. Just as there's more to a marriage than just saying vows before a Priest or Priestess. Speaking of which…" Derik said, then cleared his voice, making Ezra look back up at him. "Would you marry me, Ezra?"

Ezra found herself completely speechless, just as she heard the Goddess chuckle again in her mind.

::My pleasure.:: The voice of the Goddess again rang clearly in her head as Derik leaned down to kiss her. All thought raced out of Ezra's head just as Tala returned and she heard clapping throughout the chamber and felt Derik's arms tighten about her, holding her.

The thought of marriage sent both pleasure and dread through her.

What do I tell Baelios? was the main thought that went through her mind as she turned what energy she had towards eating her soup.

Jarod watched from across the room as Derik proposed to the Sorceress. He didn't hear her reply. He didn't see her speak. All of Captain Lita's company began to clap, along with the Tribes and the Elves. Even the Orcs cracked a smile.

Jarod pretended to be happy, but inside he seethed with anger and jealousy. He excused himself to go repair the damage done to the floors of what was now His main chambers.

When he walked in, he was surprised to find people of all races already working on it. One of the Elves was a Builder, one who designed the great palaces of the High Elves. She was directing the others, a mixed group of humans, orcs, elves and hive people in the delicate task of repairing the floor and mortaring the bricks while a second crew worked on the main supports for it below.

"What's all this?" Jarod asked as he watched, amazed at what he saw.

"We started repairing your fortress this morning, M'Lord. Captain Lita said that the Sorceress would insist that all of the damage be repaired before we all depart. So, we're doing just that, Sir," the Builder replied with a friendly smile, her long brownish-red hair tied back in a neat waist-long braid down her back. Sparkling green eyes danced merrily as she began to explain to him how they had begun the repair and how they were taking all precautions to ensure that it wouldn't collapse again. "Well, so long as another Dragon doesn't come up through it, M'Lord," she said with a bit of mirth in her voice.

"I'm sorry, I don't think I caught your name."

"Oh, it's Leasania, M'Lord."

"Well, Leasania, I am honored at the care you are taking with my home. Thank you," Jarod said with a bow to her. She chuckled and went back to work and he left to go try to find a quiet spot where he could soothe his disheveled soul.

Derik was feeling better. He'd spent five days recovering from the spell that had nearly killed him and felt all the more grateful to Ezra for saving him. He hardly left her side, but she was recovering so slowly, it was beginning to worry him. She was still too weak to get up and walk, but she kept reassuring him that she was fine.

"Once we're back in Ammora, I'll be able to recover my energies within a day or so. I'm fine, Derik. Please, please stop worrying about me," she said pleadingly when he'd suggested having the healer check her again.

"But—"

"Others are hurt still. Others still will never recover. We are lucky, Derik. Eve said she needed more bandages, maybe you can help make some. I'm sure Juktis had plenty of old sheets that Jarod would love shredding to bits," she suggested with a hint of humor in her weary voice.

"All right. I'll take the hint. But, you—"

"I'll be fine," she said gently. Derik looked around and waved to Reanalia.

"Reanalia, will you stay with her for a bit?" he asked. Reanalia gave a nod.

"Sure." Reanalia settled on a cushion next to Ezra and Derik went to go and find Eve and see if she really needed those bandages or not.

Ezra sighed, watching Derik go.

"Reanalia, you don't have to—" she started.

"It's all right. I have the feeling that he's worried if you're left alone, you'll be more vulnerable. How're you feeling?" Reanalia asked as she settled on the cushion next to Ezra's pallet.

"Tired, more than anything."

::More than tired, I'd say,:: Reanalia observed telepathically. Ezra shrugged and glanced around, then saw why Reanalia had chosen to use telepathy. Everyone close by seemed to be listening to them.

::Derik proposed.::

::I'd heard. Congratulations.::

::I'm not sure that I should marry him. It's not fair to him to tether his life to mine when my focus is on trying to keep Axrealia, and Ammora, safe. Nor is it even fair to the baby. I'm nervous enough about becoming a mother when I know that my life is dangerous. What kind of life could I give her?::

::Every immortal goes through this, or something similar, Sorceress.::

::Not every immortal has to guard against the sorts of dangers I face every single day, Reanalia.::

::True. Although, we do face danger or some sort fairly often. Comes with living forever. Most of us have magic, and those who don't are usually cursed with immortality. Usually for pissing off an immortal mage. And we have children anyway and let them grow up…and figure out their own lives as we had to figure out ours. Like mortal parents do,:: Reanalia said rather bluntly.

::Have you had children?::

::I've had two. Both fine women now and living in their own places. Both are very respected mages. You'll be fine in the motherhood department. You'll just have to spend less time studying for a while and more time changing diapers at first...then later in playing and training the little one. Trust me, you'll miss it once they grow up and move out,:: Reanalia chuckled into her mind. Ezra cracked a small smile. ::So, why do you think you shouldn't marry Derik?::

::He'll die someday. I've already mourned one husband. I really don't want to mourn a second.::

::Then why do you sound like you're about to cry? Do you love him?::

::Yes, I love him very much.::

::Then what's holding you back?::

::I'm afraid of losing him.::

::You'll lose him sooner if you don't marry him. But, there's no sense in rushing things either. Why don't you suggest that you get married after the baby's born? Give yourselves a chance to get things settled and not rush into it. If he changes his mind, then you'll feel less guilty and probably less hurt. But, if you both work towards building your life together, then you'll reap the rewards.::

::That is a good idea…although Captain Lita is already ordering people to begin planning things for as soon as we're home.::

::Yes, but you are the Sorceress of Ammora. And you just went through a very harrowing experience and you both need to recover from it. You can tell the Captain that the plans can wait a little.::

::True.::

::She'll back off. Want me to talk to her?::

::No…not yet. Besides, I have to get Derik to understand that I need time, not just to recover. We just defeated Juktis. As soon as we return to Axrealia, I'm going to ensure that Juktis is stuck in that Orb forever.::

::Good idea. You won't be tempted to use that power unless it's a big emergency. And with your task, you may need the power boost someday,:: Reanalia said with a wink.

::One can only hope that that day never comes.::

::Oh it will. We couldn't find that bastard's partner. She's disappeared. And that means--::

::She'll be back…and I'll be waiting for her.::

::We all will be. She's not going to come for just you now. She'll probably come after all of us.::

::Lovely,:; Ezra said wearily, half closing her eyes as her head began to hurt again.

::Here. Hand on the orb. Take a little of its energy to recover. A couple more days and I should be able to take you through a portal back to Ammora. Maybe with a little distance and time between you and Derik, you'll be able to look at this a little more objectively.:: Reanalia opened the bag that the orb rested in and put Ezra's hand on it. Ezra nodded and closed her eyes, drawing a small trickle of energy into herself, letting it fill those reserves that she'd spent dry.

It wasn't Ammora's power source, but it helped. Ezra relaxed and Reanalia took out a book and began to read to her. After a few moments, Ezra managed to fall back to sleep, letting the energy of the Orb slowly seep into her while she slept.

"Your color looks better," Tala greeted her as Ezra woke. Ezra stretched, feeling far better than she had before her nap.

"Mmm…I feel a little better. Where's Reanalia? And Derik?" Ezra asked, noting that Tula was sitting on the cushion that Reanalia had occupied before. Derik's pallet was still empty.

"Derik's been put to work cutting up vegetables for the cook. He's getting restless and we've made as many bandages as the healers needed. Most of the wounded are going to be able to return to duty, so to speak, tomorrow. The rest will be taken home to their families and Jarod's pledged to give them all a bit of coin to help them to recover at home. Repairs are already underway and should be finished in a day or two," Tula reported with a smile as she held up a cup of water for Ezra. Ezra sat up and drank, realizing how thirsty she was.

"Thank you. Much better," she said as she lay back again.

"Feel up to eating something better than soup?"

"Yes, oh please yes!"

"Okay, I'll fetch you something better to eat. Reanalia and Faorir have both said they want to open a portal back to Ammora to take you home. The rest of us will stay and finish cleaning up the mess here, so to speak," Tala said with a wink as she rose.

"Oh, thank the Gods. I am ready to go home," Ezra breathed, and Tala laughed.

"Well, you'll get to see it tomorrow, Sista. I'll be back with your food in a jiffy."

As Tala left, that gave Ezra time to think on it with both elation and dread.

I need to speak with Baelios...before Derik comes home. Ezra felt both guilty and sad at how she was feeling, but she needed to talk to Baelios before the wedding came up again.

And being in her nice, quiet Castle was looking better and better these days. The noise alone was beginning to grate on her nerves. The lack of privacy was also getting to her. At least tomorrow, she could retreat to her chambers, take a nice long bath...and then see to business before talking with Baelios. At least she was up to walking again.

Tomorrow, she was going home.

Chapter Eighteen

"Wait, are you sure she's well enough to travel? She couldn't even get out of bed yesterday," Derik protested as Eve broke the news that the mages were departing.

"She's starting to recover. And she's anxious to get back to the Castle, Derik. I'm sending Faorir and Reanalia with her. She'll be fine until we get back," Eve reassured him.

"How is that possible?"

"I used the orb, Derik. I'll be fine," Ezra spoke up from where she sat on her pallet. "Besides, I need to get back to Ammora before any other trouble shows up," she pointed out. Derik looked at her and saw the difference in her color. She had been paler. Now she looked as she always had, and she sat without sagging. She looked stronger again.

"I'll go with you—"

"No, you should stay here and help with the wounded and the repairs. In a couple of days, everyone should be able to begin returning home. It won't be very long, Derik."

"And then we'll begin planning the wedding—" Eve started.

"No, we will let things settle down first. The wedding can wait. I have a baby on the way. I want to slow down a little. We just defeated one of the greatest threats Axrealia has ever known. I need a little time to catch my breath, Derik," she said, feeling guilty even as she said it.

"It's okay. So, we'll take our time planning the wedding. Are you all right?" Derik looked at her, worried.

"Yes, I'm just overwhelmed and still tired. I'll be all right, but I don't want to rush things."

Derik gave a nod and gave her a hug.

"I understand and it's fine. I'll stay here if you promise to go home and rest."

"Of course. That's all I want to do right now," she said gently, hugging him back.

With both Eve's and Derik's blessing, she went to Lord Jarod to give her farewell. Taking it slowly, she walked with the Orb's bag slung across her back. She was still tired and used her quarterstaff to lean on as she walked, seeking him out. After some searching, she found his quarters. The repairs here seemed complete; the floor was back to the way it was and new hangings and sheets with blankets now graced the large bed.

And the throne, she noted with relief, had been changed as well to reflect a much lighter image. It now resembled an Elven throne more than her own, for which she felt a rush of gratitude to whomever enacted the repairs.

"Sorceress, it's nice to see you up and about again," Lord Jarod greeted her politely. She gave a nod and a small smile.

"Thank you, Lord Jarod. We shouldn't be imposing upon you for much longer. The other mages and I will be leaving today. The rest should be ready to follow in a day or two. I'm glad to see that your fortress is getting repaired. It looks like they're doing a good job, whomever they are.

"Oh, it's an Elven builder and a rather odd assortment of crew from all over Axrealia. They've done a better job than I ever could've hoped to arrange on my own. What do you plan to do with the Orb?" Jarod asked, looking at the bag with curiosity in his eyes.

"I'll protect it in Ammora. I'll keep it safe from anyone wishing to misuse it. And I'll make sure that your brother is never allowed to escape or be released. I'm very sorry that we couldn't save your parents," she offered, leaning a bit more on her quarterstaff and reminding herself that after this, Faorir and Reanalia would be taking her home.

"At least we found out what happened to them and avenged them. Perhaps I'll come and visit you in Ammora soon. Congratulations on your engagement, Sorceress," Jarod offered just as Faorir and Reanalia came in.

"Thank you," she said carefully, noting how his tone had suddenly changed. It sounded harder, cooler. She shook it off, thinking perhaps he was still recovering from the ordeal his brother had put him through.

"Ah, Lord Jarod, we're ready to go. It was nice working with you," Reanalia offered with a smile while Faorir chuckled.

"Yes, very nice working with you. I only wish it had been under different circumstances," The older Sorcerer said with a cordial smile.

"It was nice working with all of you. Hopefully we'll never face another such crisis. But, if you ever need me, send for me. I'll help you all again, if I can," Jarod offered. They gave their farewells and headed back outside. Ezra felt a little unsettled, but she shook it off.

I'm just tired and jumping at shadows. Not a good way to be, Ezra chided herself. As Faorir and Reanalia took her outside to the courtyard to build the portal, Tala and Wahya joined them.

"Sorceress, do you want us to come back with you?" Wahya asked with a welcoming smile.

"Of course, I do. But I thought you'd come back with Captain Lita and the others. I've seen you doing what you both do best; giving hope to the wounded and helping those who lost their way to find the right path again," she said with a weary smile.

"Well, true, but everyone who was lost has either been set right or has chosen their path. And Eve isn't needing as many helpers. We thought we'd give Derik a little peace of mind, Sista," Tala pointed out with a flick of her fingers going through her long blonde hair. Ezra glanced to Faorir and Reanalia, both of whom shrugged.

"Very well. Hurry up and get your things—"

"Already packed, Sista. We travel light," Wahya reminded her with a grin. Reanalia and Faorir turned as one and began to build the portal as Ezra waited, feeling the weight of the Orb against her back and side as she waited. "How are you feeling?"

"Stronger than I was, but I'll feel better once I'm home," she replied honestly.

"Ah, Derik said he thought that was why you weren't recovering. He mentioned you don't recover outside of the Castle," Wahya said softly.

"I used the Orb, just a little. I'd prefer to finish recovering in Ammora. It'd be easier," Ezra admitted just as softly just before the portal bloomed into life. Faorir went through first with Ezra hot on his heels. Wahya and Tala followed with Reanalia bringing up the rear.

They came out just outside of Ammora. With a gesture, Ezra lowered the drawbridge and began the long walk across. She was sweating as she reached the threshold at last and drew in a deep breath as her booted heels touched the marble of the Castle.

She felt a surge of power, beckoning to her from within the Castle and drew on it gratefully as she walked.

::Ezra, welcome home,:: Baelios greeted as she felt his invisible hand touch her elbow, supporting her.

"I'm going to go get a bath and seek my bed. Feel free to take whatever rooms you'd like for now," Ezra offered to the others as the portal disappeared and Reanalia crossed the threshold last. The drawbridge raised itself, much to Ezra's relief.

"Good idea, though I'd still like to have your tale for my chronicles, Sorceress," Faorir said with a smile.

"I'll tell it to you in full tomorrow, Faorir. I promise," she said wearily, feeling stronger from the power of the Castle…but yearning to go to her bed. She began to walk through the hallways when she felt Baelios scoop her up as he revealed himself, solidifying out of need as she felt the last of her energy waver. The next thing she knew, he had her in her chambers and was bathing her.

"You passed out in the hallway. You've drained yourself to nothing," Baelios chided her, not bothering to use telepathy.

"It was worth it. The orb has Juktis inside of it."

"It was worth it. But, now that you're clean, you're going to bed and I will guard the Orb until you're ready to deal with it. I'm locking it up in your workroom," Baelios said cooly as he helped her up to dry her, then dressed her with his usual efficiency before he carried her to her bed.

She felt him removing her headdress, and that was the last thing she knew as she tumbled back into slumber, feeling spent all over again.

When Ezra woke again, she felt much better. More like herself again. She stretched and rose, groaning as she felt how much more energy she had today than she had when she'd returned. Her eyes fell on her closet and she rose and went to find something that might still fit.

Her belly was starting to grow at last, stretching slowly as the child within grew. It had been four very long months since Juktis had managed to break into Ammora with his band of mercenaries. Four months since she'd conceived.

Vision of Darkness

Ezra pulled on a pair of leggings that had always been a little loose, then paused as she felt something unfamiliar about them.

"Baelios, did you alter my clothes?" she asked, noting the new panels that had been added to them.

"I did. I also made some new items while you were gone…for when you need larger clothes," the Spirit replied with an amused look on his barely visible face.

"That was thoughtful. Thank you," she said as she drew the leggings on without a second thought and added a tunic that also had had panels cleverly added. She tugged on a pair of boots, then headed out the door, using her magic to detangle her loose hair as she walked.

::Ezra, you should rest a little more today--::

::No, Baelios. I need to take care of that Orb. Then I owe Faorir our tale.::

::Our tale?::

::Yes, Our tale. No names, just…the bare bones of the story. It's time someone else knew it, don't you think?::

::Ezra, if that information ever falls into the wrong hands--::

:;That's why it'll only just be the bare bones. No names, no species, no close details. Just what happened…In case the worst happens. I'd rather that someone else knew our tale, but no secrets that can't be revealed. In the meantime,…the Orb needs to be secured. Oh…the egg I sent to you by portal--::

::It's in your workroom, Ezra. But, what're you going to do with it?::

::I have a plan. Well, part of one,:: Ezra replied as she opened her workroom door and then closed and locked it behind her.

Sitting on her altar, there was the Dragon's egg on a white velvet cushion. Next to it, on it's own cushion, was the Orb.

As Ezra reached for it, the Castle began to shake…then a doorway opened at the back of her workroom.

"It seems the Castle has a plan for it," Baelios said with surprise written on his features as he solidified next to her.

"Then let's not keep it waiting," Ezra said as she lifted the Orb and curled it in the crook of one arm, then turned to take the other.

"I'll take the egg," Baelios offered as he picked it up easily. Ezra gave him a nod of thanks and led the way through the new door. Inside a new corridor that she had never seen, lamps began to glow with an eerie magical light. She walked down the steps carefully, taking her time as this was one of the few places within the Castle that she had never seen before.

The steps wound down around in a long spiral deep into the depths of the Castle. Ezra followed it down and down until they came into a nice, warm room. Inside, a fire leapt to life within a large fireplace, warming the room. A small waterfall near that provided a nice bit of humidity to the air without cooling it.

"A new room, or a room we've never seen?" Ezra asked Baelios.

"I don't know. I suspect only the Castle does."

"If walls could talk, hm?" Ezra asked as she walked through the room, pausing as she came to a ring of deep cushions. "A nest?" she asked as she paused to examine it. It certainly looked like a sort of nest!

"I think this would be the ideal place to put the egg, until it's ready to hatch, Ezra," Baelios replied as he moved to the nest of cushions and placed the egg in the center. "I'll turn it each day and night so that the baby inside is kept comfortable. When it looks like it's ready to hatch, I'll let you know. Odd, that the Dragon's egg was in that Fortress."

"It's mother had been killed and necromanced by Juktis. He had it hidden in the dungeon right under his main chambers," Ezra explained as she watched Baelios positioning the egg so it lay on a side that wasn't caved in.

"Still, he didn't care for any other living creature. Only himself. I still find it odd," Baelios replied as he rose and then pointed over Ezra's shoulder. Ezra turned, seeing another door that was open. Inside, that eerie glowing light radiated from somewhere in the center of that chamber.

Drawn to it, Ezra walked into the chamber. The light dimmed a little as she blinked watering eyes. Then a pedestal appeared with a cupped cradle that was the right size for the Orb of Eithal.

Ezra didn't hesitate but placed the Orb in that cradle. Stone roots began to grow from the pedestal, curling around the Orb and rolling over its surface. Not to weaken or break it but touching it and drawing the Orb's power through the roots. There was another flash of light and Ezra sensed a large power boost as the Orb became part of the power source of Ammora!

Vision of Darkness

The boost of power went through the bond that Ezra shared with the Castle, and she found herself marveling at how much stronger she felt! She backed out of the power chamber and watched the hidden door swing itself shut, sealing itself with a soft click.

"Baelios, do you—"

"I'm…. stronger," Baelios said in a shocked tone of voice. Ezra turned and saw Baelios had not only become solid again, but he almost looked alive!

"It's the Orb. It amplifies magical power. It's given the Castle a very large power boost. And through the Castle—"

"Us as well," Baelios said, looking at his hands that nearly sparked with power. "I almost feel…alive."

"You look more alive than you have since the End of Days spell."

"We never foresaw this," Baelios said softly, looking at his hands still. Ezra sighed, feeling dread as she put her hand on his shoulder.

"I don't think anyone foresaw anything that we've been through in the past few months. And, I need to talk to you…about Derik."

"What about him?" Baelios asked as he turned with her to walk towards the staircase.

"He proposed after the last battle," she paused, her hand on the wall and one foot touching on the staircase. She hung her head, feeling both elation at the thought, and guilt.

"I see. Do you love him?"

"Yes, I love him. I love him as much as I once loved Bael."

"Ah, I see. You're worried that I'll be jealous or angry."

"Aren't you?"

"No. Ezra, you need someone in your life. Someone to make you happy. Someone to bring you balance. This past thousand years, you've spent doing nothing but study, train, and prepare for the Darkness. These past months, since Derik came to stay with us…you've come back to life. You laugh and smile far more easily now than you have in years. Bael intended for you to live, not merely to exist. Until now, you've existed. Now…now you're living again. I couldn't be happier for you," Baelios said gently as his hands came to rest on her shoulders.

"I wish I could know what Bael would say—"

"Bael is part of me. Whenever you talk to me, you speak to the entire Wizard's Council."

"I wasn't married to the entire Wizard's Council, Baelios."

"No, but Bael was part of it. He's proud of you. And he's happy for you, too. He wanted you to live, to have children, to have a life. Marry Derik, when you're ready. We're all happy for you, Ezra."

"He's mortal. He'll die one day—"

"And you'll grieve for him, just as you've grieved for friends. And you will still have me. Not to mention the little one," Baelios pointed out as he wrapped an arm around her waist and began to lead her back up the stairs. "Faorir is waiting for you and I'll get you some breakfast and meet you in the library while you share your tale."

"Thank you, Baelios."

"It's my pleasure, Ezra," he said with a smile as they came back out into her work room. With a weight lifted off of her shoulders, Ezra went upstairs to meet Faorir.

The next couple of days was spent telling Faorir her tale. From when she had been orphaned and raised by the priests and priestesses of the Temple of the Warrior Goddess to when she had met Bael. Keeping specific names out of it, she found herself reliving those days of the past with Faorir and enjoying it. It felt good to tell someone of her journey in its entirety.

When it was finally done, Faorir whistled, looking over the journal he'd written it all in.

"Nearly filled! I'm surprised, Sorceress. Your tale was much longer than I had ever thought it might be and it's still not over," the older Immortal said in amazement.

"I'm sure yours is even longer, Faorir. You're much older than I am."

"I've managed to stay out of the world's affairs as much as I can."

"I know, but the world isn't going to let us stay out of its affairs. We're part of the world and we should do our best to do what we can to keep it safe without imposing ourselves, naturally."

“Therein lies the problem. It’s hard to help without becoming like someone like Juktis.”

“True, Faorir. But we can do what we can to help where we can. With Juktis gone, that part of the world should become a much happier place again,” Ezra pointed out with a smile.

“I think the entire world is better off without him. Were you able to put the Orb in a safe place?”

“Yes. No one will find it. Juktis will never return,” she replied, feeling relief at that thought.

Then the vision came. Ezra saw herself, running alone through the corridors, taunting someone behind her.

“Alyra, come on, can’t you catch me?” she called back over her shoulder as she ran through the work room and down into the bowels of the Castle. A dark twin of herself, the same one she’d seen rising in the cave, ran after her, nearly catching her as Ezra reached and touched the orb. There was a flash of light—

And Ezra found herself back in the library with Faorir. Ezra blinked, trying to let her heart slow down just as she felt the child within squirming and stretching.

“Are you all right, Sorceress?”

“I just had another vision. I’m all right. It’s not going to come to pass for quite some time,” she reassured him.

“You’re sure?”

“I’m positive. Don’t worry, nothing is coming today.”

“Well, except maybe the return of Captain Lita and her warriors.”

“Maybe, but without a gate, it’ll take a week or more to return. They do have their sky chariots, so at least they won’t have to walk,” she replied with a small smile.

“Well, when you and Derik marry…send for me. I’d love to come and see that, if you don’t mind, my dear.” Faorir rose with a wink. “I’ll stay until the others come back. After that, Reanalia and I should be getting back to our own homes.”

“I’ll send you both invitations, don’t worry. I’m planning on taking a while before we do get married. There’s much to do for the city and we need to start planning for the baby,” Ezra said with a bit of weariness, as well as excitement.

"You've also earned a bit of rest. What about that other mage, the one we didn't find?"

"She's retreated for now. I'll begin seeking her out soon, after we finish getting things settled here. I need to find that cave where Juktis found her and maybe get some more answers. It won't be easy to find her, I've learned that much," Ezra admitted as they began to walk down the stairs to go back to the ground floor.

"Well, if you need help with it, I'm willing to try. I do have a few tricks up my sleeve, you know," the older mage said with a wink.

"Let's get things settled before we stir it all up again. Give me a few weeks at least, then I'll send for you and Reanalia. I think between the three of us, we might be able to find her."

"What about Jarod?"

"He has his hands full with taking control over that Fortress. I'd rather not bother him until he's settled and feeling more comfortable," Ezra admitted, still feeling ill-at-ease with Jarod.

"You don't trust him, do you?"

"Not entirely. I can't explain why, it's just a feeling."

"Sometimes feelings are the only warning we get, Sorceress. Three of us working together should be sufficient to find the upstart."

"Finding her isn't what I'm afraid of, Faorir. It's what comes after," Ezra replied, feeling dread at the thought of what might be ahead.

"Isn't it always? Let's go get Reanalia and relax for a bit. Let's share some stories."

"Oh, let's invite Tala and Wahya for that. They have quite a few stories that we might all find amusing," Ezra suggested as they began to head for the dining hall.

Epilogue

Two days after the mages had left, the rest of the Axrealian forces were ready to depart. Lord Jarod was generous, giving gold to every tribe, people and company that had come to overthrow Juktis. When asked why, he simply said, "I don't wish gold gotten through evil deeds," and kept handing it out. By the time he'd paid everyone, his coffers only had a small sum left, enough to keep his fortress, with its new staff, going for quite some time.

Derik went with Captain Lita to thank Jarod again before the gates opened to let everyone out.

"My Lord, thank you again for your generosity," Lita said solemnly as Derik bowed his head.

"As well as for your help, Lord Jarod. I'm very sorry for your loss, but I'm glad that we were all able to help set things right," Derik added.

"Thank you to you both. Please give this to the Sorceress and the mages for me. They were all a pleasure to work with," Jarod offered as he handed several small boxes over to Derik. Each one was tied with a small ribbon and neatly marked with a tag.

"I'll make sure they get them and thank you. I'm sure they'll appreciate the gifts."

"I'll have my guards open the gates. Take care," Jarod said briskly before he left the room ahead of them to go towards the walls.

"He's still a cold fish," Lita remarked softly.

"Let's just go for now. He's probably yearning for a bit of privacy. I know I am," Derik said with a wry grin as they headed back towards the courtyard, where the Tribesmen, the Orcs, the Elves, the Hive peoples, Giants and Lita's Company were all assembled and ready to depart.

"As am I. I'm ready for home. I wish the journey back was as easy as the journey here, but at least we have the sky chariots. We should be home in a day or two," Lita said with a wink as they got on board her sky chariot and she stood at the controls. The gate opened to a cheer from the gathered people.

"AXREALIA, AXREALIA, AXREALIA, AXREALIA!" the combined forces chanted as they made their way out of the gates. Each set of peoples marched, or flew, out and began to head for their individual sets of homes. In the sky, the hive peoples soared through the air on their gossamer wings.

The tribesmen all set out for their own home, all except Wahya's tribe. That tribe set out for Ammora, leading the way for Lita's company. Giants walked serenely, heading for their individual homes in peace.

Derik took in a breath of fresh air as Lita's sky chariot rose into the sky. "Let's go home."

The morning dawned beautiful and bright. Ezra had woken early, eaten and taken out some of her books as was her usual routine. But, today, she had decided on a very important change.

::Baelios, I'm yearning for something green. Something outside of the Castle. What do you think?:: she sent as she opened one particular book that held a spell she had been considering casting for ages.

::The world knows we're here now. I suppose it wouldn't hurt to make where we dwell more pleasant. But the question lies in what would we gain, what would we lose? And what would we affect elsewhere?::

::Magic always has a price. But this spell would allow things to grow again outside. It wouldn't take water away from elsewhere. We get plenty of rain. It would cut down on erosion around the base for the drawbridge. And it would allow more farmers to come and settle. Cephra's farm is growing and it's running out of places that aren't in the forest. We could offer some land to her offspring to come and settle and begin their own farms, if they wish. With the city at the base of Ammora, we can't expect one farm to meet all our needs anymore,:: she replied, having thought this out in random moments over the past months.

::It would also give animals more places to come and settle, if we're careful. We must preserve the balance, after all,:: Baelios reminded her.

::Of course,:: she replied soberly.

::What do you need for the spell?::

::Water and a handful of fertile soil. We have plenty of that in the herb garden. And water from our water supply should help,:: she replied as she looked it over.

::Anything else?::

::Some seeds, any kind of seeds so long as they are ready to be planted.::

::I'll bring them up for you in a few moments,:: was the Spirit's reply as she studied the spell again. Once again weighing the good versus the bad and what they would gain or lose. When Baelios walked in carrying a tray with everything she needed, she couldn't help but smile at him.

::Thank you, Baelios. Let's go up to the parapets. We need to be up high to cast this spell,:: Ezra told him as she began up the staircase that would lead out to it. Baelios followed her, bringing the ingredients for the spell and refusing to allow her to help carry them.

Once they were there, they spent a few long moments just looking out over the landscape they had both come to know so well over the past thousand years.

"It's funny. We've been here so long and before all of this, I never would have considered casting this spell. The wasteland and dead forest were a perfect place to hide ourselves in," Ezra said softly, realizing that she might actually miss this view.

"We were found anyway. Now the world knows we're here. No reason to hide anymore, Ezra," Baelios pointed out as he placed the bowl of seeds, the bowl of earth and the goblet of water on the stones before her.

"And no reason to be missing all of the things we've yearned to see," Ezra said as she took a breath and centered herself. She grounded herself quietly, making sure she was ready and began to draw on the power within herself and within the Castle.

It was like touching a lightning storm now! Wild and unpredictable, yet it calmed tamely when she reached out with mental hands to touch it. Drawing it up into her, she allowed it to flow into herself and began to chant softly, letting the power flow out to touch the three things before her.

Then she poured the water into the soil, then added the seeds. As the magic poured through her, she let it touch everything in the bowl. Then a whirlwind formed and rose up out of the bowl, lifting the water, soil and seeds up into its small maelstrom, then it rose higher and higher into the sky. Ezra brought her hands up together before her, then gestured, sending it all flying apart to spread over the landscape.

For a moment, nothing else happened. Then she saw the trees by the base of the drawbridge moving. Not to a wind. But something green was coming out of the long-dead stems and unfurled, showing leaves. The bark turned from stone back into living bark. The soil began to sprout grass, flowers, mosses and bushes! Ezra and Baelios watched in amazement as the landscape turned green. The small flower beds that hadn't been planted in the city burst into an array of green and color as flowers and grasses grew in them. A small river appeared, flowing through a small little valley, bringing with it the promise of more as the wasteland came to life.

“That was a beautiful spell, Ezra. The best you have ever cast,” Baelios said in amazement, his orange eyes glowing with pleasure at what he saw around them. Ezra smiled and just enjoyed the scene about them.

“Thank you, Baelios. You were a good teacher.”

“You were a good student, once you accepted you had to learn.”

“I didn’t have a choice in the matter, remember?”

“True. But if you did…what would you have chosen?”

“I would’ve chosen for Bael to live and for me to have died long ago of old age as a doting grandmother. But, knowing now just how much danger our world is in…I’m glad to still be in the fight. At least we won’t be alone anymore.”

“No, we’re not. Look!”

Out on the horizon, she saw a very unexpected sight. Sky chariots were approaching and on the first one, she spotted Derik’s red hair next to Lita’s dark brown.

“They’re home,” she breathed before she turned to teleport herself back down to the entrance hall. It was faster, and easier, than running. She lowered the drawbridge and ran out just as the Sky chariots landed and Derik leapt out to meet her. He caught her halfway across and swung her around before giving her a long, passionate kiss.

“I’ve missed you,” Derik whispered as he leaned his forehead against hers.

“I’ve missed you, too. Welcome home, Derik.”

In that moment, nothing else mattered. Not the cheers of the mercenaries that had come to make their home in their new city. Not the smell of the new grass and trees. Not the small warm breeze that washed over them, nor the cry of the Falcons circling slowly overhead. Everything else fell away and all that mattered was that they were together again.

Jarod was restless, still preoccupied with the thought of Ezra and her new engagement. As the sun rose, he began to scry. Because Ezra trusted him, she had allowed him to see in where his brother never had. He watched as Ezra and Derik kissed on the drawbridge and felt jealousy twist his guts.

Vision of Darkness

"She should have been *mine*," he whispered into the darkness of his empty bedchamber. "Why a mortal? No matter. In time he'll die…and then I'll be there to comfort her. I just have to patient. I have…. *time,*" he murmured as he began to plan for that day. "By the time the years pass, I'll be such a trusted friend, she won't think twice when I come after he's *gone*. And in the meantime, I have plenty to do to be ready. One day, Ezra, you *will* be *mine*."

A hand came out of the shadows, curling over his shoulder. A woman came out, curling her nude, tattooed form into his lap, chuckling as she threw her long black hair back over her shoulders.

"Yes, she may be yours…one day. Until then, let us talk about how we can help each other, Jarod," the strange woman's voice purred into his ear, sending all thought of Ezra from his mind. Ezra would wait. He would have her. One day.

Author's Note

There's so much to say and so many people to thank. First of all, thank you to my husband, John, my kids—whom keep me busy and probably out of trouble, my parents and to my friends Aimee, Gretchen and Brenda. You guys are the ones who encourage me to write and who encourage me to never ever give up.

Thank you to Meri and Joe for being my first two readers and for being my friends—It really helps to know that my friends like or dislike what I write, but also that I really do have something to offer.

Thank you to Charlotte Burnette, Verlene Potter, Alta Dunst and Jeannine Villars for encouraging me to continue writing and never give up.

Thank you to my friends Ahrika, Anchin, Suta, Deka and Scarlet, for making me laugh on a daily basis in role play—hope you're all having fun too.

Thank you especially to Christina Pickles, Frank Langella, Melendy Britt and Alan Oppenheimer for portraying such wonderful characters during my childhood, partly of which inspired me to write and reach for dreams that others said were impossible to achieve.

Lastly, thank you to the readers. I hope you enjoyed the beginning of Ezra's story. Don't worry, more is to come.

About the Author

Dawn Wilton grew up in Colorado Springs, Colorado. She went to High School at Mitchell High and attended college at the University of Southern Colorado in Pueblo where she got a Bachelors in Music and in Mass Communications. She lives with her husband and her three children in New York State.

Made in the USA
Middletown, DE
25 March 2022